aftershock

a novel

alison taylor

HARPERCOLLINS PUBLISHERS LTD

Published by HarperCollins Publishers Ltd

First edition

HarperCollins books may be purchased for educational, business
or sales promotional use through our Special Markets Department.

HarperCollins Publishers Ltd
Bay Adelaide Centre, East Tower
22 Adelaide Street West, 41st Floor
Toronto, Ontario, Canada
M5H 4E3

www.harpercollins.ca

Library and Archives Canada Cataloguing in Publication

Title: Aftershock : a novel / Alison Taylor.
Names: Taylor, Alison, 1971- author.
Identifiers: Canadiana (print) 20200222139 | Canadiana (ebook) 20200222759
ISBN 9781443458214 (softcover) | ISBN 9781443458221 (ebook)
Classification: LCC PS8639.A91 A7 2020 | DDC C813/.6—dc23

Printed and bound in the United States of America
LSC/H 9 8 7 6 5 4 3 2 1

This one is for Sabine.

Airport.

Chloe said something, but Jules wasn't listening.

She was trying to judge, without tweaking her neck, if she could, with an adequate margin of safety, slide her Benz in between the two cabs. Partly to allow Chloe room to get that ridiculous duffle bag out of the back, partly because airports were full of exhausted, over-emoting travellers, banging around their hard-edged baggage. The Oxy cushioned a lot of things, but she still felt every threat to her car like a needle on her skin.

Mum? Chloe was digging in her "day pack," also too large and, in Jules's opinion, hideous. She'd come home the other day with the army surplus bags, monstrous vomit-green canvas things. Totally impractical. Outmoded by the army for good reason. But then, Jules didn't have to carry them. And Chloe. Well, Chloe would do what she wanted. Like her haircut. If you could call it that. Her gorgeous auburn hair hacked down to a quarter inch of bleached white spikes.

Jules sighed. Nothing was ever easy, with Chloe. The constant push and pull between them left her drained, and this horned and acid-tongued stranger that was her daughter's latest metamorphosis shredded her heart and her composure as it clawed and spit fire, refused her embrace. But letting go was still painful—like everything else these days, unexpectedly so—and the idea of Chloe leaving still sucker-punched her with the force of a car crash every time she thought about it. She couldn't bear the thought of prolonging her own metaphorical spiral through the windshield any longer than necessary. So, when one of the cabs pulled away, she slid into the gap, double-parking. Immediately, there were two young men gesturing at her madly, pointing at the Taxi Stand sign, their voices muted by the well-sealed windows of the SUV.

Better make it quick. Jules avoided eye contact with the cabbies, holding up her forefinger in the universal signal for just a minute.

Chloe looked up sharply from her rummaging. You're not coming in?

I can't park here, look at these— She flinched as the one in the turban rapped on the passenger window.

So park in there! Chloe nodded towards the short-term parking garage fifty feet away, both arms elbow-deep in her pack. Jules shuddered inwardly at the ghosts residing in that particular garage.

Chloe, I have a meeting.

This was a lie. She'd taken the day off to deal with the inevitable emotional bruising of this exact and dreaded moment. With one hand still on the steering wheel, she thumbed at her phone, pretending to check for email. Swallowed twice. Threw a glance in her daughter's direction that was never intended to land, slammed up against Chloe's glare and quickly looked away again.

Go on, I'm in a hurry. Pinched voice she hoped passed for irritation.

Fine.

Chloe punched jeans and underwear back into the top of her pack, yanked the top flap over and roughly tugged the straps closed. Jules kept her eyes pointed at her phone, tried to block out the huffing and puffing in her peripheral vision. Took deep breaths.

Pop the trunk, please, *Mother*.

Chloe pushed her door open and jumped down. The two protesting cabbies had become four. They stepped back to let

Chloe out, then moved to lean into the passenger side to talk at Jules.

Close the door, Chloe!

Jules fixed her eyes straight ahead, on nothing. Chloe slammed the door, much too hard, but not before Jules heard her say: Don't bother. She's a racist bitch.

Love you too, dear, Jules said. But the sealed car swallowed her words. She waited for Chloe to reach the back, then popped the hatch open for her. One of the men brought a luggage cart over when he saw the size of Chloe's duffle bag and helped her lift it on.

Try not to miss me too much, Chloe called up through the car's interior. I'm only gone for a year. She would have slammed the trunk closed too, and Jules felt a dark satisfaction at her daughter's frustration as hydraulics eased it shut.

Jules gave the cab drivers a courtesy wave as she pulled away from the curb. She caught a last glimpse of Chloe, in her buzz cut and motorcycle jacket, gesturing rudely at her in the rear-view mirror.

Driving down the 427, she felt totally uncalled-for tears sting her eyes. She never cried. Hated criers. What the fuck. Not getting along with Chloe was not new. But she felt worse about it than usual. An accusation that she was a terrible parent sang nastily in her brain, and she didn't even know whose voice it was.

She'd hoped to establish a truce, before Chloe left. Had meant to slip her a couple hundred bucks when she dropped her off. But, like so many of her better intentions, she'd lost her grip on it, and now it was too late.

The drive to the airport, too, had been a peace offering. Well. So much for that.

It had all started with the phone call. Jules, ear-deep in a glitchy algorithm, had only answered because it was after hours, hitting the speakerphone button without taking her eyes off her monitor.

Jules Wright.

Hi, Mum.

What's wrong? A call at work was as rare as it was unwelcome.

Nothing's *wrong*, exactly . . .

Can I call you later?

This is later. I called you last week. Remember?

Jules scanned through lines of code for anything problematic—a misplaced ampersand or asterisk could wreak havoc.

Don't whine, Chloe. I can't stand it.

The line hissed. Creating the database was the easy part, but to provide the client with live analytics it had to work fluidly with the algorithm she'd written. The whole thing was hours late going online, she'd had to wrench it away from a junior associate who'd been streamlining it towards disaster. She shouldn't have passed it off to him in the first place, but lately her workload had swelled malignantly. Still, the price was hers to pay.

I'm in the middle of something, so.

I've withdrawn from school, Chloe said, and she started to say something else, to explain or elaborate or make some kind of excuse, but Jules wasn't listening: she was imploding.

What're you gonna do, Chloe? Work *retail*?

Something non-linguistic tore out of her throat. Her hand shot out, picked up the receiver and slammed it down again.

She knew what Chloe wanted. Chloe wanted to travel.

EVEN THROUGH THE Oxy, Jules felt fresh frustration. She banged on the steering wheel, her arms dragging a half second behind her impulse. She hit the horn accidentally, swerved slightly and earned a scowl from the young man in the next lane. She gave him the finger and sped up to get in front of him.

The day after Chloe's phone call, after spending an hour longer than normal in standstill traffic on her Toronto–Hamilton commute, Jules arrived home to find her front door open wide. Already aggravated, she had the brief thought that she'd been robbed and felt the grim vindication of catastrophic expectations fulfilled. Then she heard the racket coming from inside. Not robbed: invaded. Angry female voices yelled to distorted guitars from portable speakers on the mantel, a sticker-covered cellphone lying next to them. Also on the mantel, crowding out the single photograph of Chloe in her grad robes (Here, Mum, so you don't forget me—as though she might) and the two sleek silver candlesticks, were a couple of beer cans, a pack of cigarettes (when had that started?), some keys and a pair of Ray-Bans. The matching black roller suitcases Jules had bought her the previous month—to take *to* university—were hunched together on the hearth like kids on a smoke break, everything ripped open and loose, uncontained. Black T-shirts, boys' underwear, flannel sheets and expensive toiletries all fled the suitcases in a desperate mass exodus. Some jeans and sweaters had conquered the couch, a scuffed leather jacket lounged in an armchair. Someone had pulled up all the couch cushions to look for lost change. A tower of textbooks swayed on the coffee table, topped by an empty fast-food container.

Well. At least she'd bought some books.

Jules took off her shoes and was straightening cushions when Chloe wandered out of the kitchen eating a sandwich. Without a plate.

It started like this:

You smoked in my house?

Nice to see you too, Chlo, welcome home.

Are you staying long?

I used an ashtray.

But no plate?

I've only been here like an hour.

Rod's coming over later. Think you could take your shoes off?

Well, I couldn't stay in residence. My flight's on the eighteenth.

And ended, maybe, finally, with that last rude gesture at the airport.

———

JULES SIGHED. SHE did a lot of sighing these days. She shoulder-checked so she could change lanes for her exit, craning her head around to the right, and—

Fuck.

The kink in her neck flared up, scalpel-sliced through the cotton wool of the painkillers. First the angry twist under her right shoulder blade. Within seconds, pain spiked up her neck and down her back, into her upper arm. Oh fuck. It was a bad one. She leaned over, pulled a heat patch from the glove compartment and slapped it on.

She needed more pills, and soon. Maybe Rod would show up tonight.

Departures.

———

The customs officer—who was practically my age—called me Sir, then got all awkward and stammering when he heard my voice and saw the name on my passport. When my duffle bag was three pounds overweight, he muttered something about the scale being off and handed me a boarding pass while calling me Miss at least three times in some sort of limp apology. But I didn't give a fuck. People are so attached to their genders.

Walking through the airport with just my day pack, I felt light, almost buoyant. As if I could imagine my heart back in place where Jill had ripped it out.

Fuck you, JJ.

THE LINE THROUGH security moved like held breath, a delayed moment of release. At the conveyor belt, I took off my leather jacket and my combat boots, emptied my pockets. You've been selected at random, they told me, as I watched them rifle through my pack, a guy-girl team of security officers smugly pulling out each item one by one, scanning for who the hell knew what with a beeping handheld. My paperback. My toothbrush. The emergency underwear in case my duffle got lost.

The ten minutes it took me to repack made me miss my official boarding time. I sprinted through the terminal to find my gate, swearing at people who blocked my path.

I CAUGHT MY breath and watched the world slide away, gravity pushing me into my seat as the airport, the city, the sprawling suburbs, the parking lots of farmland around them, withdrew into the distance, receded into the past. I pondered that from down there, you might only see one plane climbing into the sky, but from up here the cars on the road were shrinking into roaches, then ants, then mites, scurrying and indistinguishable. I imagined Jules pulling over on her way out of the airport, watching the plane take off, wistfully regretting our interaction. Imagined Jill, writing her exam, and hoped she could feel her own heart tearing out as the plane rose. The concrete-coloured day slid under a carpet of postcard-perfect clouds and pure blue sky.

MY FIRST STOP was to see David. My father. I had a sense of tracing a path he'd laid down years before.

When I was little, he'd been a journalist, a foreign correspondent. He was away a lot. But when the baby died, he put freelancing aside and got a job as a staff writer at our city paper. He stayed home more, started taking me to school, made me lunches, came to my atom hockey games. And Jules was around less, if that was possible. She travelled for work more, closed herself in her room whenever she was home and fought with David. Around the time I started high school, David seemed to finally concede that Jules would never come back to him, never emerge from wherever she'd gone after the baby died. He said he wanted to write a novel, but he couldn't do it there, in that house, with Jules and her grief. And me. And Lizzie's ghost, although no one ever said so.

Before I knew it, I had a new stepmother: Amanda. When Amanda's law firm opened offices in New Zealand, the newlyweds jumped at the chance for a fresh start. I was fourteen when they moved to the other side of the world. Then, a couple years ago: an unscheduled call from David. His voice wavered with excitement, not something I'd ever heard from him before, as he told me I had a sister. A *half*-sister, I thought. It wasn't lost on me that he'd waited until she was born to tell me, hadn't alerted me to any of the warning signs, like pregnancy. I didn't want to be bitter, but he was so proud, so joyful, I didn't even recognize him.

Another damned little sister, I may have said, knowing it would hurt him, but he was so elated that I don't even think he heard me.

Not that I could really blame his impulse to get away from Jules—or from our house, heavy and stale with something no one could name—to start something new. Here I was, acting on the same impulse, fleeing a continent that held too many memories in the hope that if I travelled far enough and long enough, I might somehow be able to breathe more easily. And maybe sleep better.

Hotel.

———

The heat patch was even less helpful than usual. By the time Jules got to the hotel, where she thanked her platinum card for allowing early check-in, she could barely turn her head. She took a forty of Oxy, lay on the bed as her eyes leaked in silent frustration, or maybe self-pity, and tried to relax her neck muscles through deep breathing.

CHLOE HAD DROPPED all her courses and the university had dropped a refund into her sweaty little hands. She'd booked a flight and had three weeks to get ready for her trip. So she'd come home, and they'd argued every single day of it.

Do you know how long I've been saving for your education?

Big sigh. You tell me every fucking day.

Don't you speak to me like that in my house.

Another big sigh. Well. You do.

Your whole life, that's how long. And now you want to throw it away—

I wasn't learning anything.

You wouldn't know it if you were. And you're too young.

Too young to learn?

Too young to be gallivanting around in dangerous places—

Gallivanting. Seriously.

—when you should be getting your degree, so you can get a decent job, so you can pay for your own damn trip, instead of stealing from me.

Her biggest sigh yet. Whatever. Can I borrow the car?

As if.

IT WAS CIRCULAR and stupid, and Jules knew it. Part of the problem was that she didn't have a straightforward reaction to the situation, or, really, to Chloe, if you got down to it. She was appalled. She was overwhelmed. She was disappointed. She was proud. Her heart could burst. Rage simmered in her brain stem.

IT WAS 2 P.M. The day before, Drew, prognostic as usual, had said, Sweetie, come for dinner, stay the night. Jules had said yes to the meal but opted for a hotel room because Rod had promised to meet her after his shift. We'll have a hotel date, he'd suggested, which sounded dreamlike, as in somewhat dislocated from reality, but also with the potential to be quite mundane. She wondered how late he would leave it before cancelling.

A hot shower, the pulsing water directly on her neck, the Oxy easing its way forward: the kink eased somewhat. She could still feel the knot pulling when she turned her head, but there was a bit more give. His-and-hers terrycloth robes hung from the bathroom door, matching Ss emblazoned on the shoulders. She pulled on the shorter and boxier "his" and sat on the edge of the bed.

A YEAR. SHE had, after weeks of arguing about it, come to accept that protesting was futile. Chloe was going to go no matter what Jules did. She had then used her remaining mental energy to distill her reaction into its two major components. One, she was livid that Chloe had so glibly thrown away her first year at school, not to mention the money, which was not insignificant. Two, she was terrified. Anything could happen to Chloe, the places she was going. Anything. At nineteen, she was irrational and impulsive—more than Jules herself had ever been, of that she was certain—and seemed to relish opportunities for danger. New Zealand, fine, David was there, they had *infrastructure*. Bad enough they got all those earthquakes. But India? Thailand? Poverty, tsunamis, underdevelopment, filth— these were not places for children. She didn't think she was being racist, despite what Chloe had said. Just . . . *careful*. What Chloe didn't realize was how much work Jules had put into building the life they had, with its tightly woven safety nets. If she'd seen where Jules had come from, the shitty one-bedroom over the storefront in Hamilton's north end—well, then she might be less eager to jump from the plane without a parachute. So to speak.

Jules pulled the bottle of twelve-year-old Bowmore from her roller suitcase and free-poured a "double," which meant almost filling the tumbler, leaving just enough room for ice. If she could be bothered to go get some. Which she couldn't.

Her own mother had barely batted an eye when Jules left home, university bound on a combination of scholarships and student loans. Good for you, dear, was the reaction, curdled by the unspoken undertones of, Fine, leave me here to suffer by myself. Jules, already packed, standing by the apartment door, looked at her mother's glassy eyes, the flicker of the television the brightest light in the heavily curtained room, and knew what she was working to escape. High school had been about eyes on the prize: university would save her from her powdered-milk childhood, make her life anything but what it had been, make it clean and bright and easy. Not just for her, but also for her mother, and later, as it turned out, for her children. Her child. And it had done—chronic pain aside—and here she was. And Chloe fighting against all the benefits of Jules's decades of relentless work was nonsensical, not to mention hurtful. It was like she wanted to start from scratch. What did she think the world would offer her?

Two days before Chloe was due to fly out, Jules had found her sprawled on her belly on the living room floor, poring over a guidebook for New Zealand. Her knees were bent up so Jules could see the rips in her jeans. Her socked feet kicked idly, massive headphones hugged her ears. Jules flashed on an image, that shorn bleached head trying to ask directions in the slums of god knew where, and felt a rush of vertigo, had to sit on the couch to steady herself. She watched her only daughter and tried not to panic.

How much money do you have? She wasn't sure Chloe would even hear her, but she looked up right away and pulled the headphones off. Jules could hear Bob Dylan playing.

Chloe chewed on her lip and squinted at her mother, deliberating. Just under four grand.

It was paltry, for a year, and they both knew it. The school had refunded half the tuition they'd paid. The first semester residence fees, another seven grand, were just a writeoff. At least she wouldn't have to cough up for the second semester. Jules let the silence ride while a tinny Dylan asked his unquantifiable questions about roads and seas.

She knew Chloe would never ask her for money for her trip, would never ask for help of any kind. At four, she had been self-sufficient enough to refuse help tying her shoes, even if it took her twenty minutes. She'd taught herself to read, to ride a bike, to skate. The set of her jaw was an unspoken mantra: I don't need you.

In a moment of stubborn cruelty she couldn't seem to suppress, Jules decided she wouldn't offer money. Chloe would have to ask. Instead, she offered to drive her to the airport. She remembered now the slump of Chloe's shoulders at the meagre olive branch, the pointed way she replaced her headphones to end the conversation.

JULES LEANED BACK on the hotel bed, her topped-up Scotch propped on her stomach, her neck cradled in her travel-size memory foam neck pillow. A couple of hours of flipping between reality disaster shows, weight loss shows and news, a nap, an Oprah rerun, a couple more glasses of Scotch, another forty of Oxy and a cab ride later, she was knocking on the door of Drew's west Toronto house.

Drew bellowed her name as he opened the door, his massive mouth gaping from his gigantic head. Sometimes he was such an odd mix of frat boy and drag queen. He moved, in his orange plaid smoking jacket and purple ascot, with a grace that denied his three hundred pounds and sixty-odd years. He held both of Jules's hands, kissed her on each cheek. He took her coat, then stood back to examine her outfit. She had struggled into her new olive-green suit, with its wrap-around silk jacket and pants that swirled at her ankles. She was a little worried that she wasn't tall enough to pull it off. The saleslady had assured her it was a designer original, and that it was slimming; she thought she looked as short and squat as ever. The pressure of the waistband on her midriff was a constant reprimand about how much she drank and how little she exercised. But Drew was thumbing the drape of her sleeve and nodding. He'd sent her to the store where she'd bought it, told her it was time to leave Reitmans to the plebs, honey. Which was a bit harsh, she dressed better than that, although not by much. What professional success she had was clearly not based on her fashion sense. Jules wondered for the twentieth time why she was wearing it. She felt the jacket bunching around her waist and yanked it down.

Drew name-dropped the up-and-coming designer. How chic.

It should be for what I paid. I hate all clothes.

I hear you, sweetheart. Well, you look stunning. No Rod?

She shrugged uncomfortably at the compliment and twisted her mouth at the question. Emergency at work. Obviously.

Obviously. Text message? He led her through a vault-ceilinged foyer into a huge living room where a young man in black was already seated.

What else? Jules rolled her eyes, accepted a glass of red. Rod cancelling due to a work emergency was not just common, it was predictable. There were protocols. A text message tonight, flowers sent by secretary tomorrow. The message had come in the cab on the way over. She raised her glass to Drew's and sipped. The wine was smoky and excellent.

And this is Farzan.

He turned to the man sitting on the mauve leather couch, as muted and intense as Drew was garish and genial. He was probably half Drew's age, compact and neat with sharp, dark eyes. Drew sat beside him on the couch and held his hand, just in case there was any doubt that this was his new lover. Jules perched on the edge of a velvet armchair, angled straight-on in deference to her neck. Farzan nodded and smiled and said hello. Drew beamed at him. Well, hi there, Jules said, and drained her wine. She was happy to see Drew with someone again. It had been almost five years since Mikhail died. Drew motioned to the bottle on the sideboard. Grateful, she got up to refill her glass.

Technically her boss, Drew was also her closest friend. One of her only friends. They'd known each other for years now, since he'd come on board at work, but fostering new friendships was not something she had done in earnest for a very long time and had never done easily. As she sat there in her Scotch-Oxy-wine-imbued daze, watching Drew fawn over Farzan, who was watching her silently top up her buzz, she remembered why. Even with the ones she loved, socializing could be excruciating.

She'd said as much to her shrink last week, that the rewards weren't worth the work. Dr. Morrow had in turn suggested that her lack of interest in others said more about her than it did about them.

She turned her wineglass in her hand, watched the liquid legs ripple the inside of the glass. Yeah. Might need to change shrinks.

But Drew was definitely one of the good ones. One of the best, even. Jules had trouble, sometimes, being in the world, interfacing with people. She knew that putting too much out there would bite you in the ass. Professional was not a problem. Meeting with colleagues, dealing with the partners, clients, fine. But the monthly cocktail parties always threw her into a long and repetitive loop. She knew she had to go; she dreaded it for days. She didn't know how to talk to those people. Every conversation felt contrived and hollow yet left her uneasy she had revealed too much or seemed too drunk, worried her subordinates were shooting looks behind her back, her superiors shaking their heads as she turned away.

But Drew would circulate among data miners and sales folk, an ambassador of jokes and generosity, changing the current of the room with every move he made, laughter and appreciation rippling in his wake. And for some reason, at one of these events a few years ago, Drew had homed in on Jules and in his effortless way asked how it was going. Jules had felt caught, not knowing if he was looking for a small-talk answer, which she was incapable of, or a real conversation, which filled her with a whole other world of anxiety. Do you really want to know? she'd asked him. And he'd laughed, whole body rocking back as he tipped up his head and said she could get back to him but in the meantime she looked like she could use a drink. He threw a trunkish arm around her shoulder and led her to the bar.

So, DREW SAID finally, and she looked up from her wine to see his hand resting on Farzan's knee. She's gone.

Gone and gone. She is officially David's problem. Jules raised her glass again, this time to her daughter and her absent ex. Along with his new spawn. Hope he doesn't fuck it up, she tried to joke, wondering if it was possible to fuck up worse than she had herself. Bolstered by the conversational burst, she braved ahead. Just the three of us, I guess?

Drew and Farzan exchanged grins.

Actually, no. I invited another friend.

Jules could see where this was going. Drew did not like Rod.

The doorbell rang.

Right on time! Drew was moving across the living room and into the foyer before Jules could say anything more.

To Farzan, she said, He's very sweet, but, as she poured them more wine.

It's only dinner, Farzan said in a suede-textured voice that would have worked well on the radio. I think you'll like him.

You just met me.

True. Just something about him. And he nodded in agreement with his own words. It wasn't lost on Jules that it must be something about her too.

Drew returned with a stocky, fair-haired man he introduced as Declan, who acknowledged Jules and Farzan with barely a nod, then flopped into an armchair as he commanded Drew:

A drink, sir. Required for civilized conversation.

Jules knew right away that Drew had misfired completely on this one. With his perfectly symmetrical acorn face, Declan was far too at ease with his Irish charm to ever have anything in common with someone as bitter and neurotic as Jules. If she even cared, which of course she didn't.

He took the glass of wine Drew handed him and proceeded to describe the traffic altercation he'd had on the way there. One of those stories in which the storyteller is unquestionably Doing The Right Thing, stopping to let an old lady cross the street, and provoking an Over The Top reaction of crass fury from the driver behind him, a reaction exponentially inflated when the Right-Thing-Doer repeated the Good Deed on the following block. Again, not at a crosswalk, again, holding up the growing line of cars behind, this time for a Mum With Kids. Declan got out of his chair to imitate the apelike strut of the Young Thug who had finally abandoned his Muscle Car to stalk up to the morally pristine driver, call him an asshole and ask him what the fuck he thought he was doing stopping in the fucking middle of the fucking road. At which point the Mum shot the Young Thug a dirty look and rushed her children down the sidewalk while the Right-Thing-Doer only smiled, pointed out that he wasn't the one who'd left his car parked in the middle of the street and drove off with a wave.

Drew and Farzan laughed loudly and drank; Jules smiled politely and drank. Declan noticed and shrugged at her, suddenly humble, like he knew he was a bit much. So she told him, I would have yelled at you too if you'd stopped in front of me like that.

Drew and Farzan laughed even louder, and Declan said, Well, you I would be scared of. Then she did laugh, to her own surprise, right from the belly, head tilted back.

At dinner, with only the four of them at a table that easily sat twelve, Jules found herself directly across from Declan. There was no empty chair, no fifth-place setting. Drew had never expected Rod to show up. Well. Neither had she.

Drew and Rod had first met at the obligatory corporate Christmas party the previous year. Rod thought Drew was too flamboyant. He would never admit it, but his discomfort around gay men in general was obvious. He called them homosexuals, for starters. And Drew found Rod annoying, said he tried too hard. Until he'd had a few drinks, at which point, Jules could only agree, he became intolerably pompous. Either way, boring, Drew said. But he could also be very sweet, and she'd found his oddness a good match to her own, his awkwardness easy to be around. And he was patient with her. Which, after five years of post-David celibacy (and a year and a half of peri-David abstinence), felt like her only chance at any kind of intimacy. She'd cringed when she'd explained this to Rod, hearing the language of her then therapist taking over her words, her thoughts, her self-understanding, and unable to stop it. She had emotional boundaries they would have to negotiate together if they were to navigate the maze towards physical closeness. And Rod, on this their third date, had nodded and kissed her and said good night. And then sent flowers to her at work the following day. Which made her think, I'm forty-five years old, and here's this not totally repulsive, reasonably successful man, a doctor for chrissake, who says he likes me and wants to be with me, what exactly do I think I'm waiting for? A few weeks later they did start sleeping together, and he turned out to be as shy and patient in bed as out.

He wasn't especially handsome, with hair like rough black hay and shirts that were not just out of style but lacking it completely, but he was single and appeared emotionally and financially stable, and she knew that many women, of many ages, would see him as a "catch." But his social skills were a bit off, so it made a kind of sense to her that she would be someone he was interested in. She was impatient and sharp-tongued and knew that some found her abrasive. The first time he had asked her out, she had asked him why. He hadn't even looked surprised at the question but had said she was "pretty smart" (which offended her because she was very smart and didn't need him to tell her so) and funny, which she supposed she could be in an acerbic, cutting sort of way. She'd been under the impression that Rod had no sense of humour, though, so that seemed inadequate as a selling point. But he also said he found her attractive, which wasn't something she'd heard in a long time, and it made her curious enough about this odd, skinny man to see where it would go.

After that first romp, which had been easy and pleasant and not odd at all (both a disappointment and a relief), as he lay beside her on his black silk sheets (okay, maybe a bit odd), he'd murmured sleepily that it was nice to be able to let down his guard. Jules, who felt rather attached to her guard, had stroked his hand and said nothing. She knew he was actually speaking of loneliness, and that was something she understood.

So maybe their relationship lacked a certain fire, maybe he worked a lot of long hours and had to skip the occasional dinner party (not that Jules tried to go to many), and maybe she sometimes missed what he was saying because she had completely tuned out while he was talking. Were any of these things really that much to complain about? At least she wasn't alone.

Except that now, two years later, here she was at a dinner party and she was alone, because Rod had to work, as usual, or maybe he just said that because he didn't like one of her only friends. But either way, here she was. Having dinner with a loud-laughing Irish guy with a sadness in his eyes that unsettled her deeply. Who kept looking at her sideways. Who smoked while she ate.

Arrivals.

———

There she is, Davey. Oh my Lord—she's practically bald!

Amanda's voice sliced through the bustle of the terminal. People turned to look as I leaned against the weight of my duffle and navigated the crowd. You'd think none of them had seen a girl with a buzz cut before. A woman in heels caught my eye and looked me up and down with aggressive distaste. I snarled at her. She looked away quickly.

When I dropped my bag at their feet with a bodily thud, Amanda, five feet tall and muscled like a marathon runner, shocked me with a brisk embrace. I'd always thought she hated me, but she said, Honey, look how gorgeous you are, as David beamed at me, scooped me into a tight bear hug. He felt smaller than I remembered, or maybe I'd never realized how short he really was. His faint smell of old books. I squeezed him back, surprised at my own rush of emotion, how hard it was to let go.

Amanda laughed, a warm chuckle that sounded out of character. I pulled back, embarrassed and ready to scowl at her. But she wasn't laughing at me, she wasn't looking at me at all. I followed her eyes down to the small face that peered up at me from behind David's legs, waiting like a feral kitten to see if I was friend or foe. Well, I was waiting to see too. Dark curls, cherub cheeks. Just way too fucking cute. Easy to hate.

This is your big sister, Char. Chlo.

I blinked in surprise. I'd asked to be called Chlo years ago, but my family customarily either forgot or refused.

C'mere, David said, and reached down for the small hand that was hooked through a belt loop at his hip, trying to draw the kid out from hiding. But she wasn't having any of it and retreated farther behind him.

She's no fool, I said. David laughed, and Amanda bent down to scoop up the child, who then buried her head in her mother's shoulder.

Are you being shy? Amanda asked her redundantly, and David mussed her hair.

THEY TOOK ME to their house in the suburbs of Christchurch. Amanda drove. I sat in the back seat with Char, who stared at me from her car seat. She had a floppy plush dog half her own size on her lap, and together they watched me, my very own panel of judges.

This is Spot, she told me, which was a dumb name for a plain beige dog, but whatever. He's my dog, she added.

Yeah, I said. I gave them a polite smile and turned away to stare out the window. When I glanced back a few moments later, she was sound asleep, which I considered perfect. I'm not much of a kid person.

As we passed through downtown, David catalogued the earthquake damage of the preceding year. The spire had come off the cathedral. The city's tallest structure, a hotel, had been badly shaken, then collapsed, along with a third of the city's buildings. I tried and failed to imagine the city "before," when structures stood firmly and roads ran smoothly. I couldn't picture anything but the wreckage before us.

We were really lucky, David said. Our neighbourhood was

totally flooded, a lot of people we know lost their homes. We just had to fix three picture frames and tear up the driveway.

Don't forget the water damage, said Amanda.

I didn't forget. He turned back to me. We also had some water damage. His eyes went to Char and his whole face softened. He smiled at me and I knew this was a moment when I was supposed to admire his other child, feel affection, smile warmly back at him, but I just didn't have it in me, and what played across my face was grimace at best. David turned back around, but I knew I'd hurt him.

We drove down streets lined with boarded-up windows, signs out front insisting STILL OPEN, passed vacant lots and piles of crumbly rubble. That used to be my favourite bookstore, he said, and that's where I had my last birthday. He talked about where people had been trapped; I saw the row of broken houses where a friend of theirs had been killed. Amanda told me:

Her husband is staying with us. Lance. Their house is gone, so.

We passed a school with a giant pit in the playground, the nearest brick wall collapsing into it; a suburban strip mall, cracked and caving in. Many businesses looked boarded up for good. It was hard not to think about zombie invasions.

David kept enumerating: four major quakes, seventeen thousand aftershocks and counting. The damage to property. The expense.

Lots of people have given up even trying to make repairs, he said. They just can't afford it. He reached across and rested a hand on the back of Amanda's neck.

You never know when the next one's coming. Scary times.

Unseen and exhausted by the sight of them, I looked away.

I'VE HAD NIGHTMARES since I was a kid. The previous summer they'd started to come back, and then in my first few weeks of university they'd gotten much, much worse.

They kept me from sleeping more than an hour at a time. Exhaustion filled my brain like mud. I could barely focus. Language became cryptic. I sat in the backs of classes and labs letting gibberish wash over me, white noise that lulled me to a doze, probably the best sleep I was getting.

Over-the-counter sleeping pills sometimes helped me fall asleep but didn't quiet my subconscious, and imbued the following day with hallucinatory heaviness.

My dreams felt like memories. My memories felt like dreams.

I went to Student Health—a few times—hoping for something stronger, but got laughs, lectures and flat-out nos. Eventually, I lashed out at one of the student doctors and was asked not to return until I'd checked my attitude.

My temper flared, often, resulting in my suspension from the varsity hockey team, a moment of self-sabotage that sent me further spiralling.

I spent a couple weeks in limbo, going for walks to smoke joints down by the lake, drinking cheap red wine alone in my room, going through my stash of weed and sleeping pills, and even the couple Oxy I'd pilfered from Jules. I took to wandering the halls drunk at night, thus completing my alienation from my floormates. If there were other queers on my floor, I never found them, and I became accustomed to the looks of vacant dismissal, the outright sneers. Then there was the telephone call with Jules, during which my mother was clearly, progressively, inebriated. I tried to explain that I was having trouble sleeping and was struggling with school, until she dismissively, drunkenly, declared that I didn't know what it was to have it hard.

I hung up, and the next day, on receiving back my first officially failed math test of my entire life, I went to the office of the registrar and formally withdrew from school.

With my tuition refund in the bank, I had three days to vacate residence. It was October 23, also my birthday, which meant I received my annual email from David, or more precisely from Amanda, with another passing invitation to come visit them in New Zealand. I'd been angry at David for years and had never taken these invites seriously. And now they had a new kid, like they were trying to be some perfect nuclear family, and I wanted no part of it. Except in the secret ways that maybe I did, but I would never tell them that. That night, alone on my birthday, a little stoned, a little desperate, and on a whim, I emailed back: think I need to take a year off before university, would love to come visit but don't have much money. I left it at that, prepared for disappointment. But David himself had replied right away with an offer to help me with the plane fare. It felt like a gift from the universe: a lifeboat. After that, it all just came together.

Except the part about telling Jules, who freaked about the cash.

I opened my eyes and watched David and Amanda chatter at each other in the front seat, their faces soft, the whoosh of the road fogging their words. I thought he had changed. I remembered him, from the years when he'd been working at home and we'd spent a lot of time together, as shadowy and quiet and sad. I had an image of the two of us, when I was eight or nine, reading in the living room as the daylight waned, separately but together, hardly talking until one of us got hungry enough to suggest a pizza. Then watching TV on the couch, and sometimes I would lay my head on his shoulder, and he would wrap his arm around me, usually we watched cop shows, but also anything with spies, until I had to go to bed. I didn't have a lot of friends back then. Still don't. It wasn't like I was anti-social—I played sports, played trumpet in band. I just wasn't close to anyone. Even at hockey, I was the goalie, the oddball of the team. David was my best friend for those few years, and I liked to think that I was his. Certainly, Jules was never there, and if she was, she had her own TV in her own room upstairs.

She would take all her meals there and tell us she was "sucking her thumb up in her nest" if we needed her. Which we never did. Or I never did. Even when David was away for work, it was my babysitter Maureen—Mo-mo—who picked up the slack. But then my dad left—abruptly, when I was thirteen. And now I had to suppose that he probably had needed something from Jules and hadn't been getting it. Maybe he'd needed something from me too.

From the back seat I watched him react to Amanda as he scratched at his beard. His eyes followed her gestures, traced her features as she drove. Amanda's hair was longer and redder than I remembered, her skin already brown with summer tan. She seemed to have relaxed into her life here. But David was *different*. His eyes darted around and he blinked constantly, peered out at the world with the wariness of a balding, slightly stunned, hobbit. He seemed less swaddled in melancholy, like he'd shed several layers of heavy coats and couldn't believe how much lighter he felt, how much more mobile. His movements were quicker, to the point where he was almost twitchy, skittishly waiting for the next calamity to befall him. Where he had once seemed beaten down because of things that had happened, he now seemed anxious about what *might* happen. Until his eyes fell on Char, and stillness filled him. The meaning was clear: now he had something to lose.

Jill had spoken harshly about him, even though they'd never met. She said he was, by definition, an asshole for leaving. I thought it was more complicated than that.

People leave. That's what they do. (Only now seeing the irony in my words.)

With your mum all fucked up like that? Yearly emails? Pathetic. Jill used her cigarette as a pointer, pushing the lit end towards my chest for emphasis.

We'd been sitting out behind the school, in the unofficial smoking area, fall of grade twelve. I could picture her, legs pulled up underneath her oversized hoodie on the concrete bench, her hair a shock of turquoise, half-inch plugs in her earlobes.

I'd grabbed the cigarette out of Jill's hand and hauled on it.

High expectations only lead to disappointment. You study for chem yet?

Your mum is loaded—

They all suck, we've established that.

—and he left her for his booty call.

I rolled my eyes. Who can blame him. It wasn't even a question. You coming to my game?

But the truth was, I blamed him. I blamed him *hard*, and if I was honest about it, I was probably a bit jealous of Amanda. We'd been allies under siege, comrades-in-arms, and then he'd met her and was gone.

Then the kid came along and it all made sense.

I COULD SMELL the gardens before I saw them, a sour apple and honey smell, all sweet mulch and rot. Bordering the torn-open driveway of a bungalow on a suburban cul-de-sac leered eight-foot-tall tentacled flowers, their saturated colours flaring all around us and making my tired eyes ache. Thirty-six hours of airports and airplane food and a confused mishmash of day to night and back again, the abrupt upside-downing of late fall into late spring, and now this final, unearthly arrival—I stopped on the path to the house, swaying under the weight of my bags. Hands took my shoulders with a waft of strong perfume.

Oh, there you go, let me take that from ya, hon. Davey, grab her big bag, it sure looks heavy. Then she was gone again, retrieving the kid from her car seat.

This is our house, I heard Char say.

Yep, we're home, Amanda told her.

DAVID PULLED A plate of leftovers from the fridge in their tiny cottage kitchen: cold roast lamb, bread, potato salad. I dug in, glad Jill wasn't there with her vegan guilt. I could hear Char laughing maniacally somewhere, Amanda making chasing noises. David sat across from me on the polished wooden bench, and I watched him wrestle his attention away from them and bring it to bear on me. He blew out his cheeks behind all his facial hair.

I guess you know your mother isn't very happy, he said finally.

When is she ever.

He worked his jaw in concentration. I worked my teeth on a bit of lamb.

That money was supposed to be for your education.

You would expect his voice to be rough, like his face, but it was kind of high and whiny.

That's exactly what I'm using it for.

She's worried about you.

I snorted. That's a first.

I put down the cleaned lamb bone and pushed my plate away. I was sick to death of living down to people's expectations.

That place was suffocating me. Fucking ivory tower of bullshit.

Char came barrelling into the room, stood in front of me with planted feet, her little round tummy sticking out from beneath a Daffy Duck T-shirt.

Chlo, she said. I was surprised she knew my name.

Yes?

Want to see my room?

I looked up at Amanda, following her daughter into the kitchen, and to her credit she came to my rescue.

Chlo's very tired, Charmin. You can show her later, okay?

I was pretty sure that Charmin was a brand of toilet paper but said nothing. I thought for sure we were in for some waterworks, but then Amanda produced a Popsicle, and the two of them exited through sliding doors to the backyard.

David watched them go, then rubbed his shiny head and sighed, and said he thought he could take a day off this week to show me around town.

I yawned. I'd just seen the town. It was a post-quake shithole, and I didn't need a tour guide.

David kept talking, saying the museum was partially reopened, and that the cathedral was still closed, but, well, did seeing the university interest me?

I sighed and rubbed my eyes. It did not. David's voice rose in pitch.

Well, I have a lot going on right now, but—

Dad.

He caught his breath. Yeah?

Don't worry about it. I sat back in my chair.

David had spotted me frequent flyer points for a good chunk of my round-the-world plane ticket. So, when I'd booked it, I had made Christchurch my first stop. And I had wanted to see him. But right now I couldn't wait to get away from him and his stupid perfect life. My next flight was to Bangkok. Then Delhi, and finally Paris, where I imagined drinking wine with Parisian artists and writing poetry in a tiny garret. Not that I'd ever written poetry, but it sounded good. Then maybe I'd go home and try school again. Or maybe not. But one thing I knew for sure was that Christchurch would be a short visit.

Dinner.

———

Twenty hours earlier and half a world away, Drew toasted his guests:

For making my Friday night so ripe with possibility.

They stood to clink glasses. Jules had to turn her whole body to face Drew, her neck immobilizing her again, even through the haze. Drew's mouth puckered in concern, pale eyebrows way up on his red face.

I'm good.

Jules pulled her sixth-last Oxy out of her pocket, flashed it at him briefly before tossing it back with some water. She felt Declan's scrutiny as she bent her body back into her chair.

Pain in the neck?

You could say that.

What'd you do?

Who knows. Jules waved a dismissive hand. There's always something.

Wow. Oxy. Straight to the good stuff, eh?

Whatever works, eh, Jules? Drew winked at her. He knew she had it under control.

Whatever I can get my hands on, she said.

Amen to that, said Drew. He and Farzan laughed. So did Declan, but his gaze never left hers.

There *are* better ways to manage pain.

Really? Jules said. Are there? She pretended to think for a second, then shook her head. Don't see it. But in truth, she knew the Oxy was excessive. Rod prescribed it for her to deal with her worst flare-ups, but after only a few weeks she was almost done with the latest batch of ninety. Every week she seemed to go through more than the last. Times like this, she pretended it was fun. It wasn't really.

Jules, Declan's an anesthesiologist. Drew gestured with his fork. He's a *doctor.*

She watched a clean, calloused hand tap ashes into an ashtray. Declan had barely touched his game hen. She barked a laugh, appreciating the contradiction:

Medical advice from a doctor who smokes?

His eyebrows twitched in amusement as he took another drag.

For your health, he said, smiling, and crushed the cigarette out.

Oh, well. Thank you.

Jules looked down and poked at her salad with her fork. She felt herself starting to sweat profusely. She pushed her plate away and went to the bathroom to splash water on her face. A few minutes later she heard the music start.

Back in the living room, the lights turned low, Drew and Farzan danced to the mid-nineties comeback hit of an aging face-lifted icon. Jules wasn't much of a dancer, never had been, but with Drew she could always cut loose a little. She bounced and swayed in place next to them, fist pumping as they all shouted the lyrics at top volume, making declarations about survival and love. Declan sat where he had sat earlier, stocky, square frame filling his armchair like a throne. As he lit another cigarette, he caught her eye. He smiled and she wondered if he was laughing at her.

Then Declan got up to dance too, shuffling back and forth, singing along and punching the air with a smoke-trailing hand. He tried to lock eyes with her, to sing a line together, and she suddenly felt self-conscious. Ridiculous. She sat down. Remembered that she wasn't sleeping in her own house that night. Remembered why.

She attempted the mental calculation of time zones and flight durations, but the numbers kept sliding away from her. She wanted to think that Chloe might have emailed or texted her, that they had that kind of relationship where the daughter would update the mother as she travelled, with assurances of well-being. Jules didn't want to think too much about their scene at the airport, and the kind of asshole she'd been. She realized she was getting quite drunk and thought she should get some water. Or some air. But didn't.

She pulled her phone out of her jacket pocket. She had, as a data wrangler, the technology and, as a mother, the inclination to track Chloe through her phone. But there existed several obstacles. The first, and least surpassable, was that Chloe was currently hopping on and off planes and her phone would only ping intermittently over the weekend. The second was that Chloe would never consent to having tracking software on her phone—even her FindPhone was inaccessible to Jules. Third was the more nebulous moral dilemma involving the fact that Jules had the expertise to track Chloe's cellphone without her knowledge but had promised not to, meaning she now approached a moment where she would have to decide whether or not to cross this barrier of air: to keep or to break her word.

When she'd tried to convince Chloe to let her track her phone, Chloe, who claimed she wanted to travel phoneless, had played the Don't You Trust Me card, and Jules had to say that of course she did. The truth that she trusted no one completely was irrelevant. They had negotiated: Chloe would bring her cellphone, she would keep it functional by purchasing SIM cards and she would text and/or email regularly. That'll have to be good enough, Jules, and you *know* why.

She did know why (You use your powers for evil, Chloe had

once yelled), but it didn't make it easier, in fact it made it more difficult, to now be faced with either waiting for Chloe to get in touch or tracking her clandestinely. The icons and words on her phone's screen blurred and floated. She squinted harder, seeking pixelated filial breadcrumbs.

If the music had been playing on vinyl, she would have heard a dramatic record scratch.

Jules, Jules, Jules. She looked up to see Drew looming over her, shaking his head in mock despair. Farzan and Declan stood behind him, grinning like teenagers.

She couldn't help laughing. What?

Somehow, Farzan slipped in past Drew and out again with Jules's phone in his hand.

She's on *Socialink*.

The chorus of extreme dramatic gasping made her laugh harder.

Like this is somehow shocking in this day and age? Can I have my phone back, please?

No way, said Drew.

I'll take that, said Declan, plucking the phone from Farzan's fingers and sliding it into his front pants pocket. He patted the suggestive lump it made. You know where to find it.

Really? You're going with lewd?

I am, yes. He winked at her. She felt her face burn.

Don't you like us? Farzan teased her, grinning. It's playtime! He opened his arms and shimmied his shoulders.

Jules, laughing, tried to be serious. Drew, please tell these people I have an analytics due Monday.

A collective groan.

You have got to be kidding me. Drew shook his head. On a Friday night? At *my house*?

You need to *relax*, said Farzan as Drew started the music up again. They began grinding into each other, raunchy, playful, more than a little awkward. Jules put an exasperated look on her face and watched them from the couch. Declan was back to his shuffling, saw her watching and gave a little shimmy. She crossed her arms at him and shook her head in mock disapproval. But she was also laughing, and he giggled like a kid.

She wasn't an idiot. It was obvious Drew was trying to set her up with Declan. But she was with Rod, and Rod was fine, they were somewhat committed, she loved him. Who was this guy? Some coarse and arrogant "funny man" who smoked like a crematorium? No thanks.

And yet.

She was aware that he was aware that she was watching him. She looked away every time he glanced over.

Oh so nonchalantly, whistling silently, Farzan changed the music: eighties indie Brit rock, totally undanceable, still the most convincing ploy yet to get her back on her feet. Her ass had grown roots in the couch, though, and she stood her ground. Sat her ground. She mouthed words about feeling dead while you're still alive, and her foot twitched to the murky rhythm. But she stayed put. The others were all yelling out lyrics, and again Declan opened his arms wide to Jules, tried to get her up. Jules laughed but shook her head. At this point she was a bit afraid that if she tried to get up, she might fall over. Best not to find out the hard way. She leaned her head onto the back of the couch and watched her friends and Declan through slitted eyes, expecting the show to continue, reliable as TV. But Declan stopped, dropped onto the couch next to her and pulled an ashtray onto his knee for his current smoke. Drew had said he was the only one ever allowed to smoke in his house, and only on special occasions. Jules didn't think tonight was so special. But it wasn't her house.

It's the mixture that makes you lethargic, Declan said.

The music was loud. Jules had to play back the words in her head.

Oxy and alcohol, he said.

I'm not lethargic. And my neck still hurts. So, without that . . . She spread her hands to indicate the dire possibilities, hoping it would ward off the oncoming judgment.

I have to tell you. He smiled, but sadly. You're ripping yourself off.

He leaned into her as he spoke, and Jules knew she was supposed to ask what he meant, but she knew what he meant, and she didn't want to talk about it. She could tell by his persistent exuberance that he wanted to tell her to embrace life, to try to feel more, not less, and she didn't want to go there. Not with him, not at all. That was the whole point. She'd watched her own mother's slow decline, trudging from one night shift to the next, weighed down by the chronic pain of bad hips, bad knees, borderline poverty, relentless life. This, without question, was better than that.

The couch on her other side caved in as Drew sank into it. He took a small box out of a drawer under the coffee table, removed from it a tiny plastic bag filled with white powder and a mirror the size of Jules's cellphone. He leaned his bulk over the coffee table and began to divide some of the powder into skinny rows like tiny banks of new snow.

In her final years, Jules's mother had joined some sort of independent evangelical church. A week after her final stroke, the one that killed her, Jules had gone to the sparse room in the nursing home, with its picture of her church leader on the dresser, and gone through the skinny file of financials, only to discover her mother had given away basically all of her money. She liked to make offerings, the nurse told Jules. Apparently, she thought it would help her recovery.

Drew handed a short straw to Declan, who gave Jules a twinkling smile and said, What the fuck, as he put it to his nose and inhaled a line.

Jules shook her head, thinking of her mother's sagging single bed, the lone frayed armchair, the grey, grey room. This is it? she'd asked the orderly. Where's all her stuff? The orderly had shrugged, embarrassed. She hadn't had much. What she'd had, she'd given away. It was exactly what Jules had been working her whole life to avoid: being old and sick and alone. She hadn't said it aloud, but something must have shown on her face. You can't take it with you, the orderly had said.

Carpe diem! Farzan said, snorting the third line of coke. He handed Jules the straw, moved the mirror closer to her. She hesitated. Not only had she never done cocaine, she'd never snorted anything. She knew Drew did this kind of thing all the time, but this was the first time he'd pulled it out in front of her. He reached over now and squeezed her knee.

Trust me, honey, this'll kick Oxy's ass.

The burning in her sinus lasted mere seconds. She felt like she could do anything.

Sink.

———

I woke up choking in a panic, my tongue crazy-glued in place, gums swollen, throat blocked, I couldn't breathe, couldn't call for help, I lashed out wildly and blindly—and woke up with a frantic gasp.

Daylight.

The dream was a variation on a theme, something terrible happening that I couldn't stop, I couldn't get a breath, couldn't get a grasp, and there were voices, too distant to help, too busy to hear. There was a time my parents had sent me to a psychologist, who'd spent a series of Tuesday mornings talking about childhood traumatic grief and survivor guilt, while I, at age seven and a half, lay on his couch thinking about hockey. Even then, I knew the spiel: the baby had simply died, no one knew why or could have prevented it, and no one could or did blame me for anything. I thought it was more complicated than that: something was broken in our house and I didn't know how to fix it.

But I also knew—now—that it was simple. I had control issues. Abandonment issues. Parental issues. Who didn't?

Which is why, after following a metallic racket to find a gunk-blackened David over a clogged drain in the kitchen, giving him a wide berth and going in to use his computer, I fired off an email to Jules that said—

In Christchurch. Plane didn't crash. Chlo.

—in the full expectation that Jules would not even notice the hostility, because she never listened.

Conversely, it was also why, when I opened David's web browser, I set up a user shell, so I could browse privately. No history, no trackers. Nothing flagged. Not because I was worried about David looking at what I had been doing. I doubted he even had the skills to trace my interweb activity. No, it was because of Jules that I was diligent about using stealth online. Privacy settings meant nothing where she was concerned. She paid sporadic attention to what I did, but just that she could see anything and everything—and had, once, by prying into my Socialink account, an unbelievably creepy violation that still made me seethe—was enough to instill paranoia.

It was, incidentally, how she'd found out about Jill, after which she'd fought hard to put a tracker app on my phone. I'd flat-out refused, but the discussion resulted in a hole in the drywall roughly the size of my foot. In retaliation, she forbade sleepovers at our house, even though I stayed over in Jill's basement bedroom most weekends. Guess that's over, I thought, as a memory hit me in the chest like a basketball: sitting face to face with Jill on her bed as she stripped off her tank top, her tube-thin freckled arms and chipped black nail polish, her wicked mischief grin in the light of a dozen candles.

Not under my roof, Jules had said, claiming Jill's gender had nothing to do with it. She might as well have said, Not while I'm home, though, since there were always hours after school when I had the house to myself, and Jill came over every day. We would smoke a joint and fool around on the living room couch, watch whatever videos were going around on Socialink, do our home- work together and fool around some more. Then she would go home for dinner, and by the time Jules came in the door, I'd be watching TV in my pyjamas, or in bed with my laptop. But it didn't matter now. That was over too.

My Socialink newsfeed informed me that my ex-girlfriend had been tagged in "Rachel H's Photos." I clicked on the first thumbnail, which was how I learned that Jill had already moved on, because there she was, shimmying up behind the improbably pretty Rachel—both hands on Rachel's hips, Rachel's butt pressed into Jill's pelvis, two big grins hamming for camera. Jill in her favourite Led Zeppelin T-shirt. It was a bit much.

But it wasn't a surprise. I knew Rachel. She'd gone to our high school, and even though she typically dated guys from her own, extremely fashion-conscious social set, I had been convinced for the last year that she and Jill had a crush on each other. They were both ridiculous flirts, which Jill would try to use as proof that that's all it was. But I just knew there was more to it than that. And when I found out Rachel and Jill would be going to the same university, I kind of lost my shit. I didn't mean to be like that. I hated being the jealous girlfriend. But all of a sudden Jill was texting with Rachel, talking to Rachel on the phone, going for coffee to talk about what it might be like at their new school. And I found myself going through her phone when she was in the bathroom, jumping to conclusions when she was fifteen minutes late, unable to stop myself from drilling her with questions when she finally showed up. I even followed her once, not believing she just had a dentist appointment. (She did.) It was mid-August when Jill finally told me that Rachel had invited her to be roommates, and that Jill had agreed. I was suspicious, but not surprised.

Isn't that a bit last-minute? I'd asked her.

She said, No, not really, but she'd looked so pained, so scared and guilty, that I just knew:

You've been planning this the whole time.

I wasn't sure—

When did you decide to be roommates?

I didn't want you to be mad.

You registered for residence in *May*. Did you know then?

Chlo, she's the only other person I know that's going there.

So that's a yes. Have you had sex already?

What? No!

The rest of the summer was grey with the tension between us. We went off to our separate schools and, after a few weeks of ugly unravelling, broke up.

Wallowing in misery but refusing to cry, I clicked through her photos, looking for the moment when things had somehow slipped out of place, our connection misaligned. At what point had I stopped trusting her?

I clicked on a picture from earlier in the summer. We'd done mushrooms and spent an afternoon wandering along the Mountain Brow, the edge of the hundred-metre escarpment that split our hometown in two. We'd sat on a low stone wall smoking joints, the whole of downtown laid out before us and Lake Ontario beyond, and watched the fires from the few still-active steel foundries in the north end make tracers on the sky above, the lights of the handful of skyscrapers blinking secret messages at us as dusk crept down. We had laughed so hard my cheeks had cramped, my stomach muscles ached. Everything felt loose and easy, our connection even more psychic than usual, the world within our grasp and our mistakes without consequence. In my memory it was almost dark as we floated back through the residential streets to Jill's house. Jill's parents had been away, her sister out at some party, and we'd had hours of raucous, hilarious sex on the living room floor. All in all, one of the summer's best days. One of our last best days together.

But I did the math: she'd already known, that day, that she'd be rooming with Rachel. Did she already think they might get together?

There were other pics, and I clicked through them in a daze. But I knew what I knew.

I shut down the computer. Thought, not for the first time, Fuck you, JJ.

So apparently I also had girlfriend issues. *Ex*-girlfriend issues.

DAVID'S HEAD WAS still under the sink as I slipped out the sliding doors to the patio. I slumped on a bench at the picnic table. The backyard was at least fifty metres deep, loomed over on all sides by an army of carnivorous-looking plants that threatened to consume the tent someone had pitched at the back, a human infringement in an alien world. A blue child-sized car was abandoned in the middle, like the Mars Rover after the mission had returned to Earth.

The late sun was a searing red ball. I leaned my elbows on my knees and stared at nothing.

You must be Chloe, then.

Flip-flops and ropy legs, sharp bike-short tan lines, glaring pale thighs and tighty-whiteys. A large brown bottle in one hand, two glasses in the other. A smoke between his teeth.

Chlo, yeah.

Lance, he said, stepping up to sit on the picnic table. I moved up to sit beside him and get his balls out of my face. He handed me a glass of beer, and as we clinked our glasses together I remembered Amanda saying her friend had lost his house in the earthquake. And his wife.

So that's your tent?

Yep. He lit one cigarette from the stub of another and nodded slowly. Till my house is rebuilt.

I recognized him then. Not him, but the tone of his voice, the slackness of his face. I took a deep, slow breath, felt my chest inflate with emptiness. I wanted to say more but knew the triteness of words.

The world tilted.

I lurched to catch my balance, grabbing the edge of the table as it started to shake, the beer bottle shuddering across it, a deep rumbling like an underground train threatening to burst through the surface. Lance caught the bottle. Something smashed in the kitchen behind us.

Just a glass! David called out.

It was over in a matter of seconds. My heart pounded, my whole body flooded with adrenalin like I'd slipped on a cliff edge and almost gone over it.

Fuck. So I guess that's an aftershock?

Ah, your first one! Lance said.

He produced a joint from somewhere on his brief-clad person—it was best not to think about where—and licked it.

Feels like the end of the world, hey, he said, lighting up.

Yeah, kinda. I tried to laugh, still catching my breath.

Lance drew in smoke and held it.

In fact, I'd spent weeks feeling like my world was crumpling in around me like a paper bag, and this moment, following actual planetary shaking, was one of exhilaration and relief, vertigo turned to glee.

Chlo! The high voice preceded running footsteps, and Amanda's louder voice.

Lance! For god's sake, put some pants on.

Amanda came out of the house with a shopping bag. Char came running up to me, then got suddenly shy and stopped, staring at us. Lance had disappeared his joint and raised his glass to me.

I'm offending sensibilities. Hey, Char-bar, he said, and she climbed up to sit between us, held on to his arm. She looked like a zombie who'd feasted on someone's chocolate throat.

Did you have some ice cream? Lance asked her.

Char gaped at him in astonishment. Yeah! How did you know that?

Someone swam all by herself today, Amanda told us with an expression that was both wry and proud. She let go of the side of the pool and made it the whole way across.

Aw yeah! That definitely deserves ice cream!

It's been a thing, Amanda said to me.

But how did you *know* about the ice cream? Char had grabbed

Lance's leg and was leaning way up into his face. I appreciated her tenacity.

It's all over your face, I told her.

Char turned away from Lance as she remembered I was there, and scrutinized me for a long moment, leaning in close.

What's on *your* face? Char countered, trying and failing not to smile.

Uh, my nose?

Char's eyes went wide and she looked at Lance to see if he'd heard it too. He was grinning at her. She looked back at me with a big smile and laughed like a maniac.

Here, Chlo. Amanda handed me a small package. Is that the right kind? But she didn't wait for an answer, she went back into the house to reprimand David for the mess.

What's that? Char asked.

It's a SIM card, I said. I turned the packaged phone chip over in my hands. It's so I can use my cellphone in New Zealand.

It was exactly what I'd requested, but after seeing Jill's photos, I didn't want any contact with my former life. Not even a little bit.

A fat bee flew by my chin, circling. I reflexively planned a route to the EpiPen in my toiletry case.

So, how long you here, then? Lance asked.

I rolled my eyes and shrugged. Not too long.

Heh, said Lance, like he knew exactly what I meant.

I tracked the bee as it bumbled from bloom to bloom, down past the tent at the back of the yard.

Chlo? Char was searching my face for something, who knew what.

Yes, Char?

Wanna see my room?

Porch.

Drew had a backyard with a pool, dry now for the season. Motion activated lights as they stepped outside. Summer had sent a damp breath from the past, and leaves plastered the wooden deck. Somehow Jules found herself standing next to Declan, very close, as he passed her a joint. Their fingers touched.

Now the health expert smokes, he said quietly.

Totally different, she said. Medicinal.

Drew caught her eye and winked at her. He and Farzan had pulled out a couple of chairs from the patio table, and Farzan had his feet on Drew's lap.

Better than that other shit, for sure. What doc is even giving you that?

My, um . . . Rod. You don't know him, she added, cringing inwardly. Her mouth had gone dry. She told herself it was from the pot and the coke and took a deep drink of her wine.

Rod? Not Rod Scott? Julie—

That's her boyfriend, Drew interjected, and Declan closed his mouth and nodded.

Jules. It's Jules. Boyfriend? Really?

Amidst laughter, Declan put up a defensive hand.

My bad, he said. *Julie* doesn't have a *boyfriend*. *Jules* got a *lovah*.

Sounds so dirty when you say it like that, she said.

44

The truth was, Rod's bashful and restrained bedside manner had become, in the context of actual bed, more annoying than comforting, like he thought she was some fragile paper sculpture that he might crush. But Jules had a hard-enough time feeling, and his delicate touch just made him seem far away, like a timid knock on her fortress wall. It also didn't help that, if she was honest about it, Rod wasn't really the same person she'd met two years ago.

Do you love him, though? Declan was asking now.

Jules blinked at the sudden turn from joking to probing. She shrugged. I don't know. He's okay. I don't know yet. Why are we talking about this?

There was an awkward beat during which Jules started to sweat again, and then Drew was leading Farzan by the arm into the house.

Jules's daughter just left to go backpacking, he said over his shoulder as they passed. She has an empty nest.

Jules thought about Chloe, the previous morning, dragging her ridiculous duffle bag out to the car. Her gaze drifted up into the void beyond the glare of the porch light.

Eventually Declan said quietly, An empty nest. So you don't live with your not-boyfriend or unloved lover.

A car alarm, blocks away, stopped, making her wonder when it had begun. The sky became bigger and blacker, and their island of light felt warm and close, the only bright spot in a universe of night. She sighed.

Nope. Now it's just me.

Just the one kid?

Jules's lips folded in on themselves, her jaw tensed, an ingrained reflex of thought suppression. She nodded, tried to stay in the moment.

Europe or something?

What? Oh god. I wish. New Zealand, and then who the hell knows. She's "only a text away," though. So.

She folded her arms over her chest.

But, she added, shrugging and at a loss.

Declan moved around and leaned on the deck railing, facing Jules. Shook out another smoke.

Sounds like you're worried about her.

Does it? I guess I just don't know what she might do.

Oh yeah?

The porch light was hitting Declan's face at a sharp angle. He looked sinister and strangely beautiful. Jules swallowed.

People can be unpredictable, he said.

There'd been a time, way back at the beginning of it all, when Jules had felt like she knew Chloe, inside and out. When she'd sat with her for hours in the evenings when her own work was done, revelling in their shared love: math. Even at age four, when she could barely read, Chloe knew her numbers, could count to a hundred and was getting the hang of basic addition, counting it out on her short little fingers. By the time she was six, she was learning her times tables. Jules was entranced by Chloe's curiosity, her excitement at finding a solution, her satisfaction at understanding the basic rules. She had watched her daughter learn and been filled with love and awe.

There followed complicated years when life had intervened, and distance and walls had grown between them, but even though Chloe was not an easy teenager to live with, Jules had always assumed a certain consistency, that her daughter was still the child she'd known.

When Chloe met Jill, her flannel pants had torn away, her button-downs had come untucked, revealing ripped jeans and vintage rock T-shirts like a secret identity. She started to go out on weekends, came home late and spent evenings chatting online in her room. She wanted more money for her cellphone. She smiled more—never at Jules, but still.

At a low point she could barely bring herself to recall, Jules had back-doored into Chloe's social media account to figure out what had brought about these changes—was it simply adolescence? should she be worried?—and she'd seen pictures that made her more curious rather than less. Pictures of Chloe and a pierced, turquoise-headed girl around her age. Jill, she knew now. And in the photos, Chloe looked like a different person, one Jules barely recognized: she looked *happy*. She'd tried to casually ask Chloe who she was hanging out with, but her daughter had seen right through it, started spitting livid words about "violated privacy." Which was true. Jules winced at the memory and shoved it aside. What mattered was that Chloe so obviously starting to thrive had been a sign that things could change: a lifeline for Jules. Even if it meant her daughter wanted less to do with her than ever. Even if Jill was flaky, a bad influence and sometimes mean.

Jules felt herself getting maudlin, which was annoying, so she turned the tables.

What about you? You have kids, or a partner?

Smoke plumed and dissipated.

Nah, Julie. No partner.

Jules took a stab at the dark. But . . . you did?

Declan nodded. She fought for a long time. Until . . . she just couldn't.

Something resonated in Jules, underground thunder vibrating in her bones. A distant awareness of profound loss, buried somewhere underneath all the layers, all the years, of drugs, depression and denial.

She moved around to lean on the railing next to him, putting him on the side away from the pain in her neck.

That how you met Drew? She knew Drew still went to a grief support group.

Aye, he said, a soft almost-growl. They both held the rail that supported them, the edges of their hands barely touching. They stood in silence for more than a minute. Then Declan said quietly, Drew thinks it's time I moved on.

Clearly, they both knew Drew had arranged this.

And what do you think? In a way that could have seemed inadvertent but wasn't, and not even sure herself what she thought she was doing, she leaned on her hand so that it pressed into his more firmly. Just a little.

And he didn't pull away, but he didn't answer, either. He never got a chance. The back door opened, and when Rod stepped through it, they both dropped their hands from the rail.

Neptune.

W hen a kid invites you to see their room, it's like being invited into their mind: you have to pay it the reverence it's due. And you can't say no. Unless you hate the kid. Which I apparently didn't.

As Char took my hand and led me through the house to her room, Amanda called out that I shouldn't judge her by its state because she tidied it every evening but then Char happened every morning. I heard Lance telling her she should just blame it on the earthquakes.

The room was a mess, but I'd seen worse. I thought it was probably genetic.

Stuffed animals crawled over piles of books and blankets, and the dog I'd met earlier (Spot) sat at a toy piano. A princess castle dominated one corner, which made my lip curl a little, but the whole centre of the room was cleared to make room for a pad of paper as long as Char when she lay down beside it.

Sit down here, Chlo. She pointed to a spot beside her. I moved to sit close by. No, not there. Here.

Okay, I laughed. I'll do what I'm told.

Yes, she said. Here, you can draw with this colour. She handed me a blue crayon. Over there, she said, pointing to one corner of the paper.

Okay, I said. Not really knowing how to act around kids, I found her instructions quite helpful. What should I draw?

Char looked up at me for a few seconds, thinking. Can you draw . . . a dog?

I think so. What kind of dog?

Um . . . the kind that rescues people.

I looked at her, remembering the torn-apart buildings of this city she lived in. That's bleak, kid.

She nodded.

Okay. And what are you going to draw?

She looked down at the paper and started sketching a shape in purple. I'm going to draw our spaceship, she said.

Our spaceship?

Yes. We're going to go to Neptune.

I froze, watching her, a whorl of forces scrapping it out in my brain, my chest, my stomach. Love, kinship, jealousy, resentment, fear. At Char's age I had a favourite game, invented by me and my father. He would smooth out the sand in the sandbox in our backyard and draw a rocket ship in it, big enough for us to sit inside its outline, me in between his legs, and Lizzie, a few months old, propped up between mine. He'd already taught me the names of all the planets, we'd paint them together, uneven splotches of colour across a page in the order of their distance from the sun. Neptune was our favourite destination, the beautiful purple-blue jewel that called to us, invited us to go as far as we could, and then farther. David would make some sound effects while I narrated our trip through the galaxy and Lizzie giggled and gurgled in my arms. I knew he would look after us, and we would both look after her, and we would adventure together every minute we could before he went away again for work. And then it would just be me, keeping my sister safe.

Char looked up from the very not-aerodynamic shape she'd drawn, saw my blank corner of the page. You're not drawing, she said. Draw! But I couldn't.

I left her there looking confused, and I felt even worse. But I wasn't about to get too attached.

THE PRESSURE FROM Amanda didn't help.

I knew she was just trying to make me feel welcome, but her approach was all wrong. First there was the conversation where she asked me if I would babysit while she ran errands.

I don't babysit, I told her, thinking of Mo-mo and how that turned out.

But she's your sister.

I barely know her. I'm not good with kids.

Well, you'll have to learn sometime.

Why?

Don't you want kids of your own?

No.

You'll change your mind.

I don't *like* kids, I finally said.

But she's your *sister*.

And maybe I would have caved, just to be nice. The truth was, I found it hard not to like Char. But then Amanda called her in from the backyard, where she was terraforming with her mini-bulldozer, to the kitchen where I sat reading at the table.

Wouldn't you like Chlo to stay and play with you while Mummy goes out for a little while? As she talked, she bent over, wrapped her arms around her daughter and nuzzled her face into her curls.

Char's face lit up. I closed my book.

I wish I could, I lied. But I'm still so jet-lagged. And I went to the guest room and shut the door, trying not to hear my half-sister crying in the kitchen.

I felt bad, but I hate being manipulated.

SECOND WAS OUR conversation when we went out for dinner the next night:

Well, *I* think education is very important. Amanda had Char on the seat next to her and watched her colour as she spoke, but her words were clearly aimed at me.

Now she's in the school of life, Lance said. Seeing the world and all that.

David, dragged away from his ongoing kitchen-sink project, rubbed at his forearm where he'd missed a spot of dirt.

Remember the last time we saw her, Davey? She was, what, fifteen?

I can't believe how grown-up you are, David agreed as he inspected his other arm.

She had those chubby cheeks, and such pretty hair. Amanda lightly pinched Char's cheeks as she said it, making her giggle and squirm away. Then Amanda eyed my bleached brush cut. Hope it grows in okay.

That's what hair does. It grows.

Amanda tugged a few of Char's curls as though unsure.

Part of the whole gay thing, right? David could have been confirming the weather.

What? I choked out.

The haircut, David clarified.

I gaped at him while I searched for words.

Amanda was still scrutinizing me. Should I take you shopping for clothes?

What's wrong with my clothes?

No need to have you in ratty T-shirts all the time.

I looked at Char, who seemed to have nothing but pink in her wardrobe. But she also had untameable black hair and a tummy no T-shirt could contain, and was never unmarred by streaks of Magic Marker and her latest meal. Amanda clearly chose her wardrobe, but Char resisted with all available materials.

You have such a nice figure, sweetie. Don't you want to show it off?

I stood and drained the end of my pint. I needed to get out of there. Out of the pub, out of their house, out of this fallen-down town.

I need some air, I said as I not-quite-slammed my glass down, grabbed Lance's cigarettes from the table and walked towards the door.

Chlo!

I kept going but heard Amanda behind me asking why I couldn't take a compliment.

Outside, I lit a smoke and looked up into the sky at the completely unfamiliar stars. The air even sounded different here. No bass drum of distant highway. The crickets sang a half-tone high. My head rushed with nicotine, a free fall of galactic disorientation. My heart pitched. I leaned against the wall and stared at the empty parking lot, trying not to hyperventilate.

I'll have one of those, said David, settling in beside me. I gave him a smoke. I don't usually, he said. I quit. But. Special occasion. He inhaled deeply.

It was a quiet night, but maybe all nights here were quiet. The Firkin Forget It was squished between two other shops on a tiny parking lot. A single car went by in a breath. Faint laughter and old rock gave the pub a heartbeat.

David stared at the woods across the road. She's just trying to be nice, he said.

Stepping away, I kicked an army boot at a crack in the asphalt. I know, I said. But you could all try a little less. A tiny shard flew off and bounced against the pub's wall.

Next door was a hastily boarded-up bakery. Nice Buns, said a dangling sign.

It hasn't been easy, though, this past couple years, I'll tell you that. The quakes have us all walking a tightrope, twenty-four-seven. And with Char to worry about. Every moment is just . . . waiting.

Graffiti-marred boards in angry red, partially blacked out: *God H---s F--s.* I shivered in my leather jacket.

Could be the next big one, sure, David was saying, as though I'd asked. Or could just be all the books falling off the shelves again. Or maybe the ground opens up one morning, just by dumb luck right under where you're standing. And you know it could happen, because it's happened to . . . He waved a hand around. People we know.

He rubbed his bald head, looked tired and sunken. But somehow, Amanda and Char are always this good thing I find at the end of the day, that tells me I'm still here. Still waiting. But still here.

I heard his adoration, and his terror that something might happen to his little girl. The fault lines in his voice as he thought about the happiness that he needed to protect, and the people who shared in that happiness, who made it possible.

He paused to take a long drag off his half-finished smoke before stamping it out. Terrible things. But something's gonna kill me, right?

He stared down the road into the darkness. I pulled my eyes away from him, looked back at the bakery. Spidery cracks of windowpane crept out from behind the boards and terrified me.

David searched the ground, mustering. I'm really happy to have you here, kid.

Um. Yeah, me too. I'm happy to be here, Dad. To . . . see you.

But as I said it, I knew it was a lie, and realized I wasn't at all happy to be there, in a place so insidiously hostile.

It hurt, in fact, that David would want me there, in such a place. It hurt to be around him and to feel so disappointed in him. He'd historically been the soft parent, steady and reliable, holding my hand as we walked to the store, obediently driving me to hockey practices. Jules, by contrast, was the storm front that regulated our lives, filling every horizon with roiling dark clouds and forks of fire whenever she was home, a humid and heavy vacuum of anticipation when she wasn't.

I'd thought David would thrive in his new life, burst out in colour like the Dr. Seuss flowers in his yard. But looking at him now, shoulders rolled forward from a submissive life, I wondered if he was just weak.

A memory chased itself across my brain, Jules's voice thick and wet and threatening to burst, *Are you really that spineless*, the lower buzz of David responding, barely interrupting her messy and deteriorating rant about the time she'd had to spend alone with me, alone with a dead baby, alone in the house when he should have been there with her. Jules slamming out of their bedroom, the door bouncing in its frame. David on the edge of the bed with his head in his hands.

I shifted around him to go back inside the pub, to move past this moment.

I'll really try for that day off, and we can do something. Whatever you like. Hey, I don't even *know* what you like.

I sucked in a deep breath. I need to go, Dad, I said.

Go?

Yeah. Like, *go*.

I saw his face start to fall, saw him catch it before it hit the ground.

But he said, Okay, and heaved the pub door open, attempted an awkward arm around me as I squeezed past him.

It's okay, kid.

I saw that he meant it, in fact I sensed his relief, that the pressure my presence caused would soon be easing.

As I went back inside, the world tilted and rocked.

I DREAMED ABOUT Lizzie, as I so often did. The sister that wasn't. The sister that was. The sister who haunted me, aging in parallel, skipping around time in my mind:

There she is as a baby, gurgling in the air, in my father's upstretched arms, spitting and drooling as he brings her to his face—

I stand on the porch and hold her hand as we watch a cab drive our father away. I look at Lizzie, imagined as a fairer version of my tweeny self, shorter and girlier, already showing curves I still don't have, but also bookish, a tight ponytail and glasses, plastic dolphin earrings dangling, and she smiles a crooked smile at me. Could have been you, she says—

Carpet, scratchy as grass, prickles the backs of my legs, the wall behind my head as immovable as stone, my mother sitting on the floor of her bedroom while my grandpa and my grandma Nan stand over her. She shouldn't see you like this.

If my mother raises her head, she could meet my eyes.

I try to call out, I have something to tell her, but panic blooms as my throat closes, my lungs rattle their cage—

I woke gasping and sat straight up. My body pounded with my heart. The old clock radio was buzzing, insistently. It was 4:34 in the morning and I felt like shit.

The house was quiet. Lance would be up soon, but I had some time before we left—we both needed out of there. I dressed in the dark, padded to the kitchen and poured myself a glass of water. I slid open the door to the backyard and stepped out, anticipating cool mulch smells and crickets, wincing instead in the sudden glare. A motion-controlled light made sharp bed-headed shadows of the grass. I sat on top of the picnic table and tried to become invisible until the comfort of darkness blinked back. Moon- and city-glow dimmed all but the brightest stars. The silver fly of Lance's tent shone like a ghost.

One thing my dad and Amanda both needed to understand: I knew how to look after myself. I'd been doing it long enough. Jill called it Selective Parenting. Most of the time Jules didn't give a shit. I did my own groceries, my own laundry, got myself to school, arranged my own rides for hockey, and had since the day David left when I was thirteen. And other than the ban on sleepovers with Jill, I had a lot of freedom: I never had a curfew, I got a weekly allowance for food and clothes, and Jules had no say in it when I came home with my hair dyed black and blue in grade eleven. (In fact, when she saw it, she just rolled her eyes and kept watching TV.) Or when I got my tongue pierced in grade twelve. (Try not to drool, dear. And when I took it out because I was drooling too much: See? You should always listen to your mother.) But it also led me to joke—in that funny-because-of-how-true-it-is way—that my mother would rather take the Benz to a car wash than watch one of my hockey games.

That was one good thing I had to say about David. In the years before he left, he never missed a game or a school concert, and even managed to drag Jules out to one once. It wasn't his fault she answered a work call at full volume in the middle of Marci's trumpet solo; he still got major points for effort. After that, I figured it was better if she didn't come. But it still hurt that she never even wanted to. Then David had just left. Jules was in another world, and now he was on the opposite end of this one. At first he wrote, called, tried to keep up regular contact, but after a couple of years of my tepid responses, he'd basically given up, his efforts tapering off to Christmas and my birthday. It wasn't supposed to happen like that. He was supposed to read into my silence, sense my anger and pain, and respond to it. But he didn't. I'd been sulking and it backfired. And now I had become peripheral. A stranger in his house. An intruder in his life.

WITH A RUSTLE of cloth and the soft scrape of a zipper, Lance emerged from the tent at the back of the yard. He approached the house, re-triggered the security light and shielded his face from the glare. He was fully dressed. He dropped his hand as his eyes adjusted, saw me and nodded.

Ready already? His voice was low and rough, misshapen from sleep. He had a knapsack over his shoulder, smokes in his hand.

Couldn't sleep.

Lance nodded, dropped his smokes and knapsack on the table, went into the house. He reappeared with a brown bottle and two glasses.

One for the road, yeah? He poured us both some beer.

Bit early. But I took a glass.

Heh. Heard that before. Could be part of the problem, I s'pose.

He moved to sit beside me. I side-eyed his profile. I wondered if he had nightmares about his wife dying. When I'd re-entered the pub the night before, swaying to yet another aftershock, Amanda had been telling Lance it was time to get his shit together.

You seem fine to me.

He did his customary half-snort laugh, like things were equal parts funny and sad and he couldn't believe no one else saw it.

Yeah. Well.

His gaze fixed in an outward-inward stare of psychic scab-picking.

We all deal with loss in our own ways, I said. This was the main thing—really the only thing—I remembered from grief therapy. But it was a big one.

Lance's eyes flashed, but I couldn't tell where he looked or what he saw. You know something about it?

I thought about Lizzie, and how much of my life was scaffolded around her memory, and nodded.

Anyway. You should meet my mum. Cheers.

Lance tapped my glass with his, swallowed a mouthful of beer. Your mum's a boozer?

Among other things. When I was a kid, she was a real mess. After Lizzie.

Lizzie?

My baby sister. She died.

He looked at me for a long moment, I could see him in the corner of my eye, but I kept staring into the depths of the garden.

I did not know that, he said.

Yeah. What I didn't say was that after David left, it seemed like Jules had managed to put some of her pieces back together, to become more functional as a person if not as a parent. But when I got home from university, I was alarmed at how quickly she had reverted. Now it seemed that maybe the intervening years had been just that—an intermission from a life of sedation, rather than a period of sedation in an otherwise engaged life. But I didn't get into that with Lance.

Nor did I mention the guilt that weighed me down, even now.

A whispering crowd of flower heads on skeletal stems shifted in the night garden, pockets of deep black darting through with the breeze. It was time to get out of there.

So . . . Where's your boat?

Aw, Kiri's boat, yeah? 'Bout an hour's drive. You sure you wanna come?

After a quick imagining of how Jules would have reacted (Oh, an overnight ocean sail with a virtual stranger in a foreign country? That sounds safe.) I'd packed my bags before going to bed.

Oddly, the one thing that gave me pause was Char. She would probably be disappointed, but I reasoned she was better off without me.

So I told Lance: Oh, I'm sure.

Aw, go on, then. Grab your gear.

Bed.

———

I'm tired, said Jules. My neck hurts.

Alright. Rod slid his hand out from under her shirt, rolled over, took his glasses off and turned out the light on his side of the bed.

Jules was left in the light from her own bedside lamp, a circle of yellow cut out of the dark hotel room, making the walls seem close, the shadows cavernous.

Already, Rod appeared to be asleep. She shouldn't be surprised. He had worked an eighteen-hour shift before heading to Drew's. And her saying she was tired and aching was a clearly defined signal that they would not be having sex. She didn't even feel like being touched right now—by him—and she knew he was just respecting that. All the same, she felt let down by his half-hearted effort.

She turned off her own light, slid down in the bed, lay with her eyes open and space between her and Rod.

Declan had set her on edge, at first, with his unpressed button-down, his nicotine-stained fingers, his too-easy laugh. But then something had shifted, and she'd glimpsed depths behind his veneer. The warmth from the edge of his hand had spread up her arm like a blush, into her cheeks, her chest.

Then Rod had arrived, saying, Did you get my text?

And Jules had said, No, because her phone was in the front

pocket of Declan's jeans, which she wasn't about to explain, and anyway she'd given up on Rod hours before, when she'd gotten his first text, saying he couldn't make it.

Promised you a hotel date, didn't I? He'd smiled as he walked across the back porch to where Jules, feeling caught, stood leaning against the railing next to Declan. He kissed her on the lips, right there, a foot from Declan's face, and Jules felt like two people trying to occupy one body, she was both in the moment and watching it from the outside.

But she kissed him back. That was what he expected, what was expected of her. You greet your lover with a kiss. But she kept it short, a cursory brush of the lips. She could feel Declan watching.

As Jules pulled back from Rod and looked over, Declan flicked his glance away, turning around to look into the empty swimming pool and the dappled darkness of the garden. Rod kept his hands on her hips, searching her face as he pressed his lips together, analyzing flavours.

We smoked some pot, Jules said.

They spent the last hour of the evening back in the house. Drew and Farzan sent Jules significant looks she tried to ignore, while she and Declan made periodic eye contact, taking turns at being the first to flinch away. And Rod did not let go of Jules's hand until Jules said she wanted to go. She felt hyper-aware of Rod's hand in hers, his presence shadowing her. She knew he was uncomfortable, could see him starting to compensate by espousing "expert" knowledge on every subject that came up, and she knew the others could see it too.

I've been to Ireland, he told Declan. Couple times. Frankly, I think the whole country is overpriced for what you get.

Oh yeah? Declan drawled over a cigarette. This was one of the times he raised an eyebrow at Jules, his response and his disbelief clearly less about what Rod was saying than about the fact that Jules was with him.

I mean, it's pretty enough. And the whiskey is okay. But I paid five hundred bucks for a room in a hotel that didn't even have an *elevator*. If they're going to stay competitive, they'll have to update all those old buildings.

And to Drew he said:

You know your house is right near that slaughterhouse that burned down. Said matter-of-factly, not as a question. Now that was a big mistake, zoning for new residential right beside a pork factory. No wonder someone torched it. And I guarantee it was someone living on your street. Had to be. But I guess you don't mind having an arsonist for a neighbour?

It was all true, but Drew was not to be baited.

For all you know, Rod, it could have been me who started those fires. And where is it you live again?

Which is when Jules said she wanted to go. After all, it was 3 a.m.

On their way out, Declan embraced her, slipped Jules's phone into her purse and said, It was nice meeting you, Julie, right into her ear. His breath gave her goosebumps.

And so they left, took a cab back to the hotel. Alone together, without a group, Jules could appreciate Rod more, was able to remember: she *did* love him. At least, she thought she did. She had no reason not to.

He waved off the doorman so he could open the door for her himself, held her hand as they walked to the elevator, put his arm around her shoulders and kissed her on the temple on the ride up.

I'm glad you had a fun night, he told her as they got ready for bed.

Did I?

Seems like you did. With Drew and Farzan. That Declan fellow's kind of off.

Jules's heart jumped like she'd heard a bump in the night.

You sure seemed to get along with him, though.

What's that supposed to mean? She spoke to the almost closed bathroom door, behind which Rod was doing whatever his private nighttime ritual was. Flossing his teeth? Having never witnessed it, she could only assume it was something so benign.

It means, it seems like you had fun. It was nice to see you making friends.

I have lots of friends.

She pulled on her nightshirt and slid under the covers. Rod didn't answer her. They both knew it wasn't true.

Then Rod came out of the bathroom, got into bed and started kissing her. And though she could occasionally feel the mechanical needs of her body, it was more often hard to reach herself through the numbness. On the rare occasions she did feel desire, it felt important. But this was not one of those times. Kissing Rod felt inert and lifeless, his hands on her butt and belly nuisance groping.

So she said, I'm tired. My neck hurts. And he left her alone. When he started his quiet snoring, Jules took another Oxy, then tried to read a novel on her tablet while she waited for the pill to kick in.

She knew she was probably self-sabotaging again, taking this perfectly acceptable thing she had with this basically presentable and decent guy and doing what she could to turn it into complete shit. Acting out in irrational ways, testing to see how much damage her life, her relationship, could take.

Old habits resurfacing. She'd been in love, once.

She sighed under the weight of that resident ghost, the pocket of anxiety and regret that never actually left. That had started, temporally, with the birth of her second child and the postpartum depression that came with it. And that six years later, five years after Lizzie's death and the grieving, the heartache and the long, slow spiral of depression had only ended, finally, when David left. It ebbed, stopped descending, stopped taking her all the way down with it, but it didn't go away, not really, just withdrew and took up quiet tenancy in a backroom of her brain.

She rolled towards Rod, snaked her arm around his bony back to his concave tummy, settling her forehead on the back of his neck. But his antiseptic hospital scent put an acrid, chemical taste in her mouth, so she rolled away again and went to sleep with her back lightly pressing against his.

Minke.

———

The drive up the coast was a series of hairpin turns along cliff edges, the rocky coast and booming surf hundreds of metres below, and Lance casually yanking the steering wheel back and forth. He was six-four and folded into his vintage Bug so his knees hugged the wheel; he used them to steer while he rolled a joint, reaching out a hand to jerk the car around each turn. I was sure we took some of the curves on two wheels, I felt them cutting like skate edges. I was high and awestruck, the world rushed in at me, and I grinned to taste it.

A friend of Lance's had a place on a river, and the boat was moored there. Lucky, he said, as the first quake had torn up the Christchurch marina and left sewage hemorrhaging into the surf.

A thirty-foot cruiser with a reddish wooden hull and a metre-wide steering wheel of polished steel, *Minke* creaked her ropes in greeting and rocked gently as we climbed aboard.

We motored along the river, past landscaped shores, riverside houses and flats of pale-green farmland, until we finally surged over a rushing, watery speed bump at the river's mouth and emerged onto the ocean. We hauled up sails, cloth snapping and glaring in the sun, and *Minke* came alive underneath us. We tacked north, sometimes skimming across the tops of waves, sometimes slicing and pounding through them, as *Minke* hammered on the ocean with a force of her own. I stood with Lance behind the wheel, buoyed and flying.

We might run into some orcas, Lance said, tapping the face of the compass in the steering post. The analog dial looked like an old watch, all carved wood and brass inlays. Beautiful like an antique, which it probably was. I wondered if he had a GPS.

Wait till you hear 'em sing. Touch you right here, believe me.

As he said it, he reached out and prodded my chest gently, over my heart.

I nodded. It was like he'd punched me in a bruise. Suddenly all I could think of was Jill.

WE'D MET AT my first hockey party. Not that Jill would be caught dead playing hockey. But her sister, Marci, played centre. I'd been the only tenth grader on the team, and I was awkward and shy and possibly a bit unusual to begin with. So, faced with a room of clamouring eleventh- and twelfth-grade jocks and "cool kids," I'd edged into a corner by the punch bowl. The sugar in the fuchsia drink coated my teeth, something in it burned my throat, but out of boredom or anxiety or both, I kept drinking it down.

Then she'd appeared, black plugs in each of her ears and black hair straight out of anime, a shock of turquoise down the middle of it, like a skunky Smurf, or a Smurfy skunk. She'd walked right over and sat on the straight-backed chair beside my own.

You're Chloe Wright. Jill Proust. She stuck out a hand, fingers splayed wide.

Chlo. I know who you are.

We shook: up, down, up, staccato movements that made me blink, amused.

Jill motioned for my glass of punch and, armed with an imp grin and a silver hip flask, set about turning us into friends.

When Jill's flask was empty, we went upstairs to refill it from her mum's liquor stash, locked in the master bathroom for the party, and then went down to Jill's room in the basement to look at her comic books. Somewhere over her first-edition *Ghost World* we started kissing. We never agreed, later, who kissed whom but decided it must have been our souls colliding, willing us together with unseen force. And it made sense.

I was where I was supposed to be. Everything else fell away.

After that, holding her hand, and being out and known as one of the queers at school, that made sense too. Some people gave me strange looks, or made comments, but when hadn't they? Some people seemed to hate me more, but others, oddly, less. I was still That Goalie. I had more friends on Socialink, and people said hi to me in the hallways. And I had Jill: my best friend, my soulmate. My anchor. It all made sense.

Then, three years later, just as our first university assignments were coming due, one night over video chat, Jill had called it off. It was too hard to be together but apart, she said. She just needed to devote herself to her studies, she said. Which was so completely out of character that even if I hadn't had my suspicions, I'd have known she was avoiding some kind of truth. I came right out and asked if it was because of Rachel, but she denied it, looked me in the camera lens and said they were just friends. When I saw the pictures on David's computer, I knew she'd lied to me, and somehow that made sense too, a horrible, sick-feeling sense.

I was hunched over in a bolted-down, low-slung chair on the foredeck when Lance dropped sail and anchor, sat down beside me and handed me a beer.

I popped the tab and we touched cans.

To the beginning of your great adventure.

To saying Fuck It.

I drank in the salt air, the warmth on my face. Closed my eyes and yelled wordlessly into the wind.

Lance nodded. Shake it off, mate. Exactly why I come out here.

We were a couple miles offshore, with mountains in the distance to port, ocean forever to starboard. The beer rinsed away the bad taste in my throat, and now the rocking relaxed me, the rise and fall, rise and fall, slow and deep planetary breathing, my own chest moving in sync.

Kiri—my wife, yeah? This was her boat. She would have liked you.

Yeah, I'm pretty fucking great, I said, understanding: he was as alone as I was.

Tacking in and out of the wind up the coast, I'd been goosebump cool, but now, drifting under the noon sun, I felt smothered and hot. Shedding my hoodie was like emerging from years in the dark, the pores in my skin hungrily opening to the light.

Lance handed me a bottle of sunscreen and asked if I wanted fish for lunch. Next thing I knew, he was showing me how to remove the hook from the mouth of a flopping silver body as I tried not to see accusation in the steel-grey eyes that couldn't blink. Lance put the fish out of its misery with a hammer blow to its head, and then put the knife in my hand and walked me through slitting it along the belly (shiny skin splitting to wet red flesh), scooping entrails (long spiny bits, globs of intestine) overboard.

Just the thing to take your mind from your troubles, he said. And he was right. Feeling the wetness, the slippery blood and fat and skin on my fingers, even the way it made me gag a few times, shifted my position in relation to reality. I was in it. Really *in* it. I'd been numb for weeks, everything distant and remote, my own movements underwater slow. An intestine curling over my wrist and sliding across the deck of the boat was a moment of sharpness, cutting through, placing me there, where I was.

LANCE COOKED THE fish in the galley kitchen while I looked around the yacht's cabin of gleaming wood. Everything was bolted down or stowed in compartments beneath benches. Framed photos were nailed in place on the panelling.

Is this your wife? Lance stood on a marina dock next to an onyx-skinned woman even taller than he was.

Aw yeah. That's my Kiri.

Her cheek was tilted so it brushed against his wind-mussed hair. They weren't quite smiling, but they looked happy with their whole bodies. Their bare feet.

For minutes there were only the sounds of the water against the outside of the boat, the hiss and sizzle from the pan on the stove. I sat on a bench and stared out a window where the line between ocean and sky rose in and out of frame.

He rattled the pan. Fish is ready.

KIRI, A MARINE biologist, had outfitted the underside of *Minke* with an underwater microphone: a hydrophone, with a speaker inside the cabin. After lunch, we sat at the tiny navigation desk with its ancient radar system and scanned through the airwaves of ocean. Until Lance raised a finger to say, Listen.

I heard clicking. Rhythmic and guttural, totally inhuman but speaking to me on another level. A call, loud and close, followed by a response, much quieter and farther away. Echolocation, Lance explained. Sonar navigation. Every pod has its own dialect.

Dialect, I repeated.

Aw yeah, they're calling out their names, hey? To see if they know each other.

Thinking that kind of linguistic interaction seemed unlikely, I suggested it was more like dogs knowing each other's scents.

Lance gave me a hard look and clicked the speaker off. Not exactly. Come meet them.

OUT ON DECK, I watched a triangular fin cutting towards the boat, a slick, oily shadow ghosting along underneath it. At ten metres away, it did a slow roll, black-and-white body shining as it curled through the air, tail sticking straight up to give a wave before it dove, only to reappear beside the boat moments later. There were three, four, then five of them, circling *Minke* in formation, rolling, diving, resurfacing.

Orca pods are maternal, Lance told me. This is probably a mother and her offspring. They're very co-operative, yeah? Take down a whale bigger than any of them, or a seal. Surround it like a death squad.

A couple of them started jumping, flying out of the water, sleek power twisting around before splashing noisily down again. It was impossible to think of them as *fish*.

I couldn't help the grin that hurt my face but tried to tone it down. Pretty cool, I said.

These are Kiri's. They know our boat.

The orcas played in the water around *Minke* for a long time, long enough for Lance to go below decks for a while and come back with red eyes.

Silly buggers. His voice was hoarse and torn.

MUCH LATER, LANCE said, So, tell me about this girl who's broken your heart.

The sun had dropped behind the mountains on the coast. The sky closed in, the air cooled. We sat in the cabin and drank wine by candlelight.

Jill. Her name was sawdust in my mouth. I told Lance how we'd left notes in each other's lockers and texted at night, how we used to make out in the girls' bathroom, and about the time we almost got busted together for shoplifting T-shirts from a vintage store. How we'd done everything together since grade ten.

Then the horrible breakup over video phone.

Lance cringed as he emptied the bottle of wine into our cups.

You're the one who wanted to go *there*, Jill had said, referring to my university in the eastern part of the province. Jill was studying art history, and much closer to home. You could have come here, she said, but it wasn't good enough for you. (She wasn't wrong. The math program at Jill's school was a joke.)

I love that you're so open about it all, Lance said. That you're like, fuck it, this is who I am. He gestured to indicate my whole person.

Well. It is, so.

It doesn't cause you problems? Like, at school? Can't be easy.

Being queer?

Or with your pals?

They wouldn't be very good pals.

Maybe so, he said. But I still think you're brave.

A PORTHOLE ABOVE the table captured within its frame multiple layers of light and reflection: a diffused crescent of moon against a new-blue-jean sky, the shifty flames of three mismatched candles, the shiny curves of wine in cups and the pale shadows of our hands on the tabletop. All sliding and overlapping, doubled by the two panes of glass.

I loved my Kiri, yeah? Still love her.

I stared at the glowing end of the joint in my hand, the flaked green nail polish from another lifetime, as Lance told me how he'd been in his office at the university when the 6.7 quake hit. Kiri, at home on the first floor, had been crushed by the weight of the second collapsing onto her. Their street had flooded, preventing rescue or even retrieval for seventy-plus hours.

I should have been home, he said. Not . . . with a student. The way I was.

He turned his cup in his hand, stared at the thumbprint pool of red in the bottom.

It's not an easy thing, to admit that you've done something you can never apologize for.

His eyes had a liquid gleam. His inner forearm bore a faded tattoo of an anchor.

Forces you to live in the real world. And that's the challenge. Living with what you did. And what you didn't do.

I'd spent a lot of time in my life feeling both very alone and responsible for it. Something about Lance, and the weight of loss that followed him around, made me feel like I might not be the only one who assumed that when bad things happened, they were at least partly my fault.

THE SKY BEYOND the portholes was deep black. We smoked the rest of the joint in silence. Something splashed nearby.

Oi, we should go look at the stars, yeah?

THE NIGHTTIME OCEAN stunned me with its endlessness. Lance stood behind me and pointed out Alpha Centauri. The stars may have been sharp and clear, but I wasn't able to focus on them. They drifted in their halos. My legs wobbled from the wine.

And that there is Beta Centauri. You can't see the Southern Cross this time of year, but those will always point you in the right direction.

Ha. My phone has GPS.

He leaned with his forearms on the rail beside me. Yeah. Mine too. But that's just the thing. You don't need to know anything anymore. You don't even need to *see* anything anymore. Just look it up on your damn phone.

Hey, I agree with you. That's why I'm here, on this trip.

Oh yeah? To get away from it all, is that it?

Well, yeah. Some kind of, I dunno, freedom? My mother's a freaking data wrangler, did you know that? She puts people's lives into algorithms. Everything they do online—profiles, location data, likes, friends. So she can exploit it. So her clients can make money off it. So. Yeah. Trying to un-map myself, I guess.

But—you're keeping in touch, yeah? They can still track you through your phone. You're not *really* free. Right? None of us are.

Don't remind me.

Ha. Yeah. Fuck technology. Except for the head. 'Scuse me.

Alone on deck, with the breathing and creaking of ocean and boat, the deep silence of space, I felt the vastness of the sky crack open in my chest, like my ribs were peeling back, painlessly, to let it in. I imagined myself drifting among and between the stars, tasting and touching with my mouth and all my skin the fabric of space-time.

I pulled my day pack from inside the bench where I'd stowed it, dug out my smartphone and gripped it in its battered plastic case in one hand. Thought about all the texts I'd sent Jill. And all the ones I would never send now. The only people likely to contact me now were my parents. Thinking about Amanda's concern and the quiet expectation in David's eyes, that I be a certain kind of person, dress like a girl, smile and act nice, the hurt on Char's face every time I disappointed her, gave me an almost physical longing to make some kind of sweeping and dramatic gesture to mark the moment. To definitively commit to my journey and separate the past from this new future.

I stepped up to the rail, drew my arm way back and launched the phone as hard as I could. It arced up and out, caught on an ocean breeze and curved slightly, disappeared into the void and made a tiny splash I could hear but not see.

What did you just do?

Lance, frozen halfway out of the hatch. There was shortness to his words, they were clipped and tight, threatened to squash like a bug my sense of lightness and liberation. But the deed was done.

It was done and I knew I'd done something horribly wrong, something I wished I could take back but would never be able to. Gravity was like that. Things fell.

Let's just say I cut the cord, I said. I made a throat-slicing motion with my hand, hoping to turn it into a joke.

Wow, he said. He had a bottle of wine in one hand and our cups in the other, but with his rangy hands he could still climb the ladder onto deck, still gesture. He walked to the rail of the boat, looked into the darkness as though he might see my phone out there. His easy posture had sagged, defeated. He looked at me in a way that made me wonder if we ever would have really been friends.

Why would you do that?

His disappointment crushed me. Unreasonable thoughts went through my head. The night held me in place, there was nowhere to go.

I just really needed to get rid of it.

Wow, he said again, shaking his head, slowly, side to side.

I just don't want to talk to anyone, I said, but my words felt weak.

You know what kinds of toxins are in those things?

Toxins? The whole framework of the conversation collapsed under me. It's just a phone, Lance. One phone. You're the one who said fuck technology.

He started for the back of the boat. Heavy metals, radioactive shit, plastics that will take centuries to break down—

There was a horrible moment where I thought he was going to cry again, only now I was the one making it happen.

I'm sorry, I tried to say, but he didn't even acknowledge it.

I'm going to bed. Drop you in the morning, yeah?

He disappeared down the hatch. I heard wood sliding, and a slam. And that was that.

I WOKE UP to sunlight beaming through the porthole over my bunk, searing my eyeballs. Rolled out of my sleeping nook into an empty cabin. I took a piece of cold, crispy bacon from the pan on the stove and climbed up on deck. Lance was sailing, looking distant and at home, his eyes watching the horizon, the sails, the waves, his movements relaxed and sure. I sat on a bench right in front of him. He didn't look at me, didn't speak. I commented on the temperature, which was mild, and the landscape we passed, which was rugged. Lance answered, agreeable but monosyllabic, and kept sailing.

He was nothing like me after all, I decided. If anything, he was more like Jules, with secret rules he expected me to follow, self-medicating to avoid dealing with his heartbreak. Forever disappointed by what he judged to be the failings of others.

Eventually, we approached land. A few small, wind-rattled buildings clutched at the shore, harsh coastal cliffs rising like rogue waves behind them. Way up the coast, tiny figures cut in and out of rolling surf. They looked like a school of fish, and for a moment that's what I took them for, dolphins playing in the tide. But then they would stop, their movements suddenly less fluid, more human, as they inched their way out from shore, only to catch another wave and ride it back in. *Surfers.*

Lance lowered the sails and steered in by motor, swung around until the starboard bumper nudged the end of a long wooden quay that jigged and jagged up to a scrap of beach, rocking on floaters. He jumped out, secured a rope, then jumped back in.

There you are. He pulled my duffle bag out of its storage compartment. His tone was cool and civil and his eyes hid behind shades.

What—*here*? We were nowhere, or maybe somewhere, but without my phone I had no idea where that was.

You wanted to be free, yeah? Independent? You don't need anyone? There's a town with a hostel over that hill.

I looked up at the cliff wall, whiplash switchbacks of road cutting across it.

I tried again: I'm really sorry. I didn't mean to offend you.

He tossed my bag onto the floating pier and everything recoiled as it landed. I automatically bent my knees into hockey stance for balance.

Nah, *I'm* sorry, Chloe. Shouldn't've lashed out at you like that. It's just sacred to me, yeah? The ocean. Beings, intelligent, sentient beings, *live* down there. I thought you got that. You're a nice kid, but . . . Anyway. I just got upset.

I still couldn't see his eyes, but I knew he wasn't looking at me.

You can call your dad, let him know where you are. Guess you'll have to borrow a phone.

Lance hopped onto the dock again and started untying the ropes. Meantime, I gotta be alone. Got to find myself some peace. Get my perspective back. Finally, from his crouch on the dock, he pointed his face directly at me. I felt caught, paralyzed by guilt.

And you need to figure out your shit. Now get off my boat.

Drive.

————

Drop me at the hospital?

Rod had left his Porsche at work in Hamilton the night before and had taken the commuter train in to Toronto.

I thought we might get into our cups last night. Didn't think I should drive.

Jules nodded as she sipped her coffee in the hotel's restaurant. She was trying to think of how to broach the subject of needing a refill for the pills. A re-pill. Rod would not be impressed, would say she was taking too much. And maybe she was, but when she had a flare-up, of her back or her neck or her shoulder or hip, they were the only thing that made it bearable. And the last few weeks had been one long, slow fireworks show of pain.

It wasn't that she wanted to take the drugs. In truth, the drugs, even as they softened the signals to her pain receptors, made her feel like crap. Weighed her body down like sodden and stained clothes she couldn't remove. If she hadn't needed them the way she did, she never would have taken them in the first place.

This is where she was, where she'd been. A gruelling pregnancy, an abysmal postpartum depression, the baby dying and everything that came after had cumulatively amounted to three and a half Very Bad Years. Her default mode became—after she'd moved into the spare room, and when she wasn't at work—lying in bed and watching TV.

David, the love of her life, had been worried. She saw that. Chloe was maybe seven or eight by then, and she often looked worried too. David had strongly and repeatedly suggested some kind of therapy, but Jules thought she needed to get out of her head, not further into it. She knew he was suffering alongside her, knew she was making it worse, but couldn't stop herself from wanting to burn it all down.

Then one day Jules saw a show about a woman whose son had died. In her long depression afterwards, the woman had gained three hundred pounds, and she was now subjecting herself to televised fat-shaming: "to get my life back," she cried.

Jules didn't approve of these shows, of all that newfangled reality television in general, of weight loss shows in particular, and *this* show she thought was the worst of the worst. She could not imagine willingly undergoing such humiliation, having struggled with her own body image for most of her life. She flipped onto the show by chance but ended up watching the whole thing in what began as morbid fascination and ended in tears of catharsis as she recognized herself in the fat woman's narrative.

The trainer on the show got the woman to start running on a treadmill, and by the end of the hour she was running two kilometres, a hundred pounds lighter and *smiling*.

And Jules thought, well, alright then, and started running. A lot. Obsessively, according to David. Five days a week, six in the morning, forty degrees or twenty below, it didn't matter. It helped like nothing else had helped, thinned the impenetrable murk of her depression to a light haze of realistic pessimism. She had more energy, dropped twenty pounds, felt comfortable in her skin. Drank less. Had to buy new clothes—and shopped for them without emotional breakdowns. Sex, for a while, was almost appealing again. She measured her week in miles and minutes, the looped distances around parks. It gave her life structure, and purpose outside of work and David and Chloe—whom she saw more than before but still kept at a distance. They were too hopeful, too doe-eyed, too expectant. Like they were waiting for something she couldn't give them, which really meant they were waiting for her to fail.

Then one day she lifted a box of files onto her desk at an awkward angle, and she felt something give. It didn't hurt, but she felt *wrongness* ratchet up along her vertebrae. And then it did hurt. By the next day she couldn't get out of bed. She'd blown a disc: major herniation, they said, probably from the impact of running with a weak core. And that was that. A year of physio, a lot of time spent lying in bed or doing exercises on the floor, and now her life was measured in counts of ten, the road to healing much longer than any she had run.

Two years later, when she finally felt as if she could run again, she was "strongly advised" against it. So she walked. A lot. Pulled her groin; returned to physio. After the groin, it was the hip, then the shoulder, then a second disc above the first one, then her groin again. Just as one thing was healing, something else would go. She was on and off various pain medications, forever increasing dosages. Her mood, her spirit, fell, like a stone through the ocean, sinking, plateauing and sinking further, an inexorable journey towards an unseeable bottom. After much pleading by David and her doctors, antidepressants were added into her daily cocktail. Those years blurred for her now. Exercising when she could (less and less), drinking heavily when she couldn't (more and more) and always returning to the spare room, the flickering blue light and the bottle of Scotch. It was a bleak time for her, for all of them in the house of loss, each of them shrouded in a private grief.

And then David left. The baby had been dead seven years and Jules was still in mourning; Chloe at thirteen was almost self-sufficient, and he had met someone else. Those were all the reasons he gave her, not that he needed a reason to go live his life, since they clearly weren't living one together anymore. Although she initially panicked at the idea of it, of having to look after Chloe and the house and herself without the crutch that was David, she quickly found that a great strain had eased. Chloe was furious with her for letting him go, for pushing him away, for not even trying to stop him from leaving, and she raged about it, frequently, for six months (or was it twelve), but Jules didn't think it was her fault or her problem to solve. It was simply the way things were and they would have to carry on without him. Her injuries, her discomfort, continued, but she was able, slowly, to reconstruct a more functional persona, was able to move, however slightly, out of crisis mode. Pain became more about management than simply suffering. With a tentative new optimism, she sought out new doctors, new treatments, new exercises, new explanations. Had her failure to do some basic physical activity left her weaker than everyone else her age? Was it a genetic deficiency? Or some kind of disease? Someone had to be able to tell her, to find out what was wrong and fix it. But no one could.

She still wasn't much of a parent, she knew, but Chloe seemed fine. She played hockey, got herself to games and practices, kept her marks consistently decent, did very well in math and computer science. It was only later, after Chloe met Jill, that Jules started to get calls about skipped classes, and even then it was put to her as a discipline problem, not an academic one. In general Chloe just didn't seem to need much parenting, although Jules could now sometimes admit to herself that it was very convenient for her to view it that way.

Finally, maybe three years ago, after almost a decade of chronic pain, one particularly alert nurse practitioner looked at the size of Jules's file and actually clucked. She referred Jules to a pain clinic at the university hospital, where she said they would have a team of doctors and research physicians who would approach Jules's case from different angles and share information. With their combined resources, they might figure out what was going on.

So, you couldn't say she hadn't tried. Over the years, she had seen them all—doctors, physiotherapists, massage therapists, acupuncturists, chiropractors. At the pain clinic she added to the roster an occupational therapist, a naturopath, a kinesiologist, even a psychotherapist and a psychiatrist—she'd spent years on Paxil, still took Celexa every goddamned morning—and now, a neurologist.

She'd been waiting in an examination room, leaning against the grey padded treatment table, watching white coats walk back and forth outside the open door. She heard him before she ever saw him, whistling down the corridor, some kind of jazz tune, full of vibrato and perfectly pitched, a musician's whistle. In he walked with her thick file in his hand, and right away she could tell he was different from everyone else who worked there. Most of them wore jeans and T-shirts under their lab coats, it was a casual, team-oriented kind of place, and here was this six-foot-plus, stick-figured fortyish man in a pricey but ill-fitting suit. Jules worked with men in expensive suits, and they almost always had hidden agendas and vile attitudes towards women behind their smooth demeanours. She was leery.

But he was lanky and nervous and avoided eye contact for a couple of minutes at least, as he flipped through her file. Finally, he said, still looking down,

I'm Dr. Scott. Rodney Scott. Rod. I bet you're totally fed up with guys like me.

As he shook her hand, finally looking at her, Jules thought he meant she must be sick of men in suits, which she was, chronically. She gave him half a smile.

Too many doctors, am I right? And he smiled back through thick lenses. His black hair looked shocked, stuck out in all directions. From his swivel chair at the desk, he gestured to the armchair beside him. Jules shook her head.

No sitting. My L5 has flared up.

Lower lumbar. That's no fun.

He stood back up, leaned against the desk to face Jules at her level.

We all sit too much anyway. So, Ms. Wright, tell me your story.

She'd just watched him read her file. But he had her tell him anyway, in her own words.

Feel like I bought a lemon, Jules said forty minutes in. Everything breaking down all the time. Wish I could just upgrade my body.

Rod glanced up from the note he was writing, said, I've seen worse, and then immediately went bright red.

At that moment, she felt she was in good hands for the first time since she'd lifted that box of files. Maybe even since she'd had Lizzie. Or gotten pregnant.

Then he said he wanted to run some tests.

A STRANGE DUET made her lift her gaze from her coffee cup. Rod's high-pitched guffawing playing against a husky laugh. He had gone up to settle their bill and was leaning way over the counter beside the cash register. He was tall enough that his head and shoulders were level with those of the middle-aged woman he spoke to, a brassy, short-haired blonde, her apron cut low, the loosening skin on her neck and chest well tanned, her arms a collage of tattoos. Jules had thought her stern-faced and sour, assumed she was jaded from decades of restaurant work. But now the woman was giggling at Rod, one hand fluttering a white receipt at her cleavage, one hip cocked, and Jules knew, just *knew*, he had mentioned his Porsche. Since they'd started dating two years ago, his social confidence had for some reason ballooned, and she'd noticed this a few times lately: Rod trying to flirt. He was terrible at it, in Jules's opinion, and she'd more than once heard him throw the car in to try to up his game. It didn't always work, but this woman clearly knew how to read her clientele, and which ones would tip for attention and flattery.

The woman's eyes darted in her direction, sizing her up. Jules gave her a half smile and three-fingered wave, wondering how much of the sarcasm in her brain was showing on her face. Quite a lot, she guessed, when the woman finally extended the bill towards Rod as she might offer him a Christmas firecracker to pull. Jules hoped he at least tipped her well.

After mere moments in her car, the hot, sour smell of restlessness wafted off Rod's body from the passenger seat. Nine a.m. on a Saturday morning and the expressway was moving at twenty miles an hour.

Shall we have dinner later?

As they merged from the on-ramp, he craned his neck around from the passenger seat to check for oncoming cars.

I have to check on a patient this afternoon, but after that . . .

He opened her glove compartment and started rifling through it. It was one of his more annoying mannerisms, to fidget with anything within range of his long arms. He wasn't very good at sitting still.

Jules made a noise that implied consent. She was concentrating on the densely packed highway, trying to get away from a little white hatchback that was dogging in and out of her lane. The young man driving it passed her, then pulled in ahead of her, then changed lanes to pass someone else, but his new lane slowed and he fell behind Jules again. Casually, like it was half a thought, she mentioned to Rod that she might, possibly, need a refill, if he didn't mind. She changed lanes, away from the hatchback, but it followed her over.

Rod had found the package of random snack food from her last flight from New York, stashed in there for emergencies. He turned it over, looking for the ingredients. He matched her tone of nonchalance with one of absent-minded distraction.

Hasn't been that long. You sure?

Pretty sure, yeah.

Hmm.

He lifted up the little cellophane flap on the wrapper. The ingredients were hidden underneath it in tiny printing. He squinted at them.

Well, I don't have a scrip pad with me. Anyway, I've been meaning to talk to you—

No rush. Tonight's fine.

Right, he said. He held the package up to the window, angling it in the light so he could read it better. Oh, wait, I can't. Forgot, I told Corina I would help her study.

How paternal of you.

His assistant, a nurse in her late twenties, was preparing for the MCAT as a part of her application to medical school. Jules pictured her as pretty, knew she was smart, and couldn't help imagining her as idolizing Rod. As unlikely as that might be.

The white hatchback behind her swerved out of their shared lane, he was going to try to pass her again. She tried to slow to let him pass, but he kept pace with her, right in her blind spot.

Paternal? Oh, I don't know. Smart kid. Jules, have you seen what's in these? Lila would have a field day.

Lila was a patient, a young—Jules assumed she was young— nutritionist with debilitating nerve problems in her legs. Rod said he had been asking her questions about her hospital food, trying to establish a rapport, and she had told him to start reading the back of every package he purchased. Jules suspected there was some teasing and flirting embedded in the exchange. Rod had kept that out of his version, but how he talked about his female patients sometimes felt a little close to home.

Rod succumbed to the need to pull out his glasses. This was another new thing. He'd replaced his thick glasses with contact lenses, but his prescription was such that he still needed readers.

MSG, for starters. Monocalcium phosphate, disodium guanylate . . .

He continued down the list of Latin compounds.

Jules had been going to the pain clinic for months before he'd asked her out.

He'd had them test everything. They scanned every bone in her body, trying to find something set in its socket wrong, or insufficient bone density, an obscure heart condition or different leg lengths. They ran blood tests for autoimmune conditions like lupus and fibromyalgia, tested her thyroid, ran tests of her nervous system and pain receptors. They looked for anything that would explain why she had spent interminable years going from one injury to the next, no matter how many core-strengthening exercises she did or how many hours of physio she crammed into a week.

They found nothing.

She got better, got worse, got better again, as each injury went through its cycle of flare-ups and partial resolution.

Finally, when she went in with her back worse than it had been to date, Rod suggested a discography. He would inject contrast dye into the discs in her back, check for irregularities and ruptures, get a detailed picture of each one.

She lay on her stomach on the treatment table, her head in the hole, in a gown that opened up the back. Her arms hung over the sides, the left one stuck with a needle and taped to the tube of an IV: a mild sedative, a pain reliever. The right one absently draped on a metal crossbar under the table. Rod swabbed her back, said the cold she was feeling was a local anaesthetic.

Then the needles started. Vertebra by vertebra, Rod worked his way up the discs in her spine. She felt the needle puncture her skin, felt the pressure in her back as each disc swelled slightly with the added fluid.

She was to tell him if it hurt.

The third needle slid in.

JeezusFUCK. Her eyes popped open, her teeth clenched. She felt the deep, radiating pain that had held her in its malicious grasp for so many years, the sizzling live wires that twisted around her spine, wringing her out. Sparks fired down her left leg, the sciatic nerve shrieking, torqued. She clutched the cold metal of the table legs, her fingernails pressed white.

Well, that gives us something to work with.

Rod calmly moved on to the next disc, which was just as bad.

In all, he found three discs that caused her significant pain under pressure. By the time he was done, Jules had bitten a hole in her lip and had decided she pretty much hated this Dr. Scott, with his warm, soft hands and his reedy voice. Right there, things could have been over before they even got started.

Okay, Jules. He laid a blanket over her back and gave her the good news:

The bulging on those three discs is very, very slight. Quite mild herniation.

The downplaying was uncomfortably familiar. She turned carefully onto her side, tucked her right arm under her head.

That's good news how exactly?

Well, they're not ruptured, they're unlikely to rupture, and really, with physio, they should be resolvable.

At this point, drained from the procedure and already struggling to maintain composure, Jules started weeping. This was the same thing she'd been told dozens of times over the years. It did her no good. Rod touched her: laid a hand on her shoulder. Leaned his head down towards hers and spoke gently.

The bad news is that it doesn't really explain the scale of your pain. And since physio doesn't seem to be working for you, at least not in the way we would typically expect, it doesn't leave us with a whole lot of treatment options.

You can't help me. What a shock.

He pulled his head back but kept his hand on her shoulder.

Well, frankly, I was hoping there was some micro-tearing on a disc, something that could be treated surgically. Or that there wouldn't be increased pain on any disc in particular but on all of them, or none of them, suggesting something neurological, which would indicate for a different approach altogether.

But that's not what happened.

No.

So where does that leave me?

Where indeed, he said.

HE SENT HER for more massage, told her to stay vigilant with the physio—because it can't hurt—and prescribed her two weeks' worth of OxyContin.

The Oxy didn't make her pain stop, but its resolve softened. The parasitical claw loosened its grasp somewhat, dulled its talons, and sometimes it would even let go of her spine, drift along beside her like a scratchy shadow.

She knew the reputation Oxy had. She'd seen a documentary. It was basically heroin made in a lab, they said. Highly addictive, they said.

She was careful, took it only when she really needed it, and never more than the recommended dose.

She saw Rod every week for the next few months, and they could both see that she was improving, which in turn was lifting her spirits. When he finally gathered the nerve to ask her out, she was feeling positive enough to say yes.

WATCHING HIM NOW out of the corner of her eye, as he scrutinized the package of snack food, she wondered if she'd been too grateful, if she had confused her confidence in his medical thoroughness for an attraction she was no longer sure she felt.

Silicon dioxide as a "manufacturing aid"? What does that even mean?

And then:

Watch out!

There was a loud metallic scraping as the left front bumper of Jules's SUV ground into the right rear corner of the white hatchback. A blaring of horns, the SUV lurching violently as Jules slammed on the brakes, Rod yelling, Stop! Jules, STOP!

They spun sideways across the road.

It was quiet, for a beat, and then people were standing at her driver's side window asking her if she was okay.

Stunned, Jules mentally collated the events of the last thirty seconds.

She had grown tired of Rod's voice, annoyed that he didn't want to renew her scrip—and irrationally hostile about the young nutritionist who she was sure had wrapped her hot little mouth around Rod's gnads, or at least made clear her willingness to do so—and frankly, she was pissed off that she might have to get through the weekend, including writing a report, without more pills. In a rash and defensive gesture Jules had reached across the over-wide SUV, popped the glove compartment open and grabbed the package of snack crap out of Rod's hand with the intention of throwing it back in.

Unfortunately, as she leaned across the car, her steering wheel drifted to the right. Sensing this, Jules jerked it back to the left. Also unfortunately, that was the same moment that the white hatchback chose to slide into her lane right in front of her, with scant room for error, and when Jules corrected her course so quickly, the hatchback was right there, in the space she was trying to fill.

You're lucky, someone said moments later, as they got out of the car.

That could have been a lot worse, someone said.

And this was all true, but Jules didn't feel very lucky.

Didn't you see him? Why weren't you watching the road? Rod's face was drawn and grey. His hair looked more surprised than ever.

An older man in a jean jacket and earrings was reprimanding the hatchback driver. You could have killed someone, son. The hatchback was somehow facing backwards beside a twist of guardrail.

Hey man, *she* hit *me*.

Damn it, Jules, I'm going to be late. Rod's hands shook as he pulled back a sleeve to look at his watch. Jules heard a distant siren and saw, back down the highway, a flashing light.

Cops are coming, she said. She looked back at her car. Guess I'll need a tow.

The front corner of her Benz was mashed in, part of the bumper dangling onto the ground. She sighed. She loved that car.

That's going to cost you. Rod nudged at the loose bumper with his foot. A small piece of metal fell off, clattered onto the road. What were you thinking? Opening the glovebox on the highway. His eyes widened over the rims of his glasses. I hope the cops don't give you too hard a time. He hugged her with one arm, kissed her head. Jules pulled away from him, walked over to the shoulder by the mangled hatchback and sat on the ground. Rod followed her.

I'm really sorry, Jules. But I have to go. You'll be alright?

Jules shrugged and nodded, thinking: What a fucking day.

I hate to leave you like this.

He walked over to the single lane of traffic now creeping past the accident scene and waved a hand in the air. The cops were making slow progress up the narrow shoulder.

Rod, wait. She got up and walked over to him. I'm a bit . . .

She gestured loosely at the cars, hers and the hatchback, that blocked half the westbound highway.

Maybe I could see you after you help Corina? Or before? It doesn't have to be dinner.

Rod turned and looked at her, blinking. What, then?

What?

If not dinner, what? What do you want to see me for?

Jules took a step back.

Look at my car.

Yeah. You'll have to take it in.

She stepped back in towards him and lowered her voice.

I'm pretty upset, Rod. And my neck hurts. I think I need some
. . . something.

Are you really that transparent?

I'm really that upset. Why do you have to make me feel bad
about it?

Yeah. Look. I won't do this, Jules. Please don't ask me to.

Do what?

But he shook his head. I know I wrote you a scrip for ninety
tabs just a couple weeks ago. Your back flared up, you asked me
for them, fine. But if they're gone already— I'm a doctor, Jules.
Not your dealer.

Two cop cars arrived. One radioed in that it was a "fender-
bender." Call off the bus, they said. Send a tow truck. As one of
the police cars made to leave again, Rod played the I'm-a-doctor-
and-need-to-get-to-the-hospital card, and the next thing she knew
he was kissing Jules on the cheek.

Call me when it's me you want, okay? Love you.

Rod got into the cop car, and though Jules could see him,
talking and texting on his phone from the back seat as the driver
talked on her radio, it was clear that, in his mind, he had left the
scene. She stood and watched him, and tears finally started to run
down her face as the shock of the accident subsided, or maybe as
it set in, and still, she did not once see him look in her direction.
Finally, the cop car pulled away, crept up the shoulder past the
now-gridlocked traffic.

The remaining cops looked at the front of the SUV and the
back of the hatchback and declared the damage too minor for
police involvement. It was up to Jules and the young man to settle
it between them (along with their insurance companies). The older
man with the earrings, hearing this, proclaimed that the young man
should be charged with reckless driving. The cops looked dubious

but proceeded to ask another hour's worth of questions before letting Jules leave in the cab of the tow truck. They were still only a few minutes outside Toronto, so she told him to take her to the Benz dealership, where she waited another two hours while they looked at her car and gave her an overpriced estimate of more than a week. They provided her with a rental car for the interim, and Jules drove the hour back to Hamilton, finally arriving home a mere eight hours after she had left the hotel room that morning.

THE HOUSE SAT in darkness, the street light throwing sharp monochromatic shadows at the living room furniture through the bay window. The house was waiting for her, Jules thought, waiting to show her how empty it was, but she didn't feel ready to see it. She didn't turn on any lights, felt her way up the stairs to her bedroom and left her suitcase unpacked in front of the closet. She docked her phone in the speaker on the bedside table, stripped and got into bed.

She was almost asleep when she realized she hadn't checked her email in hours. Moaning in the knowledge that she now, compulsively, had to check it if she hoped to sleep, she grabbed blindly at her phone. In among all the crap, there was a message from Chloe. Six terse words, including her daughter's name. Plane didn't crash.

Well, good.

Jules rolled over to try again for sleep, but now she felt the ache sawing its way up the base of her spine and out her left hip, and the kink in her shoulder twinged. Her mind went to the nearly empty bottle of pills in her toiletry case, and before she knew it she was digging through her suitcase, layers of clothes spilling onto the floor, the crumpled suit, its empty garment bag, the two-thirds-empty bottle of Bowmore. She found the pill container, its sparse rattle; she didn't need the light on to know it was her last one. She swallowed it with a mouthful of Scotch and went back to bed.

Lee.

———

She sat on the front steps of the hostel with a book and a coffee mug, watching us pull up. Timing, I realized later—much later—is everything. Mona, who ran the place, climbed out of the car and called to her.

Alright, Lee? How was it?

Fuckin' rad. Sweet offshore.

Reaching to get my duffle bag from where it had rolled off the middle bench of the minivan, I was still processing the fact that the floor under it was wet when I saw Mona taking a box of fish out of the hatch at the back. Literally, a leaky wooden box piled high with shiny silver bodies. I sniffed my duffle, wincing at the smell.

Found this one up the road a ways. Show her round, yeah? Mona took her dripping load around the side of the rambling, once-white house. A formerly colourful hand-painted sign that said Kaikoura Backpackers was nailed over the front steps. Lee came over, picked up the bag I had dropped onto the ground, grimaced and leaned against its weight. She was tall, freckled and fair, with wildfire hair and aviator glasses. Her ropy left bicep was completely covered by a majestic arching wave, a tiny surfer about to be engulfed by it.

Blimey. Got a body in there? Ugh, kinda smells—

She froze, her shades all smoke and mirrors.

Not a serial killer, are ya?

Embarrassed to be giving a first impression involving excessive and foul-smelling luggage, I grabbed it from her.

It's heavy, I said.

You think you're stronger than me? She pulled her sunglasses back onto her head, quirked an eyebrow. She looked pretty strong, actually.

It smells like fish.

Right. She held up her hands. All yours, mate.

THE DUFFLE BAG itself was the worst; the clothes inside were still quite dry. After I dumped them out onto the bed Mona had assigned me and shoved my passport and moneybelt into a shoebox-sized locker, Lee took me around back, where I draped the duffle over a rack in the sun next to wetsuits that dripped on the grass.

In the kitchen, I made myself a cup of instant coffee from the hostel's supply. Chipped floors and grungy walls, shelves overstuffed with bread, pasta, tubs of protein powder, each compartment labelled with someone's name. Lee cleared out a shelf labelled Delphine and said I could use it.

Yeah. She won't be back.

Back out on the front steps, Lee drank tea. From Manchester, she was following surf seasons around the world.

Ruled by the waves, hey.

And even though she'd been on the water that morning, she grew wistful, her eyes on the ocean directly across the street, tracking back and forth like she was scanning a crowd for a friend.

Her book had returned to her lap, draped over a pale knee. I read the title: *Rogue Wave*.

It's about these massive waves, yeah? Hundreds of feet high, they can wipe out entire ships. Just make 'em disappear. There's more of 'em every year, and these surfers go lookin' for 'em.

They want to surf tsunamis?

She barked a loud, husky laugh. Ha! You make it sound crazy. But yeah. You wanna know what's happening to the ocean? Ask a surfer.

That explains why you never hear about it, if it's a climate change thing, I said. That's the kind of shit they cover up.

Got that right. Lee marked her page and set it aside. So, no stick? You a squid?

What?

Surfer, yeah?

Oh. Me? No.

No? Don't get many of you. What the hell you doing *here*?

I didn't want to talk about David, or get into the whole thing with Lance. I wanted to seem like I too was unshakably independent, roaming the world as a free agent, getting by on my wits and not participating in my parents' middle-class mores. So I made up a plan on the spot.

My ride dropped me off here. I'm on my way north. To go hiking.

I'd read in my guidebook about a three-day "tramp" that sounded pretty easy, which was good because I'd never done much hiking at hockey camp.

Lee gave me a long look, then nodded slowly.

Later, surfers started appearing from all directions. Dawn surfers, who'd been napping for the afternoon, came out of dorm rooms, and bodies in board shorts and flip-flops spilled out of Jeeps and pickups—roof racks piled high with boards and damp wetsuits. Carrying their boards up from the nearest beach were the "squids," or beginners. They're not really surfers yet, Lee said, but everyone starts somewhere.

As she introduced me around, I found myself repeating the idea of the hike, and the nods of respect and acceptance soon had me deciding that not only was it a great idea, it had been my plan all along.

In all, there must have been about thirty surfers. The driveway was almost full when a pickup pulled up, squeezed into the last of the space, and a very dark, very tall guy jumped off the back, bounded to the porch, roaring—RaaaHhh!!—and picked Lee up in a bear hug. You fuckin' *iced it!*

He turned to me, to anyone in range.

Carves up this *sick* A-frame, *aerial 360s*—then she's like backhanding into this *perfect* fuckin' barrel—what?

I got that Lee had done something pretty cool but had no idea what. Lee looked embarrassed by the praise. She jostled me with an easy arm around my shoulders.

Sean? Chlo. Favourite Australian surfing buddy. Canadian kook.

He looked between us a couple times. He was even taller than Lee, and in a room of golden tans the two of them provided the only contrast, him with a handsome black sheen, and her moon-pale behind her freckles.

Ah. Well. Shit, Lee. *Bad. Ass.* Now, time to pour a couple pitchers down my throat.

I understood that well enough. But Lee shook her head. Offshore at dawn, you not comin'?

Aw, yeah. He sighed, miming dejection, looked to me as though for sympathy. Slave to the waves, right? Just one, then. He gave an exaggerated wink.

Most of the surfers had already gravitated into the hostel bar, like a choreographed school of minnows, buying beer, drinking, circling, embracing, their animated interactions as loud as a waterfall.

I stood with Lee, apart from the group, which was my go-to in these situations, but I noticed that most of the surfers who looked more hard-core—the ones with the deeper tans, more tattoos, the ripped frames of extreme athletes—all made a point of at least greeting her, some offering to buy her a drink, which she declined. A couple asked if they could go with her in the morning.

Yeah man, you're my crew, Lee said, which seemed to make them very happy.

I felt awkward beside her. Lee, in some ways, reminded me of Jill, with her self-assurance and her easy charm. But she was also quieter than Jill and stayed by my side instead of circulating in the crowd and using me as her home base, as Jill would have done, sometimes all too obviously trying to make me jealous.

Sean emerged from the fray with a couple bottles, handed me one. I tried to give him the four dollars but he waved it away.

Welcome to Kaikoura, Gidget. Get me next time.

We drifted out to the screened-in porch that wrapped around the hostel. It was quieter, the smell of weed on the breeze, bodies in hammocks and slingback chairs. We settled around a card table where we could watch the ocean across the road. The shadows were lengthening, the tide rolling way, way out. What had earlier been a narrow strip of sand had become two hundred metres of flat beach stretching towards the water.

You a tourist, Chlo? Here to whale-watch or something?

Lee punched Sean on the arm. No! I told you, she's a hiker.

Okay, okay. Sean rubbed his arm. Ow.

I cast a look around the porch. But we're all tourists, aren't we?

They both hissed at me, playful but serious. We're *surfers*.

You're lucky we let you stay here, said Sean.

Yeah, with no board? Lee jerked her head sideways. Get out.

But I mean, no one here is *from* here.

We are not here to *wreck* everything.

Isn't that just what humans do? I pictured my phone, arcing into the darkness.

Sean pulled out some weed and papers. Girl has a point.

She does, Lee agreed. And it kills me, like, half of these squids don't give a god*damn* about looking after shit. She gestured vaguely at some Belgians who were huddled over a tablet, a few kids studying their phones farther down. They ain't even *lookin'* at it.

They could be anywhere, I nodded.

And by shit, you mean . . . Sean was smiling affectionately.

You know what I mean. The water, mate, the ocean—the freakin' *planet*.

But you give a damn.

He was focused on the rolling paper bent between his thumbs and forefingers, a thin line of broken grass lying in its cradle. He darted a look up at Lee and back to his hands. By his teasing, I knew they'd had this argument before.

How you even asking me that?

Just making sure. Because, you know, without all those tourists . . . Who do you think stays in this hostel when it's not surf season? Half of us have jobs in hotels over there. He nodded towards the main part of town. If there weren't tourists, no hotels. No whale watch, no tourists.

Shut up. I still hate them.

Okay, but—

They're *dirty*.

Sean sighed. That they are, love.

He rolled the paper into a fat and tight joint, massaged the slight bulges in it between his fingers, working it into the perfect shape.

Where you in from, Chlo?

Christchurch.

Ah, Christchurch, Lee said. She had taken off her shades as the sun went down. The sky behind her was the whole spectrum of pink and her red hair blazed. Would love to surf there sometime. Hear it's a mess right now, though, she said.

I thought of roads split down the middle, a church steeple lying on the ground.

They got raw sewage pumping straight into the ocean, Lee said. My dad used to tell me about Fistral Beach, in Cornwall, back in the nineties. Pads and tampons, diapers floatin' up on surf beaches. Fuckin' sick shit. Could still be like that, who knows.

Doubt it. SCAB is all over that shit.

Scab? I asked.

Surfers Care About Beaches.

Your dad's a surfer?

Yeah. Well. He was.

Lee's face shut down as a draft of sadness crossed it.

You gonna pop Gidget's cherry, or what? Sean asked.

Lee leaned back to scan me critically, down and then up. Met my eyes.

Haven't decided.

Pop my what?

Delph left her old wetsuit out back. Probably fit her.

Sean lit the joint, passed it to Lee. They both looked at me, and I realized they were waiting to see if I understood yet what was being proposed. Lee grinned.

Oi, Gidget, can you swim?

THAT NIGHT I dreamed of the park.

Mo-mo, my babysitter, sitting on a bench with her boyfriend, faces wetly conjoined for long minutes. Play with Lizzie, go play with your sister. I push the stroller around and around the dry concrete wading pool, faster and faster, up and down the banked sides, Lizzie laughing and laughing and banging her arms, a faint warning from Mo-mo, Be careful, Chloe, Lizzie turns around but it's not Lizzie, it's Char, let's go on a spaceship—

And I trip, let go, the stroller careens, spirals into the air, up over an ocean that roars in protest and pain and utter disappointment, as it sucks the air from my lungs and I'm sobbing and gasping and fighting for breath, alone in a hallway watching my mother sink lower against the wall while my grandparents talk at her, argue at her, the baby is dead and I know I'm the problem now, I can't speak, my hands clutch at carpet, a shadow moves across, a face—

A face I know.

Hey.

My own face.

Hey. Chlo.

I opened my eyes. A line of silver hoops glinted along the edge of Lee's face as she leaned into my lower bunk, whispered.

Right then?

S'goin' on? I tried to mumble, to sound still half-asleep, because Lee, so close, on my bed, in the dark, brought me very awake, made my heart pound, hard.

You're dreaming, I think. Y'alright?

I nodded, holding my breath.

Don't wake 'em all. C'mon.

DOWN IN THE kitchen, Lee fed me a bowl of oatmeal from her own supplies. She crackled with energy, good-natured but impatient. Out behind the hostel, she spun the combo on one of a long bank of lockers, dug out a wetsuit and handed it to me.

Should fit ya.

She pulled another one, still damp, from the drying rack where my duffle still hung. She made a face as she squeezed water out of neoprene. Shoulda just slept in it.

Upstairs, as the darkness paled, we stripped down, put on bathing suits under the wetsuits. I didn't know if Lee was looking at me or not, I only knew that I had my own eyes locked on my pyjama pants as I took them off, on my bathing suit as I pulled it on, on the borrowed wetsuit as I worked it over my legs, unrolling it upwards. I zipped up the front, turned around. Lee's eyes ran over the wetsuit. My body within it.

Fits, hey, she whispered.

Um. It's good, yeah. I'd spent a lot of time in locker rooms. I'd played on my first hockey team when I was six. I'd literally been stark naked with hundreds of girls. But Lee made me nervous. Good nervous, maybe. Definitely. But still.

We went back out, to racks off the side of the building that held a few surfboards with room for thirty more. Lee pulled a sleek six-foot board from a top slot like it was nothing, an extension of her arm, and with her foot nudged a longer, thicker board that lay near the bottom.

That foamie was Delph's, grab it.

It was about eight feet long and heavier than I thought it would be.

Learner board, hey. More stable.

We walked, in our flip-flops and wetsuits, across the road and a quarter-mile down to a quiet little beach where low waves rolled slowly in. The sun was struggling to rise from behind clouds on the horizon, the breeze damp and cool on our faces. The salty air coated my skin, the ocean's heavy breath. Lee called the day perfect, direct sun left her pale skin in flames. Another reason she preferred the early surfs.

First, she had me do pop-ups. I lay face down on my board on the sand, and Lee showed me the best place for my hands.

Okay, now jump up to your feet.

She demonstrated, stomach to standing in one fluid spring-loaded movement.

Land in a squat, like. And try not to use your knees on the way up.

This was easy. Popping up was a goalie move. The only difference was feet went forward and back on the board, instead of squared in the net. And I was lighter and nimbler without goalie pads and skates. I did it fifteen times in a row with little effort and was rewarded with a wry smile.

Not bad. Now stand on your board and balance. See the wax, those sticky patches? Kind of grip 'em with your feet.

As I did this, Lee walked around the board, using her foot to rock it from different angles. She rocked it harder and harder, then started pushing me, laughing, saying, Don't fall, Gidget! Don't fall!

I didn't fall and was even ready for the bodycheck when it came. Lee was several inches taller, but I bore down and leaned into the impact.

Don't fall—*umf!*

We crashed hard. Lee bounced off me. I held my stance and grinned. She looked a bit surprised as she rubbed an elbow. Alright, Gidget, let's see what you can do on the water. Grab your stick.

We started down the beach, which was now, with the tide flowing in, reduced to half the width of the night before but still a good hundred metres that stretched from road to water. A few of the young guys from the hostel were nearby, looking unsure on boards in hip-deep water, falling and laughing.

I wondered if the waves were even big enough to surf on.

Big enough for you, Gidget, trust me.

Okay, seriously. Why do you keep calling me that?

You like Barney better? Or Kook?

Not really.

Just means newbie. Got worse words for it. Okay, walk out to like chest height, and then—see that line of white, where the waves are just starting to break? Get on your board and paddle to just outside of it.

I did as I was told, walked out through the breaking surf until the water was well above my waist. I jumped up, belly-flopped onto the foam board and promptly went right over on the other side, the board flipping on top of me.

I came up sputtering to the sound of Lee's barked laughter. I clenched my teeth and growled.

The second time, I slid the board under me and managed to keep it there. I rocked it cautiously back and forth, testing for the limits of balance. Lee was already paddling out ahead of me, moving her arms like she was swimming the front crawl. I followed her, and when we were out past the white water, she told me how to watch the waves, what to look for in the texture of the water as it swelled and bent and rolled.

But no one can really, like, you either feel it or you don't, hey.

I'd forgotten to attach the board's leash to my ankle, so I did so now, nearly falling off again in the process.

If you're gonna eat it, just bail, stay behind your board. Alright?

Alright. I had playoff nerves, ramped up.

When you see a wave coming, get in front of it, paddle fast, fast, fast and then ride it in. Do that a few times before you try to stand up, just ride in on your tum. Got it?

Okay. I saw a cluster of waves moving towards us.

That's all there is. You'll do great. Here—get this one—paddle! Paddle!

I saw the swell coming, turned my board around and paddled towards shore as hard as I could. I felt the board surge up, rising, accelerating, I whooped with adrenalin as I coasted with the top of the wave on my belly, there was air beneath me and I floated, my arms spread wide. Then the wave bottomed out and I grabbed the sides of the board in an instant of panic as I dropped, almost fell off, recovered, splashed down, then coasted into the shallows. Lee was right: these waves were higher than they looked.

I turned around to paddle back and saw Lee farther out and off to my left, cutting in, crouched on her board. As I watched, she twisted up the lip of her wave and flew, board first, several feet in the air, twisted around again and cut down onto a curl of surf, her body almost horizontal but her feet on her board, her crouched stance intact. She slid down the inside of the wave and sliced her board in and out across the breaking edge of it as she rode in towards the beach, standing more upright as the water flattened.

Holy fuck, I muttered, grinning into the wind.

I paddled out past the break point again, turned to watch the swells roll towards me. I thought they were already bigger than a couple minutes ago. At what point does the tide turn, I wondered? Was this a safe time to be out here? Weren't riptides something people frequently died in? But the moment I recognized Jules's voice in my head was the same moment I heard Lee yelling, Go! GO!

I turned my board around, started paddling furiously, again felt the swelling ocean buoy me up, saw the nose of my board come out of the water, point straight forward as I rose and rose. Fuck the baby steps, and I popped up to my feet, left foot in front, stayed in a squat—

And I flew, I was flying, the nose of my board sliced only air, the wave lifted me, the ocean embraced me, beneath me, behind me, pushing me, following me, exhaling—

A shadow to my left dropped in fast on the wave—*my* wave. I tried to swerve and felt my balance go, the board left my feet, I saw pale sky, felt the leash pull my ankle, couldn't breathe, couldn't get upright, grasped for the surface, blue light, white shadows, an underwater voice that might be my own—

A sharp pain behind my left ear and a flash

Neck.

———

Jules woke up Sunday morning with a sense of dread, of deep regret, with the knowledge that something was terribly wrong. The right side of her neck. Yesterday it had been the left side of her neck, twinging when she turned her head in the wrong direction, disciplining her like an invisible electric fence.

But this was different. There was no escaping this long and unrelenting twinge, this ghost made manifest. The screeching hellmouth in the middle of her back ripped along her nerves, in under her shoulder blade, up her neck, into the bone behind her ear.

She thought about calling Rod. Maybe she had some kind of latent whiplash from the accident yesterday. But she didn't feel up to negotiating his hidden labyrinth of expectations, making fake apologies as part of some unspoken bargain. She pushed herself out of bed, fell back with a gasp as her shoulder seized. The *whump* of a flame as gasoline hits it.

She had protocols for moments like this. Jules made it downstairs to the fridge for an ice pack, slipped it into the cotton sleeve, used its hook-and-loop straps to wrap it around her back and shoulder. Got a glass of water and went back up, into the bathroom.

Out of Oxy. Right. She rummaged for some old Percocets, came up short. But she had some Tylenol 3s, so she took a couple of those. Better than nothing. Then she went back to bed, lay there

with the ice pack and felt some of the burn seep out, the fires of
hell cooling into a hard knot, intense but inert. Back downstairs,
she switched it to a heat pack. She went back up and lay there for
another hour or so; some of the spasming loosened, uncramped.
Repeat: ice, heat, ice, heat. Eventually she could lean against some
pillows comfortably enough to watch TV. Cop shows, lawyer
shows, extreme weight loss shows. Reruns flickered past her, for-
mulae numbing her with spectacular predictability. Rape, murder,
torture. Bodies punishing themselves.

When the codeine started to wear off, she took two more. She
did some gentle stretches, tried to move around a little. Took a hot
shower. Around three thirty in the afternoon, she poured herself a
Scotch. There was only one way to survive days like this. Just get
through it.

Six a.m. Monday, her alarm rang. She went to sit up in bed and
pain shot down her back. She swore, but it felt limp in her mouth.
Nausea made her stomach cramp fiercely. And she was now out
of Tylenol 3s.

She dug around in the bathroom and found some regular-
strength ibuprofen. Wouldn't help her stomach, but you do what
you have to do. She took four.

She stood in front of her espresso machine, made and drank
three single shots in a row. Somehow, she had to get to work.

She texted Rod:

Meet me for coffee? 8 am at Café Au Lait?

She named the little place right near his hospital. She thought
that, as text messages went, it managed to sound contrite while
remaining succinct.

She took a hot shower, which loosened her up enough to get
dressed.

By the time she got out, he had answered:

C U there.

Jules always took the time to write out whole words like "see" and "you," but Rod prided himself on using the short forms popular with Chloe's generation. Even though he eschewed much of said generation, really, and quite probably Chloe herself, although he knew better than to go there with Jules. But if—when—Jules complained about her daughter, he never hesitated to agree that Chloe was being horrible, or selfish, or rude, or foolish.

The new suit she'd worn to Drew's was crumpled on the floor and reeked of cigarette smoke, so she was back to the navy blue blazer and pants, which she had always thought was her most comfortable work outfit, but today, under siege from her own body, it made her feel old, dumpy and underdressed. It was the very jacket that had made Drew send her shopping: "grotesquely unfashionable," with a boxy cut that hung tentishly over her wide hips and protruding tummy. But Rod's eye for women's fashion was non-existent, and at the moment she didn't give a shit.

THE COFFEE SHOP smell, usually a boon to her morning senses, brought fresh bile to the back of her throat. She spotted Rod sitting at a tiny round table at the back, cupping his Americano in his hands and searching its depths. The café was noisy with hospital staff, greeting each other and joking around as they came off night shift or fuelled up for the long day ahead. Rod sat in the middle of the bustle, a charcoal-suited stone in a field of green scrubs and white lab coats.

He looked up as Jules reached his table, stood to touch her lips with a kiss. She lowered herself into the seat across from him. Her lower back felt stiff. Her neck was winched in spasm. Come to think of it, her whole body was aching like she had the flu. She really needed her meds. But looking into Rod's face, she saw she'd made an error in judgment.

When did you run out?

Jules deferred answering by ordering an Americano and a croissant from the gum-chewing pre-med waiter. It hurt to look up at her.

I just wanted to apologize, she said.

It was noisy enough to feel private. Striations of worry lined Rod's forehead.

How much have you been taking?

Jules's croissant arrived. She had ordered it out of habit, but right now it looked like shiny plastic, the sight of it made her stomach cramp. She pushed it away.

Not hungry?

Jules shook her head. She felt feverish, septic. Her coffee came, and she gripped the mug tightly with both hands to hide their shaking.

I really did something to my neck when that car hit us. Pain's making me nauseous.

You should probably get that seen to.

He tracked her movements diagnostically. But his shoulders were pulled back, his mouth a hard line.

You're still mad.

Well. I'm trying to figure out if you're lying to me, lying to yourself or just stupid.

His voice cut and she flinched. She felt pathetic, suckered in. He leaned forward.

Look at yourself. You're sweating buckets, your hands are shaking, your face is *green*. I'll bet all your muscles and joints hurt, right? Couldn't sleep last night? Stomach cramps?

He was smug as he detailed the symptoms of her misery.

What's your point?

You're in opiate withdrawal, Jules. I'll ask you again: how much have you been taking?

In the last two weeks she had been more than quadrupling the prescribed dose. So she told him:

Maybe double? My neck really hurts.

Rod sat back again and looked at her skeptically. And is that the only reason you wanted to meet me? He folded his arms across his chest.

No, I told you, I wanted to apologize.

For what?

Jules took a long, deep breath and stared at a spot over his shoulder. The truth was, she didn't really want to apologize for anything specific. She just wanted to make everything okay again, put it back the way it was so that she didn't have to explain and Rod would just refill her prescription and go back to work. She tried to think of what she should say to make that happen, what vague blanket apology would appease him.

Right, Rod finally said. Well, you think on that for a moment.

He got up from the table and took the few steps to the door marked Men. An intern stepped out and they talked for a moment, the younger man paying him obvious deference, wide-eyed and nodding repeatedly. Jules cupped her coffee in her hands, steadying herself with its warmth. She noticed Rod's lab coat, draped over the back of his chair. His stethoscope was curled up in one pocket. In the other, on the side opposite the men's room, the top edge of a small pad of paper.

Time slowed as she realized: his prescription pad. He had it with him. Reflexively, she glanced over at Rod, who simultaneously looked over the shoulder of the intern, trapped her stare in his.

There was a lot of understanding in that moment. Rod's face was lined with palpable concern, and a sadness that she could disappoint him so much. He felt betrayed, probably, or used. But it wasn't like she was some kind of addict. Lots of prescription meds came with withdrawal symptoms if you came off them too quickly. That's why you tapered off.

Maybe if she told him she wanted to come off the Oxy, that he was right that she was taking too much, maybe he would give her a little bit, so she could come off it more slowly—not right away, maybe, but once this thing in her neck calmed down.

But as Rod broke her gaze and went into the bathroom, the thick door closed with a clicking thunk behind him and that, somehow, brought home the realization:

He would never give her what she wanted.

The young intern, abandoned mid-sentence, made it back to his table with a smirk and an eye roll to comment to his colleague that Doc Scott had his panties in a knot, to which the second intern replied with brutally accurate mimicry of Rod's voice, That's why he talks like this.

And it was the aggravating laughter that did it.

Jules leaned over in her chair, as if to rummage in her bag, but then she remembered she didn't have a bag, so she pretended to tie her shoe instead. The pockets of Rod's lab coat reached the floor. The one holding the prescription pad was inches from Jules's hand. She couldn't twist her head around much, but she sort of jerked it, chicken-like, in either direction, to make sure no one was watching, before reaching over and slipping her hand into the pocket. She felt for the bottom of the pad then peeled back a sheet, but the top page stuck to the ones underneath, so she ended up with a small wad. She quickly ripped the whole thing off and pulled it out in one smooth motion. Under the table she saw the bottom of the men's room door swing open. She yanked up her pant leg and stuffed the blank prescriptions into her sock, gave the laces on her loafer another unneeded tug and sat up. Slowly, one hand supporting her lower back.

As Rod sat back down, he grimaced at her obvious discomfort.

Don't worry about it, she said.

Anyway, I've been meaning to tell you—they're taking it off the market.

What—just like that? What am I supposed to do?

Well, you know, there's been some controversy, so. They're replacing it with this OxyNEO. Same drug, but it's supposed to be tamper-proof.

Tamper-proof. She knew what that meant, but it had never occurred to her to do it herself, grind it up and snort it or whatever.

Also supposedly not habit forming.

Oh, come on, it's not like I'm a *junkie*.

The paper in her sock poked, making her itch urgently. She made fists under the table, dug her nails into her palms. Rod tilted his head at her, his mouth a grim line.

Yes, well. We need to get you off it. Supervised. One pill at a time. He'd gone into Sympathetic Doctor mode. Sympathetic Boyfriend seemed to have slunk away, but the Doctor was always on duty.

I'm fine, Jules said, suddenly worried he would pull out his prescription pad and notice that it was significantly thinner. It looks worse than it is.

He reached across and squeezed her arm. Pale, uncalloused fingers.

You could get much sicker before you get better. Let me help.

His eyes went to her forehead, she was starting to sweat and wondered if the sheen of it was visible.

No, really. Jules pulled out her wallet and rifled through it. I'm sorry for putting you in this position. She figured her bill at seven dollars, but all she had was a ten. She put it on the table. She was grossly overpaying for something she hadn't even enjoyed, but she didn't care.

That's what you wanted to hear, right?

The words pushed him away with a physical force. He fell against the back of his chair, his face looked slapped.

The two young interns at the next table got up to go, and one of them shot a look her way, and the look was full of pity. And all of a sudden, or maybe not so suddenly at all, Jules needed to get away from Rod, away from his guilt, from his condescension. She stood up.

You're the one who prescribed them. If I'm some kind of addict, whose fault is that?

I didn't call you an addict.

But you think it.

She turned away, too quickly, winced as her neck punished her.

You just need to— Jules—

He could see that she was leaving, and she could see that it made him uneasy that the situation was slipping out of his control. She wondered how she had gotten under this particular thumb in the first place, how she had ever thought that this—any of this, the intertwined relationship between her body, her boyfriend and his pills, its laced and hidden trappings of guilt and dependency—could be something that she wanted. She turned back, gritting against her body's response to her imperfect angles.

Forget it, Rod. That's it. Cold turkey.

Pharmacy.

———

But Rod was right about one thing: she felt worse and worse. The hour commute to Toronto usually passed in that semi-aware state unevenly divided between preoccupation with the day to come and reflexively avoiding highway collisions. Today, every second slammed her between the ears, throbbed out to her fingertips, making her fervently wish she could curl into a ball. Even at the excruciating twenty-five kilometres an hour, she was gun-shy behind the wheel of her rental and tried to avoid changing lanes.

She could have tried to get more meds at a Hamilton pharmacy, but she was already running late. She also thought she had a better chance of passing off the forgery in the bigger city. Farther from Rod's hospital.

Forgery. She said the word in her head and let herself fully, consciously admit to herself what she intended to do. Wondered: Had she really come to this point? Did she, in fact, have a problem? No. Well, maybe. But we all have problems, and some are bigger than others.

She had meant to go to some out-of-the-way drugstore in a less affluent neighbourhood of Toronto where she imagined illegal prescriptions might slip by regularly. But when she hit her first exit for downtown, it was already five to ten, her stomach cramps were intensifying and her joint pain seemed to be empire-building, colonizing elbows, knees, wrists. She craved the solace of her private ensuite bathroom, so she drove straight to her office, sweating through every intersection.

There was a pharmacy on the ground floor of her office tower where she had been many times, and she hoped that, because they knew her, they wouldn't look too closely at the scrip. She sat in the rental car in the underground garage and practised a few times in a notebook before taking the wad of blank prescription sheets and doing her best imitation of Rod's illegible scrawl. Took her empty pill bottle up to the pharmacy.

The pharmacist, an affable young guy named Po, who had filled this very scrip many times, squinted at it and gave her a puzzled look, and she nearly panicked. She pulled out the empty bottle, tried not to let her hand shake as she handed it to him.

I know, his writing's impossible. It's just a refill of this one.

When Po read the label, nodded and said, You got it, fifteen minutes, Jules gushed inwardly with relief.

In the elevator up to her tenth-floor office, she leaned against dark leather, eyes closed to the sepia-toned mirrors.

Sometimes it threw her a little, when the elevator door opened and she was confronted by the sweeping mahogany reception desk, the lushly carpeted corporate hallway receding behind it. Closed oak doors, expensive abstract art. It was quiet, muffled. Sterile. There was nothing messy here, no place for actual bodies. This was where she tracked numbers, applied algorithms, extracted information and compiled it into tidy charts and graphs. That the numbers represented people, their likes and dislikes, habits and relationships, reactions, patterns and preferences, was an abstraction she deliberately ignored. But today it struck her how unlikely it was that she worked here, doing this, being this person. It was a long way from the one-bedroom apartment she'd shared with her mother for sixteen years. The convenience store open twenty-four hours, buses stopping out front all night, the building peeling and cracking inside and out, stained in ageless grime. Their apartment stale with smoke and soured by the active volcanoes of dishes and laundry, the pungent hormonal smell of under-washed sheets. And her mother, a stagnant body of sadness, cleaning offices by night and drinking on the couch by day, passing out to *Days of Our Lives*. Jules would come home from school and wake her up, feed her dinner and send her back to work. Cleaning offices much like these.

She felt nauseous.

The receptionist flagged her down on her way by. She had hoped to slip into her office unnoticed and was holding herself together until she could get behind her closed door. But this secretary was new and young: nervous and vigilant. She called her Ms. Wright, said good morning and held out a meticulously aligned and stapled pile of pink message slips. Which was ridiculous. They were a knowledge management firm. Data miners. Everything they did was computer-based. To even have a receptionist was sheer pretense, in her eyes. But the message slips were particularly redundant. There would be voice mail on her phone from whoever called, a log of the callers who hadn't left messages and probably an email from Amy or Annie or whatever her name was—she was really very new—repeating same. Quite possibly whoever had called would have emailed her as well. It all amounted, in Jules's opinion, to too much communication.

She grabbed the slips from Annie or Amy and tried to make it look as though the jerky movement of her hand was due to gruffness and rushing, not the uncontrollable whole-body shaking of possible opiate withdrawal.

She forced herself to walk down the hall with aggression in her step. If Annie/Amy spread the word, as she inevitably would, that Jules was in a bad mood, everyone was more likely to stay away. She closed the door with a solid clunk, leaned back against it, disassembling.

She glanced at the messages—three of them, almost identical, all from her ex-husband: "Mr. Wright called at . . .": 9:05, 9:22 and 9:46 a.m. Nine in the morning here was one in the morning in Christchurch. She recalled Chloe's sullen email from . . . Saturday, wasn't it? *Plane didn't crash.* So that was something. But the message slips were inert and unforthcoming. She shoved them in her pocket.

She made her way to her bathroom and dry-heaved the breakfast she hadn't eaten, then sat on the toilet and emptied her guts out that way. Splashed cold water on her face, went back into her office and lay down on her couch, the cool smoothness of the green leather soothing under her cheek.

The phone on her desk rang. She wondered if it was David again. She knew she should answer it, but she just couldn't.

Instead, she shivered with fever as she contemplated the effort it would take to draw the blinds on her half wall of window, the dazzling blue sky that filled it from her low-angled perspective. It seemed like her worst days were always the sunniest ones.

The day Lizzie died: the phone call from Maureen.

She'd stared out her window as she listened, watching a summer-jobber with his bucket and pole scrubbing down the Sir John A. Macdonald statue in the park below, going down and up and down the arms, like he was giving a toddler a bath, while Maureen's voice quavered and stammered and snivelled, you'd think it was her child who'd just stopped breathing.

There was a knock at her door. Go away, Amy, I'm busy. The words dry in her throat. But the door opened.

Actually, I think her name is Ashley. Drew, filling her doorway. You look like shit.

He strode across to the chair beside her, lowered himself into it. Today he wore an enormous pink suit and lavender tie. Jules turned onto her back and put an arm over her eyes so she wouldn't have to look at it.

Rod says I'm in withdrawal. I think I have the flu.

Get the fuck out. Drew was in frat boy mode, probably had a partners' meeting at lunch and had started early. This is from the Oxy?

It's horrible.

Jeezus. How much did he have you on?

You can't blame Rod.

Like hell I can't.

No, really, I was . . . upping the dose, I guess. He didn't know.

But he does now?

He does now.

Her cellphone buzzed, across the room on her desk. Drew reached behind him and grabbed it, glanced at it as he handed it over.

He's not giving you more, is he?

It said *Bay St. Drugs* on the screen.

Jules shook her head as she answered. It was Po, affability stretched thin. Ms. Wright, I can't fill this. You can't bring this to me. Each word spoken like a drum hit, short and sharp.

What's the matter, Po? But she knew, of course. She sat up, wincing.

I only caught you because they're pulling it off market, right? I stopped restocking it. So I called Dr. Scott, see what he wants me to do, maybe switch to the OxyNEO—but he didn't write this! It's not— You can't bring me this, I could lose my licence—

Po's voice had risen, frantic and pinched. I'm supposed to call the police.

Jules pressed her thumb into the bridge of her nose, thinking: Fuck.

Dr. Scott told me not to, but Ms. Wright, I think I have to. I gotta cover my own ass, right?

Don't worry, Po. Just rip it up, okay? Void it.

That's what Dr. Scott said.

Jules held her breath for the long pause, awaiting Po's judgment.

Okay, Ms. Wright. You're really lucky, okay? This time. But don't come here anymore. I can't have this, right? Dr. Scott's real angry too—

I bet he is.

—he said you were—

I'm sorry, Po. You have a good day, alright? Jules hung up on him.

The email icon on her phone had a red number on it: twenty-two messages. She tapped it and glanced at the list of headings. Mostly progress updates from the project managers she supervised. A couple from clients that didn't seem urgent and could easily be off-loaded to said project managers. And one from David. She wished he would just fucking deal with it. Whatever it was.

Drew was now sprawled back in the armchair, his jowls spilling over his pink-and-lavender neckline, making him look like a giant worried cupcake.

Problem?

She lay back down and closed her eyes. She couldn't remember the last time she'd felt this sick. There was no way she could get any work done today. She wanted Drew to go away and let her nap.

Don't take this the wrong way, but did you need something?

Drew waited a long moment before answering, she could sense him assessing her condition, trying to determine how worried he should be. He knew Jules had chronic injuries, that she had physio once a week or more, that she often had to take pretty heavy pain medication. But as a PR exec who partied like an intern, he probably ingested more substances than she did. So he wasn't really in a position to judge. He'd come to work with hangovers that looked worse than this.

Two things. Came to see if you had fun on Friday.

Subtle, she said. But if she'd felt better, she would have smiled. Instead, she draped her arm back across her eyes. Great dinner. Farzan seems nice.

Another long silence. Then:

That's it?

Alright, alright. I didn't hate him. But it doesn't really matter, does it?

She didn't want to talk about Declan. It was such a small thing, but it had played in her mind off and on all weekend, between bouts of sickness and mandatory naps, how she had come to the point of manoeuvring her hand closer to his like a lovesick teenager. One moment she couldn't have said she wanted that to happen; the next, made it happen. She wasn't ready to unearth, out loud, the ambiguity of her actions, or her emotions. So she told him:

Stupid kid in a hatchback side-swiped me on the way home Saturday.

Holy shit! For real?

Oh yes.

What— Are you okay?

Peachy. Car's in the shop, though. She sat up, clenched her teeth against the rush of wooziness. It's also possible I broke up with Rod.

Whoa. Because of Declan?

Don't be ridiculous.

She opened her laptop on the coffee table, followed the bookmark to the medical website she relied on for self-assessing new aches and pains. She did a search on "opiate withdrawal," found a list of symptoms.

Sweating, shaking, nausea, aching and cramping. Check. But seizures and convulsions? Surely it wouldn't get that bad. She closed her computer, laid herself gently back down on the couch.

Oh, sweetie. You want me to call him?

It's just the flu, she said. She'd forgotten Declan was a doctor.

Drew dialed his phone.

Jules would never know how that conversation went. Dry heaves sent her scrambling for the bathroom. When she emerged a few minutes later, Drew was writing something on a Post-it Note on her desk.

He'll see you on his lunch. One o'clock, at his clinic. He moved towards the door, a fuchsia silk ocean liner on fast-forward. I have to get to the partners' meeting.

I have to see him? He can't just call in a scrip somewhere?

'Fraid not. But he's very good, Jules. Number and address are on your desk. Oh, and the second thing was that analytics report, but I'm guessing you didn't get to it?

Oh shit.

She sank back onto the couch. A condo developer had hired them to track the next best areas for twenty-five- to forty-four-year-olds who enjoyed indoor sports and would pay nine dollars for a latte, were likely to have one but unlikely to have two children in the next ten years and disliked gardening but loved small dogs. She had the data ready but had to synthesize it, make it presentation-ready.

I'm so sorry. I was in bed all weekend. Think I did something to my neck in the accident.

Shit happens. I know Raj is keen to see it, but I'll buy you some time. Wednesday, okay?

It was eleven fifteen when Drew left. Jules spent the next hour trying to convince herself she was feeling better rather than worse. When it didn't work, she dug in her jacket pocket for more sheets from Rod's prescription pad and came across the pink message slips from David.

She sighed in annoyance and shoved them back in, worked instead on a new and improved forged Oxy prescription. When she was fairly satisfied, she hunched her shoulders and scowled to project a carapace of hostility as she marched down the hall towards the reception desk. On her way by, she handed Ashley the Post-it with Declan's number on it. No way she could see him like this.

I have an appointment with this guy at one, cancel it for me, please and thank you.

And she kept going, right into the open elevator.

SHE FIGURED THE Parkdale pharmacy would be much easier. For one thing, she now had the drug right: she'd done a blanket search for OxyNEO and found its spec sheet with available dosages on the manufacturer's website.

For another thing, it was Parkdale, a neighbourhood, if you could call it that, notorious for its poverty, its crackheads, its former mental patients. Not so different from Hamilton's north end, where she'd grown up. Surely a well-dressed, middle-aged white woman like herself would fly well under the radar as a risk for passing illegal prescriptions.

But driving over, she realized condo-fication was in full swing there. It was kind of like seeing her past and present worlds overlaid on each other. Tidy, stylish signs of new "hip" restaurants, called things like Slaughterhouse Five and Yes, hung between older ones, hand-markered, chipped and misspelled, for places like Happy Noodel and Budget Super Saving Discount. Shiny windows showcased vintage clothes between exhaust-encrusted storefronts that sold knock-off electronics and shoes, or were blocked out completely with plywood. Like Hamilton's north end, this had long been a community of immigrant families, the number of places For Rent, For Lease or For Sale demonstrating the current pace of change.

Chloe didn't know how good she had it, didn't understand where Jules had come from or how hard she'd worked to leave it behind. How close she sometimes felt to the precipice that would lead her back there. Back here.

A battered grey sign that might once have been white read Marky's Drugs in uneven black letters. The window below the sign was barred, and behind the bars was an awkward display of bedpans and a cheap mobility walker. A couple of rough-looking men were hanging around out front. They spat on the sidewalk, drank from a paper bag they passed between them. Eyed her with what she read as hostility mixed with covetousness as she parked the rental at the curb and approached the pharmacy door.

Inside was a starkly lit arrangement of three short and understocked aisles. Jules walked past an assortment of laxatives, diapers and the most basic of painkillers on her way to the phone booth–sized prescription counter at the back.

The pharmacist darted her eyes around suspiciously as she took Jules's prescription, and Jules looked behind her. A couple of teenagers were lingering in the centre aisle between a huge rack of condoms and a slightly smaller one of pregnancy tests. She idly wondered which interested them, and sent a silent thanks to the universe for making her daughter a lesbian.

Hey, you buying something?

The pharmacist had Jules's scrip in her hand but hadn't taken her eyes off the teens.

Hurry, she'll kick us out, said the girl, who was probably Chloe's age, way too skinny, with shoulder-length blond dreadlocks.

The boy, whose jeans were filthy and full of holes, squared his stance, pre-emptively insolent. We gotta right to shop. In-spect the merch, yo. His lower lip was pierced by two silver hoops that made it look like he had fangs.

The pharmacist, who couldn't have been over thirty, flattened her lips into a tight line, kept glancing at the teens as she entered Jules's name and address into her amber-screened computer. She disappeared behind the high counter with its bulletproof glass panels to find the prepackaged vial of thirty tabs of OxyNEO that Jules had prescribed herself.

Jules waited in a chair with a backrest strapped to it and tried to relax. Breathing in, breathing out, in and out, in and out, breathing through the nausea and the aching and the sweating. Moments, she told herself, in moments she could take a pill and start to feel normal again. Her neck was so bad she worried she'd injured yet another disc. But if she could just have something to cope with the pain, then she could get herself to a doctor or someone to take a look at it. Not Rod or Declan. Maybe a clinic.

The teenagers came back around the condom aisle, and Jules watched as the young woman shoved a couple deep-purple boxes under her shirt. The boy grabbed a couple light-blue ones, shoved them into the front of his jeans. He had walked to the door, keeping an eye on the backroom while he waited for his girlfriend, who grabbed a couple boxes from the rack of pregnancy tests—and who saw Jules watching and glared back at her defiantly. She kept glaring as she backed away down the aisle towards her partner in crime. Jules could see over her shoulder as she approached the door.

And at the same moment that it occurred to Jules that the pharmacist was taking far too long to retrieve a prepackaged prescription, she saw the blue shadow of a uniform darken the doorway behind the boyfriend.

Concussion.

———

Sensations garbled, blue-and-whiteness, light curving into bubbles, deep gargling in my ears, the oddly calm awareness of breathing water, liquid inside my body inside liquid and then, a second or minutes later, choking over the sand, coughing and sputtering, my head roaring in pain, Lee rubbing my back and yelling down the beach, her face stricken grey. One of the Australians tearing towards us across the sand, somehow he had gauze, bandages.

And then they were putting me into the Australian's car, taking me to an emergency room where a matronly nurse shaved the hair behind my left ear—there wasn't much to begin with—and a darkblack doctor with gleaming white teeth said, Concussion, and put in five stitches under flickering fluorescent lights as my body vibrated with elated relief that this was the worst that could happen.

Keep your head out of the water for a week till these dissolve. And best to stay put for a bit, yeah? Where there's folks that know ya.

Already I was finding the headache crushing, but he wouldn't give me anything strong, narcotics might make my brain bleed.

I was willing to take the risk, but he still refused.

So, there I was, stuck in a surf lodge and barred from the water, with a raging headache that made me wince at the light and an untouchable raw and puckered golf ball behind my ear. I wasn't used to this, to my body turning against me on so many fronts: nauseous, sore all over, constantly chilled. I'd managed to badly bruise an elbow, and all my muscles and my whole left side were wickedly stiff, like they'd seized when I fell.

A conversation came back to me from one of those frustrating nights when I'd tried to get Jules to admit that her level of intoxication was too high, again, again. And Jules, slightly slurring her words, had tried to tell me that her body was, at best, when she could manage it, a remote machine, clunky and malfunctional, tolerable only with tinkering and troubleshooting, coaxing as you would a rundown jalopy or a stubborn mule, and that much of her waking life was devoted to maintenance that usually felt futile.

I lamented the pills I'd stolen occasionally from her Oxy supply and wished I hadn't wasted my last one on a particularly nasty dorm room hangover. All I had was sleeping pills, but for once sleeping was not the problem.

Vivid near-drowning memories flickered though me at random times, awake or asleep, a pirate signal, static in my brain, swirling old nightmares of hyperventilating alone in a hallway, Jules almost catatonic as Nan berated her, my stuffed elephant Eloise still in my hand, its damp trunk the only thing left of the baby. The sound of someone close by, keening.

I SPENT THE first couple days in bed, watching the sky change colour, struggling, when it got too bright, to find comfort without lying on the swollen side of my head. My brain had been given a good shake, and I found myself thinking things I'd never thought before: is this what Jules feels sometimes? And even: what would Jules do now? Not because I saw my mother as a role model, or wanted to be like her in any way. But because I couldn't deny the ways in which I *was* like her, the tangible imprint Jules had made on my life, my coping strategies, probably even my personality if you wanted to get super dark about it. And it somehow made her less the demon who had sold her soul to the evil empire, and who had completely shut down her ability to feel. She was still all that, no question, but she was also human: fallible and fragile.

LEE BROUGHT ME meals between surf sessions, sat on the end of my bed and played cards with me, or Jenga when I felt like getting up, providing stable islands of clarity and comfort. And distraction. Right about then I might have sorely regretted not having my phone, if I hadn't had her trash-talking me as we played euchre, forcing me to fight back the laughter that made my head roar.

You blamin' that hand on a head injury?

Um. I am, yes.

But Lee's attentiveness had a nervous edge to it. A couple days later, when I'd made it out to the porch to smoke a joint with Sean, she was checking out my stitches, and even as she joked about possible permanent brain damage, she was practically clucking, and I felt compelled to reassure her that it wasn't her fault.

It's my own fault. I didn't see that Belgian kid coming. Maybe partly his fault. But not yours. Just bad luck, really.

When I was very little, I had gone to the pool with Mo-mo, watched her swim lengths up and down while I clung to the side in the shallow end, still deeper than I was tall, the pool edge chafing under my arms. Older kids flying over my head with jubilant hoots, splashing into the noisy expanse of chlorine-blue pool. It had all been unfathomable to my five-year-old self, and irresistible, and eventually I worked up the nerve to throw myself into the fray. In the bath-warm water I sank like a drowning kitten, thrashed and sputtered and my feet touched the bottom of the pool, but there was only water above me, a murky light. Until a hand grabbed me, pulled me back to the safety of the wall. Some other girl, my age and also clutching for safety, had just reached out and dragged me in. Mo-mo, steady and sure and unreachable on the far side of the pool, propelled herself up and down a marked-off lane and made it look easy.

I told Lee and Sean the story, and tried to explain how once again I'd underestimated the water and overestimated myself. Lee paused her fussing and rested a light hand on the side of my head. I should have told you to lose your leash.

Yeah, and then we might not have found her so quick. Or the board might have hurt the other kid.

Sean gestured down the porch to where the three Belgians were sequestered in a corner. One of them had a nasty sand rash on his face.

Anyway, you *did* tell me to.

See, there you go, it's a judgment call, if you keep the leash or not, and it was her first time out. If you're not ready to get rag-dolled, don't get wet.

You just seemed so confident. Lee gave a gentle squeeze to the back of my neck, then moved to the slingback chair in the centre of our trio.

Seriously, though. I've been slammed into the hockey net so many times. Shit happens.

Wearing loads of gear, though, yeah?

Plus, I loved it. I can't wait to try it again.

Yeah, that's it. Sean nodded his enthusiasm. Back on the horse, yeah?

Lee snorted. Great. She got up and went into the hostel.

It's just a couple stitches, I said. *Mild* concussion.

She just forgets. In her blood, yeah?

Oh, right—her dad was a surfer?

I thought about my own parents, what activities we shared. Drinking, maybe.

Big-time, Sean said. Famous, like. Travelled for tourneys, took her everywhere. Got her started when she was wee. She never had to *learn* like the rest of us. Sean ducked his head. And then he died, of course.

Died. Died surfing? Light moved upwards behind my eyes, blue and white and airless, liquid panic.

You didn't know? Sean looked uncomfortable. Any surfer over fifteen's probably heard about it. He just hit the trough, right? At Pipeline. Hawaii. Solid wall just took him under.

Sean depicted how this could happen with his hands, a huge rounded claw of wave crushing everything in its grasp. I pictured Lee's tattoo, the wave that wrapped her bicep, the tiny surfer cutting through it.

And she was on the beach, yeah? Saw it happen. Little nine-year-old Brit junior contender. Stayed away from the media after that, though.

That Lee might have a terror of history repeating, and the possibilities for self-recrimination, resonated deep in my bones.

IT ALSO MADE me question all the time Lee was spending with me. I wanted desperately to believe that the connection I felt with her, the excitement that made my stomach tighten every time she looked at me, was two-way. But it was difficult to ignore the worry that off-gassed, palpably, whenever she saw me take an ibuprofen or close my eyes for a few seconds. I tried to quiet the voice that made me doubt that she just liked me and wanted to hang out with me. I didn't want her to feel like I needed looking after. I worried that getting injured my first time out had somehow diminished me in her eyes. We weren't even together, and I was waiting for her to leave me.

AT SOME POINT, I used the hostel phone to call David's house in Christchurch, just to check in.

Oh my god, Chlo! We've been worried sick! What's the matter

with your phone? Amanda was so much more direct than David.

Lance didn't tell you?

All he said was that you'd call and you never did. Now he's up in Wellington helping with all those beached whales.

I had heard about this. Pilot whales, hundreds of them, had committed suicide on sandbars off the coast. Some scientist on the news had called it a harbinger of another "big one," an earthquake to dwarf all the recent aftershocks.

Well, my phone's gone. Anyway, I had a bit of an accident—

Gone? Should we try to—what's it called? Clean it or something?

Wipe. Remote wipe. No, there's no point.

Doesn't it have one of those tracking things on it? We could—

No, you can't track it.

I lost mine once and we tracked it—to the trunk of the car! She laughed, and I had to laugh with her.

But I know where it is.

You know where it is? Where is it?

Well . . . the ocean floor?

Oh, sweetie. How are we going to keep track of you?

Aw, don't worry, Amanda. I can keep track of myself.

IT WOULD HAVE been a satisfying conversation, a firm drawing of boundaries with parental units, if Lee had not overheard it.

So you *did* have a cellphone, she said when I hung up and turned around to find her sitting there.

I did, yeah.

And you threw it in the ocean, she said, not as a question, her voice steeped in disbelief. You're not one of these climate change deniers, are ya?

No, of course not! I tried to sound scornful, but the shame in my gut weakened my words. I just needed to get away from them, I explained.

Lee was skeptical. Who's "them"?

So I told her about David and Amanda and my not-so-new half-sister, thinking she would understand my annoyance with people trying to control me, trying to rope me into family bonds that I wasn't ready for, wasn't sure I wanted.

But as I finished talking, she was shaking her head a little bit sadly. I found being an only child unbearably lonely, she said. I might never understand you North Americans.

My face burned with all the ways I felt myself lessening in her eyes. I wanted desperately to tell her that I'd been lonely too, and that even though I'd only known her just over a week, I felt like she *got* me. But I wasn't ready to put either of those things into words.

SEAN, LATE ONE too many shifts, lost his dishwashing job in town. We were out on the porch, watching the tide ebb at twilight, when he told us he was going to go work on a farm on the North Island. Lee looked alarmed. Sheep, he added. Up near Auckland.

Can you surf up there? I asked.

Lee shook her head. No, he cannot.

But it's close to Piha. I need the place to stay, love. Not all of us have trust funds.

Sod off. I hate you for leaving.

Why don't you come with me? Nationals are next month anyway. You can't stay off the radar forever.

Watch me.

Aw, c'mon.

Nationals, mate? Fuckin' zoo, that. Everyone just wants to talk about my pops. It's exhausting.

Only because you're as good as he was.

I'm *better* than he was. That's why it's annoying.

Okay, okay. Well, you'll just have to hang with the guys here, then. Or get this one up to speed faster. When can you swim again?

Stitches are gone, so. Tomorrow, I guess. Technically.

See? She doesn't even want to surf.

No, I do, I'm just . . . going hiking, remember? Maybe you should come with me?

But Lee would not commit. Maybe, she said. Maybe.

A FEW MORNINGS later, I heard Lee get up before the daylight and go downstairs for her wetsuit. I would follow in a couple minutes, go with the Dawn Patrol guys, her early morning crew, to wherever the surf was up. I loved watching them. Watching Lee.

But Lee came back, dropped her wetsuit in a pile beside her own bunk, sat next to me on mine. Sean's gone, she said.

He'd left her a note and taken the overnight bus north.

Don't find many friends like him, travelling all the time. He's a good one for sure, she said. I thought she might cry.

I spent the day trying to cheer her up. We played some pool, walked along the beach, read and drank tea on the shaded porch. For hours she hardly spoke. Finally, as the sun weakened over the mountains, I tried one last thing:

How about another lesson?

Lee looked dubious. Then she smiled, and I couldn't believe how happy it made me.

We donned wetsuits and flip-flops and once again padded down the road a few hundred metres to the somewhat protected bay with its smaller swells.

But as I approached the surf with my board, I found my feet moving very slowly, and when I was within three metres of where the water was just barely licking the sand, I stopped.

The waves looked rough all of a sudden, not just white along their crests but churning and writhing with veins of foam. A noise came out of my throat, not quite speech.

Lee, already up to her knees in the soup, looked back. Alright?

Was it always like this?

Like what?

It's like . . . stormy. I was also noticing for the first time the sharp rocks near shore, looming serrated edges of black boulders beneath the waves.

Lee walked up out of the water, stuck her board in the sand, stood beside me. We watched the surf for a while. I tried to imagine paddling out, waiting for a swell, turning around, riding it in, standing . . . I shivered, convulsively, once. Visualizing the way I did for hockey was not going to work here. I'd swum most of my life. I'd never imagined I could be afraid of water.

It's okay, you know, if you don't want to.

There was so much understanding in Lee's voice, so much tenderness, that I had the absurd thought that I loved her. And that I didn't want to ever let her down.

I do want to, I said.

But still I couldn't move. After a moment Lee sat down on the sand beside me. Reached up, grabbed my hand, pulled me down and didn't let go.

I pretty much forgot about surfing at that point, all of my psychic power directed at the grasped hands on the sand between us. The fear in my stomach didn't go away but became less mortal terror and more cliff-jumping adrenalin. I thought about kissing her. I really wanted to. Out of the corner of my eye I could see her staring steadily out at the surf. But her eyes weren't tracking the waves, so I knew she wasn't really watching them. Was her heart pounding the way mine was? If I tried to kiss her now, would I be wrecking everything? Or would I be missing my chance if I didn't?

Then some new arrivals from the hostel, three Australian women, came over the rise from the next bay over, walking along the beach with their surfboards. Lee withdrew her hand and jumped up.

Watch my stick. Gonna see if someone'll buddy up for a bit. Don't mind, do you?

Course not.

She took off jogging down the sand. I stared after her wetsuited form, cat-burglar sleek.

I felt a tiny tear inside, and the feeling was familiar.

When Lee came back for her board then took off again to surf with the Australians, I found myself shuffling back to the hostel and logging on to the computer. Inexplicably fighting tears. The flickering screen making my eyeballs vibrate painfully.

I'd told myself not having any contact with Jill was letting me heal, but the taste in my mouth was so foul I had to wonder if the wound over our breakup was just festering, an infected open gash in my heart. Maybe I was attaching too much to Lee because of it. Maybe I was misreading all the attention, the jokes, the significant eye contact. Maybe holding hands was just her being friendly.

I HAD NO new emails that weren't spam. Jill was still *Single* on her profile, although I took the time to peruse several new photos of her with the somewhat too cute Rachel. Couple-selfies, unmistakably: Rachel's head leaning back on Jill's shoulder, arms extended out towards her camera. They were even kissing in one, hilariously looking sideways out at the lens. At me. I wondered if Jill was texting me and felt a sour gratification that no one but the orcas would even know.

There was also no email from Jules, which made me worried for three and a half seconds, and then my worry turned to deep irritation. I'd emailed when I'd landed, and Jules had never responded. She was probably trying to track me through social media. Or maybe she wasn't. It wouldn't be the first time she wasn't there when I needed her. Not that I needed her now. But what if I had?

I found myself on a web page called socialmediasuicide.com, which I'd heard about from someone at school. I'd had reason to consider the possibility once before. I entered my Socialink profile name (Chloe In Net) and password (0goalsagainst) and hit Enter. I watched animated clips of a little man in a top hat hanging himself by a noose, blowing his brains out with a pistol, dropping a toaster into his bath and slashing his wrists open, which sprayed blood all over the inside of the computer screen, as my Socialink account and all the connected accounts that made up my interweb presence were systematically deleted. Until, over the now-solid blood-red screen, appeared the torn-out black words:

CONGRATULATIONS, YOU ARE DEAD.

It was a satisfying, bitter pill.

A QUAD OF Russians had left town that afternoon, so Lee and I had the dorm room to ourselves. I stayed away well into the evening, past the time when the early morning surfers usually went to bed. After a long late walk on the beach, I returned to the hostel and changed by the red glow of the emergency exit sign.

How long do you think you'll stay mad at me?

I looked at Lee's bunk. I saw the glint of her eyes, the outline of her neck and cheekbone against her pillowcase. The shape of her, stretched out on the bed.

What? I'm not mad. Realizing as I said it that I had been but wasn't anymore. Jealousy was ugly, an insidious fungus on my heart.

Could've fooled me.

Neither of us moved. We stared at each other across the shadows.

You're so beautiful. I hadn't meant to say it, but I meant it.

Lee half laughed and rolled over, leaving me with the wall of her back.

If it's just 'cause I went surfing, we're gonna have a problem.

I stared at her dark form, my heart pounding in my ears.

I didn't want to have a problem.

A moment later I sat on the edge of Lee's bed, right beside her bare arm and back, the line of tank top across it.

Lee.

She didn't move, didn't make a sound. The distant red exit sign was a moon, refracting. I raised a hand and slowly placed it, finger by finger, on her bare skin. She didn't pull away. All breathing stopped. My fingers trailed down liquid flesh, her contoured bicep, her arm tucked against her tummy. Our hands clasped, wound tightly around each other. With a sharp inhale, Lee turned towards me. The warm brush of her hand on my cheek made me swoon. My head lost track of gravity. Lips on cheeks and tongues against tongues and eyelids and skin, salt on fingers and mouths, and Lee's hand on my bare leg below my boxer shorts. Her shoulder rose to meet my hand, and my hand slipped down under her tank top.

Suddenly there were footsteps in the hall and low voices outside our door. Lee froze, I dove for my own bunk as the door opened. The beam of Mona's flashlight showed the silhouette of a late arrival to an empty bunk.

Suppressed giggles rebounded between our beds like echoes down a lake.

Cops.

The cops scared her. She held her breath as a matched set of baby-faced uniforms walked up to the prescription counter. Jules got up casually from the chair with the backrest, as though she'd just been testing it out, started sidling down the aisle. Quickly. Don't look rushed.

One moment, ma'am, she heard the young man say, and at the same time the female cop asked the pharmacist, This person here?

Jules feigned obliviousness, kept walking. She thought her knees might buckle from fear, adrenalin, withdrawal. Take your pick.

Excuse me, ma'am. She felt a hand on her shoulder and she flinched, and the grip tightened. She turned around, felt the sweat, slick and pooling under her breasts and arms. Her palms were itching, wet and hot.

The pharmacist, young and nervous in her striped hijab, pointy features and wire glasses, handed the policewoman Jules's forged scrip.

I always call the prescribing doc on this stuff. There's too much of it on the street.

And?

He goes, Call the cops, that'll teach her. I guess he knows her. He was pretty upset.

I'm sure that's an understatement, Jules muttered to herself. The two cops and the pharmacist all turned to look at her with a humiliating mix of pity and disgust. She couldn't stand it.

I have chronic pain. Jules heard the petulance in her own voice and felt even more miserable. I need my meds, she tried again, only now, she knew, she sounded like the junkie they already thought she was. The cops exchanged a look, a rolled-eye, how-is-this-woman-such-a-cliché look, and Jules felt burning tears of exasperation. They were children. What did they know? This was all Rod's fault, and she found herself hating him with surprising ease.

The boy cop was suddenly behind her. Her shoulders wrenched as she instinctively tried to pull away. Pain whip-cracked from her neck to her elbow. Icy metal scratched and pinched at her wrists. She panicked in a full-body sweat, at once hot and cold.

Fucking handcuffs?

This made no sense, no sense at all. Her chest arced out like a bird's breast, waiting for an arrow. I haven't even done anything. Her voice high and tight as a wire.

Girlcop, stone-faced, patted her down. Boycop said, Procedure.

They each grabbed an elbow, propelled her out the door, the cop car by the curb, red light flashing. Boycop uttered an automatic spiel that may have included words like "possession" and something about the right to counsel, and a firm hand on her head pushed her into the caged back seat. She heard cackling laughter from the alcove next to the pharmacy and saw the old drunks and the young shoplifters, doubled over, watching her get taken away.

My car. She strained around to look at it, parked behind the cop car. They'll tow it. It's a rental.

Not our problem, ma'am. Girlcop drove while Boycop rummaged through Jules's purse. He found an empty Oxy bottle, turned it over in his hand, read the label. Turned and looked at Jules.

Been on this shit for a while, eh?

Long enough.

He pulled out the pink message slips, ironed them out. Who's David?

None of your business.

Right now, ma'am, it's all my business.

He opened up Jules's wallet, pulled out her driver's licence. Her head pounding, hands cramped behind her back, skin itching everywhere, Jules imagined punching through the mesh cage and elbowing Boycop in the throat as she grabbed her stuff back. Her self-image was not as someone who resented authority, but she felt like a surly teenager as she watched Boycop type her name into the car's computer console and tell his partner:

She's not in the system.

Of course I'm not. Jules glared out the window.

Boycop went back to pawing through her purse. And these are . . . ? He held up the wad of sheets from Rod's prescription pad, waved them at her through the bars of her cage.

Jules stared beyond his hand at nothing. What's it look like?

The paper stopped waving. Lady's got some attitude. He shuffled through pages, one by one, his head shaking side to side. Not good, not good at all. He looked at his partner again. Half of these are filled out. He turned to Jules. Now why would a lady like you need five hundred Oxy pills?

Girlcop whistled. That is *too much*. That much'll kill ya.

She didn't need five hundred. He'd found the pages with her rejected signature attempts. She wished she could set them on fire with her eyes. Instead, she said:

You get your training from cop shows?

See, now, why would you go and say something like that, when what I have here—he held up the wad of paper—is enough to charge you with trafficking. We've already got you on forgery. And, like, three other related charges. So, what you want to do *now*— Boycop swung around in his seat to look directly at Jules—what you *want* to do now is *not* give us a reason to make things worse for you than they already are. Got it?

Jules didn't answer.

AT THE STATION, they grabbed her elbows again, roughly steered her past people waiting in chairs for god knew what, detectives who barely glanced at her and uniforms who nodded at her captors then raked their eyes over Jules, their faces twitching in amusement or judgment, or both. They propelled her to a desk and sat her on a folding chair. Girlcop logged on to a computer terminal while Boycop hovered behind her looking smug. They took Jules's name and address, place of employment and next of kin. After some hesitation, Jules gave them Chloe's name. Chloe could never know about this. But there was no one else.

What are you charging me with? She'd forgotten, or missed it somehow, and what Boycop had said about trafficking tugged at a thread of worry in her brain.

He leaned over his partner's shoulder. Let's see here . . . possibilities are Forgery, Uttering a Forged Document, Seeking a Controlled Substance . . . Possession for the Purpose of Trafficking.

Possession? But—

Explain it to the Crown, ma'am.

The old-school wall clock read 3:20 by the time they let her use a phone. The heavy plastic handset felt sticky and smelled sour. Or maybe it was her. She balanced it in her hand for a few moments, testing its weight, considering. She couldn't call Rod. Chloe couldn't help her, obviously. So she called Drew.

They led her to a concrete cell that reeked of stale urine, where she spent an hour heaving into a seatless toilet, then finally collapsed onto the steel bench along the back wall.

Rough day, eh?

Her cellmate was a young woman in cheap office clothes, thick

ankles in bad flats, ill-fitting black skirt, dumb blouse. She gave Jules
a sympathetic look and a hanky, motioning to her mouth. Jules
touched her face and, mortified, wiped off the puke that was crust-
ing there. She would have laughed if she hadn't felt so wretched.

Just a Monday, Jules said.

She leaned her head back against the wall and closed her eyes.
This can't be happening, this can't be happening.

Oxy, am I right?

Jules cracked open her lids enough to see that The Secretary
was still watching her intently.

That's what my ex was on. Till it got too expensive. The Secretary
took in Jules's suit, rumpled and ill-cut but far from cheap.
Respectable, Jules liked to think, even though she felt like garbage.
Damn near killed him, the woman said.

Jules was then subjected to an impassioned rant about the evils
of Big Pharma, all patents and lies and manufactured addiction. She
tried not to listen. She found the paranoia exhausting. She would
have taken more Oxy then and there if she could have and really
didn't care what Big Pharma was doing.

An addict's an addict, take it from me. Oxy, fentanyl, smack,
don't matter. That shit ruins lives, and not by accident.

The Secretary's "fella" had arrived, a cop at the cage door
informed them. He blinked slowly, eyelids sliding down then up
his fishy grey eyeballs, an articulate display of total apathy. He took
The Secretary's elbow and propelled her down the hall.

After that, no one came for hours. Every fidget reverbed off
the concrete, scratched at the silence, her skin itched and crawled.
She could hear pipes running close by after periodic flushing. A
peephole of a window was cut into the concrete wall over her head.
She watched a watery shaft of light retreat from the shortening
day, almost apologetic. It got dark. She slept some. By the time
Drew showed up with his thousand-dollar-an-hour attorney, it was
nearly light again.

Lawyer.

On a dime, the cops' behaviour completely changed. They led her into an interview room with a table and chairs and brought her a cup of coffee. They offered her breakfast. They sensed power, or money, or both.

Drew gave her a hug, and she embraced him gratefully, which was a bit like cuddling up to an elephant, she couldn't get her arms around him. It's okay, honey, he said, and Jules didn't know if it would ever be okay, but she knew she needed to get the fuck out of there and he was making it happen, and in that moment she loved him.

Releasing her from the embrace, he studied her face.

You look like shit, he told her, which she knew meant, You must feel terrible, and she did, so she said, Fuck you, which made him smile.

After a short conversation with Girlcop, the lawyer told her they were holding her for a Show Cause hearing. They wanted to charge her with trafficking and determine if she could be released on bail until her trial.

Until her *trial*.

Trial?

Jules tried to stay focused on what he was saying, but the cramping in her stomach was back, and she was starting to panic that something was really wrong with her, that withdrawal had somehow triggered a burst appendix or a ruptured spleen.

I'm not going to *jail*.

The lawyer, a fortyish man named Marc with sandy-coloured hair in a perfectly tailored sandy-coloured suit, leaned back in his chair and looked at her.

Well, not if I can help it. But this is serious.

Marc was either very persuasive, very connected or very lucky. Probably all three. He found a Justice of the Peace with room on her docket and a Crown attorney who was happy to expedite matters, and by four o'clock that afternoon she was in a tiny, battered courtroom with the two lawyers, the robed woman behind the bench and Drew. They threw around words and numbers that seemed utterly meaningless—we can drop the five-one-five-six and the three-six-eight if she'll cop to the three-six-six—until Marc leaned over and whispered in her ear: plead guilty to forgery and possession, they'd drop the trafficking, and he'd try to get her probation.

She started to argue that she'd never actually gained possession of anything, but Marc shook his head. This was the deal. So, she nodded assent.

Then things started to happen very quickly. The court would allow bail. Was her bail covered? Yes, Drew Baron was providing collateral. This was news to Jules. She shot Drew a sheepish glance meant to indicate that she would pay him back, and he squeezed her shoulder but avoided her eyes.

The Justice of the Peace, mid-sixties and exuding uber-competence, glared over her wire frames at Jules.

Do you know how lucky you are?

Jules nodded. What she knew was that having ended up here in the first place made her a statistical anomaly, which, by definition, meant it was the wrong kind of luck. She was standing next to Marc, trying to stop the sensation of being sucked into a vacuum by fixing her eyes on a knot of wood on the Justice's podium.

I'm not sure you do.

Jules looked up at the Justice's scowling, slightly jowled face, her sharp eyes with lengthy dark circles under them.

I can see the shape you're in. But you seem to have friends, and resources . . . I really don't want to see you back here.

You won't, she tried to say, but it came out hoarse and tentative. But the Justice seemed to hear it, stopped shuffling papers and studied Jules for a moment.

Let me ask you this, Ms. Wright. Do you think you have a problem?

A problem?

What the hell kind of question was that? Of course she had a problem. She had a lot of problems. She was standing in court facing criminal charges, for one, fully in the throes of what felt like the worst flu of her life.

A drug problem.

Oh. Of course. Jules felt everyone in the courtroom waiting for her answer, and she really wanted to give the right one, but she didn't know what that was. It was hard to think. She started to shiver, clamped her jaw shut to hide the chattering of her teeth. But she knew she had to say something.

I don't snort it or anything, was the best she could come up with.

The disappointed Justice shook her head and imposed the following: no booze, no drugs, house arrest. We can't mandate treatment until conviction, but the court will respond well to demonstration of good intent. And I'm releasing you into the custody of your surety here, Mr. Baron. That work for you, sir?

She didn't ask if it worked for Jules.

That was the Show Cause hearing. It could take weeks or even months to get a date with a judge. It's high season, Marc said, with no apparent irony. I'll make some calls, see if I can speed it up. But at least you get to leave.

In an upstairs office, Jules signed a piece of paper that said she intended to plead guilty to one count of uttering a forged document and one count of possessing a Schedule I Controlled Substance. They would let her go. Sort of. Not home. To Drew's.

They tagged her ankle with an electronic bracelet, To keep you honest, said the cop who locked it on. Jules couldn't tell if she was trying to be funny. Other than Drew's house, the only place she could go without special permission was therapy, twice a week on a pre-approved schedule. And Drew had to accompany her. She couldn't even go home, to her own house, without registering a flight plan, and certainly not alone.

Girlcop appeared with a plastic crate and started pulling out: Jules's purse, a manila envelope with all her purse's former contents, her watch and earrings, her cellphone and a crumpled wad of the remaining blank prescriptions. Jules was surprised Boycop hadn't taken them. The young woman gave her a hard look and dropped them into a plastic bag marked EVIDENCE.

Ghost.

S itting in the passenger seat on the way to Drew's to begin what she could only think of as her incarceration, Jules leaned her head against the window and watched the darkened city slide by. Beside her own face she could see an edge of reflection, a second pale nose and jawline, cool and thin as film, as tail lights, storefronts, a million shining beacons flickered through it. Her own ghost, riding along.

Forty-seven years old and arrested for possession. And though she knew she had to come clean or risk losing everything—whatever she had left—maybe even going to jail, for fuck's sake—all she wanted was to get her hands on more pills. She'd run out Saturday, and now it was Tuesday evening: seventy hours of the opiates leaving her system, and leaving it screaming, each molecule of Oxy armed with a dagger, slashing and burning on its way out through her pores, her intestines. And the thing, the only thing, that would bring a halt to the razing was to reverse the exodus. Send in reinforcements: more Oxy. Nauseous, she rolled down her window.

How the hell am I going to get through this?

She wasn't really asking Drew so much as putting it to the universe, but he was there, and so he answered, lying, telling her detox was the hard part, everything would be easier once they got her clean.

Clean.

She wasn't even sure what that meant, or if she remembered what it felt like.

It's just painkillers, she said to Drew. I need them.

But she heard herself, and she knew.

They turned down Drew's street, detached homes on one side of the road hunkering defensively against the bare bones of row-house condos waiting for their flesh on the other. Drew hated the condos, said they made him feel dirty and cheap.

Pulling into his driveway, he sighed, his tummy hugging the bottom of the steering wheel. Looking straight ahead, he acknowledged aloud that he wasn't in a position to judge.

The security light had come on, its glare making her eyes seek rest in the stark shadows of things.

God knows, Drew said, I hop on and off the wagon a couple times a year. But, well, some people can't handle it. And I've seen where that can go.

Jules looked over at him. The light made his skin gleam, and she realized he was sweating.

Remember Mikhail? he asked.

Oh god.

One of the first times she'd seen Drew socially outside of work, maybe six or seven years ago now, she'd met his then husband of eighteen years, a professor of Russian studies. Tall and broad, square-headed with deep shadows under his eyes, like a handsome version of Frankenstein's monster, he'd made her see the more serious side of Drew—not earnest, as Drew was irreverent to his core, but down-to-earth and thoughtful. They talked about gay rights and gender inequality, living through the AIDS crisis and the backlash against feminism. Mikhail went on a rant about how they were all lobsters in the pot of climate change, and Drew said,

Sweetie, that's why we left the SUV at home.

Not so we could get hammered?

Added bonus.

Mikhail's research was about online activism in a repressive state, and they got on to discussing how social media was radically changing everything, from expectations of privacy to the nature of love.

It tries to convince us to change our priorities, Mikhail said. That our privacy doesn't matter. Our integrity doesn't really matter. That what matters is how we are perceived, that we never break character, that we look the right way and consume the right things, which means it's in our *own best interest* to have people like you guys—he waggled a finger between Jules and Drew—keeping track of what we all do in our spare time, so you can target us with marketing that makes us feel like we might get onto the next trend ahead of the curve. Get noticed for starting something. Build our brand. But the truth of it is, it's utterly meaningless. There's no long game in play.

Bleak, said Jules. But true.

We're so manipulated into complicity, it's impossible to stand against it, or to extract yourself from it.

On the other hand, Drew said with a small flourish, I am an openly gay man—loudly gay, in fact—making seven figures.

Climb that rainbow ceiling, said Jules. Or smash it. Or something.

Well, and I'm a big hashtag in Russia. So, no one's perfect.

They laughed and argued over oysters and then Scotch for hours. She could remember they ran up a thousand-dollar tab but not who paid or how she got home.

She remembered going into work the following week feeling fortified. Rejuvenated. Drew sought her out regularly for lunch or gossip or just to say good morning. She felt like she'd finally met her people. It had been more years than she cared to count since she'd had a close friend.

But she only saw Drew and Mikhail together a few times after that. She'd have seen them more, but it seemed complicated somehow. A couple times they cancelled at the last minute. The last time she saw him, Mikhail got drunk and punchy and then left halfway through dinner. Clearly something was going on with him, but she still didn't know either of them that well, so she kept her reactions to herself. That was a Friday night. Drew called her on Sunday morning to tell her Mikhail had jumped off an apartment building.

So when Drew asked if she remembered him, it wasn't so much a question as a point he was trying to make.

You looked after me, Jules. I wouldn't have made it through that without you.

I didn't do anything.

Yeah, you did. Don't you remember? After the memorial, everyone else was telling me I would get through it, I was going to be okay, I could weather the storm, blah blah blah. But you were like, No. It's not going to be okay. It's going to be super fucking shitty for a long, long time. It might never be okay. That's what you said to me. You can't fight it. You might not survive it. But you're not the first person to go through it.

She didn't remember saying any of that, but it sounded about right.

That really stuck with me, he went on. And I knew about your . . . Lizzie. And when I got back to work, every time I saw your face, I would think, She's right. This is what people go through. This is what we do.

Yep, Jules was nodding, looking out the window. This is what we do.

And you *were* right, and it's *still* super fucking shitty. But I've got you. And I've got Farzan. Dec, a couple others from that group. And that's what gets me through the day. Well, that and a few martinis. Ha. But what I'm trying to say is, you called me for help. And I can help. You're my friend, I love you, probably more than you know, and I *want* to help. If you'll let me.

He'd paid her bail and arranged thirty days of medical leave with the company and didn't see the need, at this point, to bring Raj and Simon, the other partners, in on the details.

So. You can stay here. Or you can go.

She heard what he wasn't saying. He was still her boss. Stay and follow the rules. Or leave and lose everything. Her job. Her best friend. Her life as she knew it.

It's your choice.

Is that a threat? She meant it as a joke, but it failed.

Yeah, Jules, I'm threatening to not watch you self-destruct.

He manoeuvred himself out of the car and started lumbering up the walk. Jules got as far as opening the car door, and then stalled, unsure of what to do next. She watched Drew use the reinforced railing to pull himself up the stairs to the porch. Without turning around, he called back to her.

But if you go more than a hundred metres, the cops're gonna call the house.

She felt abruptly, physically constrained.

He put her up on his third floor, a wide and airy triangular loft with sloped wooden ceilings that contained a cozy bedroom, a bright sitting room and a tiny bathroom.

After a shower (which she hoped might short-circuit her anklet, but didn't) and donning a set of pyjamas (borrowed from Farzan, who seemed to be moving in piecemeal), Jules beelined for the bar in the living room. But Drew intercepted her as soon as she came through the French doors.

I just want a drink.

I know you do, sweetie.

Jules peeked around him and saw Farzan, emptying out the cabinet of the wet bar, putting all the bottles into a couple cardboard wine boxes.

No drugs, no booze, no nothing. You can take up smoking if you want.

But I wouldn't, Farzan interjected as he squeezed around Drew, box in his arms rattling glass. Jules watched it, hope fading as it went through the foyer and out the front door. Farzan reappeared a moment later and started packing a second box. Drew moved to block her view.

My wine cellar's also locked up tight, so just forget about it, okay?

Maybe I should just go to my own house.

She knew it was too late to be thinking this and wondered why she hadn't brought it up in court when it could have made a difference. Home, where she knew she at least had a couple good single malts.

Jules, honey. You can't go home.

Drew gently took her by the shoulders, steered her to the couch. And anyway, to do what? Sulk and feel terrible? No. He sat her on the edge of the couch.

She put her head in her hands. Stared down at the electronic anklet poking out from underneath the borrowed pyjamas. Slid a finger under the edge of the band, felt the snugness of it.

Too bad you can't just take your foot off, said Farzan. Drew smiled at him, shook his head.

When you feel a little better, we'll go get some of your things.

Jules felt like crying, but she wasn't very good at it and never did it in front of other people.

I'm so fucking sick, Drew. I need something.

Drew lowered himself onto the couch next to her, making it sink down so she fell into him.

I know, honey. He draped a sixty-pound arm across her shoulders, simultaneously making her feel both protected and very small. Let's put you to bed.

Pool.

———

'm breathing underwater, currents slide along my skin and map out the murk around me, rocks and coral and darting, synchronized fish. Beside me, a pod of dolphins plays in the waves, swimming up to kiss the surface, their mighty thrashing tails sending them arcing, splashing. One of the young leaves the group, its belly upturning as it floats towards me, its skin greying and wrinkling, shrivelling and shrinking, and the surface of the water glares above me, unreachable.

I woke up with a gasp, sat up in my bunk and concentrated on breathing evenly. Low-angled moonlight cut bent squares across the dark dorm. The four bunks I could see held bodies, the mattress above me sagged with a fifth. Lee's bed was at right angles to mine, our heads almost meeting in the corner. Her legs shifted and her face moved into a panel of light. She reached a hand out between our bunks to mine and I lay back down and took it, grateful not to be awake alone.

You okay? she whispered, and I nodded. Lee closed her eyes but didn't let go. I lay for a while watching a few breathy clouds cut across a spotlight of moon, and listened to the crashing midnight surf. Until I fell asleep in a smooth dive, still holding on to Lee's hand, its warm grip guiding me safely under.

———

My stitches had healed, but I was still getting daily ice-pick head-aches, and my memories took on the quality of stand-alone episodes, narratively disconnected. The doctor said this might go on for months, especially since it was my third concussion (because hockey).

Lee started surfing every morning with the Australian women, and I spent long hours watching from a beach towel. Off-hours, when the tide wasn't right, surfers would crowd into the TV room or around someone's laptop to watch surf videos, but I still didn't enjoy screens, so I sat on the porch and watched the ocean, or went for walks on the beach with Lee.

I realized my world, in the few weeks since my concussion, had become very small. I was beginning to feel restless.

We were playing pool late one afternoon when Jansen, a South African guy who'd arrived the day before, came in and said he was going to hitchhike up north, and as someone had told him Lee and I were also travelling north, he wondered if we wanted to travel together.

No, thanks, Lee said, at the same time that I said, Sure.

He spun us a sad tale: He'd been robbed a couple days before, in a tourist town in the south. He'd gone to the bathroom while he was checking out of his hostel, left his pack by the front desk, and when he came back, it was gone. So now he had no passport, no phone, no credit cards, only the clothes he'd been wearing and the cash in his pocket. Nothing else. No witnesses: the guy on the desk had stepped away, just for a moment, but that was all it took.

I'm just so happy I had put some money in my pants pocket, or I would have worse troubles than this.

We'd moved to one of the heavy picnic tables in the common area, and as he talked, he looked more and more exhausted, sank lower and lower into himself on the bench, pitiful in his defeat and aloneness.

People suck, I said.

No shit, Lee snorted. Number one reason why hitchhiking is *stupid*.

After more than a week of spending every non-surfing moment together and trying to find a few minutes of privacy in the dorm room, Lee had finally asked me the day before:

So, where's this hike you're always on about?

Abel Tasman. Like a few hours north. I bit my lip, waiting.

And how many days is it?

One day to get there. Four days of hiking. Or three. We don't have to do the whole thing.

Lee raised an eyebrow. You don't think I can handle it?

That's not—

But she winked, tapped her tea mug against my plastic beer cup, and we both grinned.

BUT HITCHHIKING WAS apparently a game changer, and when Jansen left to use the landline—It is breakfast time at home. My father must send me money from Johannesburg—Lee looked at me in a way that sent my train of thought stuttering.

Hitchhiking? Are you starkers?

This from the girl who wants to surf tsunamis?

This from the girl who's recovering from a *head injury*? Anyway, the ocean's—

Oh my god, I'm *fine* already, would you—

—more predictable than this git—let alone whatever potential—

—stop waiting for me to break in half, you're—

—bloody axe murderer that might pick us up.

—acting like my fucking *mother.*

Which I immediately knew was going way too far. Lee's face went red under her freckles, almost as red as her hair. We stared at each other for a moment, feeling the heat of our first actual argument. Then I said we could take the bus, no big deal, and in my mind that should have put the matter to rest.

THE NEXT MORNING, I woke up to Lee sitting on the edge of her bunk stuffing her sleeping bag into the bottom of her pack.

I croaked out an unintelligible question.

Oh good, you're awake. Right, so, I checked my email this morning, and well, I can't go hiking with you, mate.

She opened the top of her pack, shoved in the tank top and boxers she slept in, her voice oddly strained and her eyes averted as she explained, rapid-fire, that a friend of hers had managed to get her officially invited to compete in nationals up at Piha, and it was a big deal because she wasn't even a New Zealand citizen, and she had this publicist back in England who really thought she should—

I finally woke up enough to say, You have a publicist? What friend?

She zipped up her toiletries case, thrust it into an outside pocket, then shook her head in an ambiguous yes-but-no. My board's already being shipped up there, she said, still not showing me her face.

I sat up in my sleeping bag. Lee?

Having run out of things to pack, Lee stood and said in a halting voice that she had initially said no to the tournament but had thought about it overnight and realized it was time for her to move on from the past.

I need to have my own life, she said. I can't let my dad's legacy keep me away from it. Plus, he surfed there, back in the day, so it seems, like, serendipitous. But if you want—

What friend? I asked again.

She frowned, surprised at the question, and I cringed as I realized how it sounded.

One of the Australians, she said. Talda. She knows one of the organizers.

Oh, I said. She seems nice. Talda was an amazing surfer, something she and Lee shared that I probably never would. She was also easygoing, quirky and hilarious. And as of this moment, I couldn't stand her. If that's what you'd rather do, I said.

Lee stared at me for a moment, still frowning. I hated how I must have looked in her eyes.

That's okay, I'm still getting over Jill anyway, I added, making it worse.

Yeah, alright, she said. So maybe it's you who isn't sure what you want.

I was sure what I wanted. Wasn't I? I thought I was. I thought I wanted to be with Lee. I'm not sure what I hoped to gain by saying:

Well, I'm sure I want to go hiking. I *thought* I had someone to go with me.

Lee swung her pack up onto her back and turned to look at me, said a sorry that sounded like a placeholder for something else and reached down to squeeze my hand. Well, anyway, I gotta go surf. I was gonna say you could come and meet me—

You and Talda? No thank you. Anyway, I just told you, I'm going hiking. With you or without you.

Her face went very still. I knew she was hurt, but so was I.

Right. Well, then. See ya 'round, hey. But her aviators hid her eyes, and then she was gone.

I listened to her footsteps fade away on the stairs, and tried to reconcile the hollow feeling in my chest with the full-to-bursting feelings of the last week.

I could still feel the pressure on my hand where Lee had squeezed it. Looking down, I saw a folded slip of paper tucked into the curve of my fingers. It had an email address on it for a *surfmonkey99*.

JANSEN WAS IN the hostel kitchen cooking eggs, German sausage and thick toast. He told me to sit, and eat, as he put a full plate in front of me along with a cup of coffee.

What the hell's all this for?

I cannot share a breakfast with a new buddy?

I was too grouchy to even wonder where the food had come from. The coffee was the best I'd had in weeks, which irritated me further.

Sorry. Shit mood. Not your fault. I picked up a fork and moved a mouthful of eggs towards my mouth. But everything looked like plastic. It felt like Lee had gone to the store for cigarettes and never come back.

Jansen, eating fast and talking around mouthfuls, said he'd seen Lee leaving.

She's going surfing, I said. I held my fork limply, the eggs falling back to the plate. I had a flash of kissing Lee in the dorm, our whispers as we listened for footsteps in the hallway. Felt myself fighting tears.

Jansen shoved half a sausage into his mouth. Are you also leaving today?

He had to make his way up to Wellington to get a new passport and retrieve the money his father was sending.

I don't know, I said. I felt miserable. Everything was falling apart. I pushed my plate away and grasped for a way to salvage something.

IN THE END, it all came down to Jules. I had spent my whole life being told what to avoid because certain things—so many things— were deemed unsafe. Running down the stairs two at a time, skateboarding, ice skating without a helmet, riding a bike with no hands—the list was endless of things that I loved doing, and even excelled at, that Jules was always trying to stop me from doing because she herself lacked the physical confidence. Likewise, Jules would never use Uber or Airbnb or eat a hot dog from a hot dog cart because she fundamentally didn't trust people: things that relied on the basic humanity of strangers, on an assumption of non-malevolence, were abundant with risk. Not deadbolting the front door when we were home during the day. Public washrooms. Asking for directions. If something bad could happen, she believed it would happen to her. So hitchhiking with a stranger she had only met the day before would have been out of the question for Jules.

Which, for me, made it an obvious choice.

Bedroom.

⎯

Detox was hell. It kept blasting away her expectations of just how bad it could get. Every time she thought she had plateaued, the bottom would open up again, send her flailing down to another level. More than once, Jules had the thought that she might actually be dying, and welcomed it. She lay in bed for what seemed like days, sweating, retching, cramps in her legs, her bloodstream a thrumming cord of ache. She wanted to rip her own skin off. She wanted to sleep. That was what Oxy had done, once: when she lay down and closed her eyes, sleep had been right there, waiting. Now, she couldn't lie still.

In a half-dream state, she convinced herself that Drew had a secret stash, and before she was fully awake, she was down on the second floor, fumbling around in his medicine cabinet, hoping for Percocets, with their meagre dose of Oxy, or the codeine of Tylenol 3s, even muscle relaxants, anything to take the edge off, give her distance from the moment, from herself.

He did have a shelf full of medication, prescription and other-wise, and Jules scrabbled through blood pressure pills, indigestion aids, allergy pills and Viagra, her anticipation mounting, her hands shaking, knocking boxes and pill bottles into the sink below with what seemed a blatant clatter.

She muttered curses, burglar nervous, hurrying to shove them all back into the cabinet, each label she checked frustrating her further, and perhaps it was the noise she made, or perhaps it was simply the state she was in, but she didn't hear the voices behind her until it was too late.

I told you, Drew. Julie doesn't want my help.

Jules stood frozen, one hand holding a few packages of pills in place on the narrow shelf, the other on the cabinet door, about to close it.

Jules? What are you doing, sweetie?

It's obvious what she's doing. I can't help someone who's not ready.

No—wait—Dec—Jules, c'mon.

Jules turned around as much as her stiff neck would let her without forcing her to release her hand from the precariously stacked medications. Drew stood in the bathroom door, and behind him Declan was already halfway gone, his solid frame barrelling across the bedroom, one hand finishing a fed-up gesture, swiping it all behind him.

Dec! Drew's voice boomed, all his weight in it. Declan turned at the door, grabbed the door frame to make a stand, but didn't look at Drew, his eyes fixed instead on Jules, and said nothing, just stood there, stubborn as a teenager.

Declan, Drew said. C'mon. As a favour to me, okay?

Declan remained silent for a long time, then relented. Alright, he said. I'll try. But—He pointed at Jules. She has to want it too. And— He tilted his finger to point at the sky. I want it on record that I'm one hell of a good guy.

Jules said nothing, even though they were both looking at her, expecting some kind of response. She pulled her hand away from the medicine cabinet, heard everything come crashing down onto the sink and floor all over again.

JULIE.

Declan said her name, his hands gentle as he took her blood pressure, her pulse, her temperature, listened to her lungs, his touch on her skin heightening her awareness of her own sour clamminess, her middle-aged flab, the vile yellow pallor that went right into her fingernails.

Alright?

He cupped Jules's face, used his thumb to pull lightly at her bottom eyelids, then the top. He left his hand there, cool on her burning cheek, for an extra few seconds, peered into her eyes with his own, dark, dark brown.

How much have you been taking, Julie?

She hated being called Julie, always had, but somehow in Declan's gravelly voice it was almost comforting. She could see the fine lines around his mouth from years of smoking, humour and scorn. Sadness. It came back to her, in that moment, the feeling of being drawn to him. She remembered the resonance between them, and a longing. But she remembered it only in that distant, intellectual way she also remembered that she had a job, a house, a car: just facts, with no bearing on her situation. Right now, all she could do was try to keep breath moving in and out of her body.

Forties. Forty milligrams. Maybe . . . eight a day. Or ten, she didn't continue out loud, or sometimes twelve. She thought she saw his lips tighten a little. His eyes searched her face for cracks.

Right. So, Rod Scott's your doctor.

It wasn't a question, but Jules nodded.

And your un-boyfriend.

Not anymore, she said. Not since . . . But she couldn't find a comfortable way to end that sentence. She pictured Rod as she'd last seen him, grey-suited and ashen-faced, adrift in a sea of scrubs as she walked away. It felt like another life, the man a complete stranger.

The tops of Declan's cheeks twitched with the possibility of a smile. Since the other night?

Yeah . . . Well, no, but. Sorry about that.

Sorry? Nothing for you to be sorry about. I'm not sorry. He focused on her face for a long moment, his eyes rippling from some internal spring, she didn't know if she was sinking or floating. Then he looked away, pulled his old-fashioned black doctor's bag onto his lap, held it there and addressed its interior.

But now you're my patient, right? He dug in his bag with his whole arm. I've met this Rod Scott before, at his pain clinic. He tell you?

He had not.

We've got what you might call some differences of opinion.

He pulled out a bubble pack, squeezed out a pill and shook it gently in his hand, like he was about to roll the dice.

And, well, let's just say he's been getting himself a rep. As in, you are not the only one. He handed Jules the pill.

The only what, Jules wondered.

Declan broke down the dosages he would use to taper her off the Oxy.

Jules looked at the pill in her hand. ON, it said, or NO upside down, instead of the usual CDN of the old Oxy tablets. She turned it over, saw the "20" engraved on it. With a sigh and some water, she swallowed it, expectations of real relief washing away to leave a bleak beach of defeat.

You're really lucky, he told her, and Jules wondered why people kept insisting on that. This would've gotten much worse, he said.

Jules lay down on the bed by simply tilting over sideways, not bothering to lift her feet from the floor. She watched as Declan walked to the armchair by the window, put down his bag and dropped in his stethoscope. His movements were slow and deliberate and made Jules think he wanted to say something. He came back across the room and sat beside her legs.

You gotta make a choice, Julie.

Jules pulled her feet up onto the bed, rolled away from him, hid her face from the light with a pillow.

Go away. Please.

The silence that followed was so long and empty that Jules started to wonder if he had left the room. She lay perfectly still, held her breath, listened for sounds of a presence behind her, but refused to turn and look in case he was still there.

Finally, she heard a sigh, and felt the mattress reclaim its shape.

Footsteps crossed the room and it was silent again.

She woke the next day around noon and numbly took in her surroundings. Stared out the bay window across the room. The giant head of a tree almost filled her view, a gnarled wizard taller than the house, a relic that had stubbornly survived the development around it. The Last Tree Standing. Thinning leaves smouldered, the sun backlighting them, mustard and crimson and fire. On some level she recognized that it was beautiful, this late fall cry of colour and light, with its suggestion of a day unusually warm.

Declan came in with another twenty milligrams. He took Jules's pulse and blood pressure again, his manner cool and professional. When Jules wondered aloud, somewhat grumpily, why he didn't have to go to work, he simply said, Workin' now, aren't I? Jules grunted around the thermometer he'd shoved under her tongue. She wasn't sure how to connect with this version of Declan. The truth was, she was feeling slightly better, her withdrawal symptoms somewhat de-escalated, if temporarily. But it still felt like someone was torqueing the nerve in her neck with pliers, so when Declan took the thermometer out to read it, she pushed:

Okay, so. If I can't have painkillers, how do I kill the pain?

Declan made a note. Jules realized with vague alarm that he'd started a file on her.

You're not *dying*, Julie.

Jules responded by craning her head to the right until the latest kink cracked its whip and made her stop.

Neck fucking hurts, though.

Declan started to pack his bag.

A lot of people are on a lot of pills, Julie, but too many drugs will only make you worse. The body forgets how to fight pain, your mind forgets how to deal with stress. Sometimes we need 'em, sure. But they get prescribed way too much.

So, you're not going to give me more Oxy.

I just did. He smiled. Twenty milligrams.

Come on, Declan. I can't *function* like this. She pointed at her neck for emphasis.

Wouldn't really call it functioning, what you're doing.

Fuck you. Jules lay back down.

Declan laughed. I've heard that before, he said. He pulled a pamphlet out of his battered bag, and a pen. He clicked the pen a few times, hesitating, avoiding Jules's eyes.

When my wife was dying, we tried this. She said it helped. But then—he paused, circled something on the pamphlet—she was grabbing at life.

The unspoken "not like you" slapped Jules across the face. Declan set the pamphlet on top of the dresser and left: the distant swish-click of the sturdy front door, the breath and hum of the house. She wondered if she was alone in it. A crow hailed autumn from a branch of the Last Tree.

It was all familiar, all too familiar. How many hours, even days—years—of her life had she spent like this, lying on a bed feeling sorry for herself, everybody telling her she needed their help. David, begging her to talk to someone; doctors, therapists, everyone pushing her towards antidepressants. Nan trying to help parent Chloe. And Jules insisting that she was fine. She'd never wanted help, never saw a reason to start wanting it. And where has it all got me? She hauled herself to her feet. Trying just took insurmountable effort.

BUT THE PAMPHLET got her back up like only over-yogaed, kale-in-your-smoothie positive attitudes could. The Whole Soul Healing Clinic claimed to house specialists from massage therapists, chiropractors and traditional Chinese doctors to acupuncturists, psychotherapists and naturopaths—all of which Jules had certainly heard of, and most of which she had tried at some point. But they also offered things she would never try, such as "Spiritual Counselling" and "Energy Healing," and a few she had never even heard of. Craniosacral? Radionics? What the fuck was *Rolfing*? What kind of shit was Declan selling?

In among all these he had circled a picture of what looked like an escape pod from a galactic spaceship, captioned: *Float Tank: Take a Sensory Deprivation Vacation.*

Road.

———

Hitchhiking, I quickly learned, is excruciatingly boring. Other than the snowy peaks in the distance, we could have been anywhere, on wide-laned roads lined with strip malls, motels and car dealerships.

We walked for hours and no one stopped. We had exactly one interesting conversation.

I found a dead body once, Jansen said out of nowhere, a thin attempt to bypass the vague hostility I was having difficulty hiding. I was grouchy about Lee, and I found him both smug and smarmy. In an alley in Frankfurt, he added. Mugging victim. Had his throat cut. Jansen sliced a finger across his own neck.

Oh yeah? I kept my eyes way up the road, listened to the timbre of his voice and tried to decide if he was bullshitting. You, like, called the cops and everything?

Of course. What else?

I took a drag of my rollie and felt the satisfying singe of unfiltered smoke in my throat. Maybe it was because he was a stranger, and I had no intention of ever seeing him again, that I told him:

When my sister died, I was there.

Your sister. Was she sick or something?

No. I flashed through memory thumbnails, my perpetual search for an ultimate cause—Mo-mo crying on the phone, Lizzie crying on the porch—but slammed into the inevitable guilt and shame and shut the whole thing down.

She was a baby. I was six.

You were a child. That is totally different.

Dead is dead, I said.

Eventually, a pickup truck pulled up beside us, and a fiftyish man in a green baseball cap leaned over and said, I can get yis far as Picton, yeah?

SQUEEZED ONTO THE tiny back bench beside an enormous bag of soccer balls, I watched as Jansen, up front, scrutinized the driver, the cab of the truck, the kid photos and business cards elastic-banded to the sun visors, and the bobble-heads of soccer players on the dashboard. Hanging from the rear-view mirror was a woody carving in a swirly shape like a tribal tattoo. Jansen reached a hand out, rubbed it between his fingers.

Are you a Maori?

Something about his tone made me inhale and hold the air in my lungs, wondering where this was going to go.

The driver, dark brown and broad-featured, may have wondered the same thing, but he handled it. He glanced at Jansen, at his hand on the carving, and grunted.

Aw, yeah. Name's Tanga. That's my *matau*. He reached up and removed it from the mirror. It was on a leather string, and he spread it out on his hand, slid it over his head. Tek it off for football, he said.

Matau?

Fish hook, like. For good luck.

He told us a Maori legend of a mythical fisherman who, using only a bone hook and a woven line, hauled a great fish from the ocean and tethered it to the South Island, thus creating the North Island.

Where do you get them? Jansen asked.

Aw, well. You can buy 'em anywhere, the plastic ones. But my wife made me this one, yeah? It's whalebone.

Whalebone, I repeated, thinking of all the beached whales, thinking of Lance and his orcas. Tanga glanced at me in the rear-view mirror.

Maori are fishermen, yeah? The ocean is everything. *Matau's* about our entwined fates. Respect for its power and all.

It is beautiful, said Jansen.

Tanga nodded, rubbed it briefly. I keep hoping it'll bring her back to me, yeah? He sort of laughed. Hasn't worked yet, mind.

I thought of the scrap of paper in my pocket with an email address on it, my own talisman of sorts. Wondered what sort of power it might have to repair the damage I'd done.

LIGHTS OF HOUSES winked on across the hillside as we followed the road into Picton. Tanga dropped us at the hostel, where Jansen surprised him by throwing an arm around the man's shoulders in an awkward but friendly embrace.

Thank you, my buddy. It is good to meet the local people, yes?

Alright, then, said Tanga. And he got back in his truck and pulled away.

Love that guy, Jansen said, but I'd already walked off.

The hostel was run by a couple, Nick and Chandra, and had cheerily coloured walls and bright pine bunkbeds. I noted it was much cleaner than the surf lodge in Kaikoura, and Jansen scoffed.

Because it's not a surf lodge. Those guys live like pigs.

Funny, that's what they say about tourists.

Jansen shuddered. Sand on my mattress.

I couldn't even look at him after that, just took my stuff to the girls' dorm. I arranged with Chandra to leave my big duffle at the hostel and packed what I needed into my day pack. The following morning, I caught the shuttle bus to the trailhead.

Hike.

—

Finally being out on the trail buoyed me. I worked my way up the first big hill, following the skinny trail through the forest, and emerged onto a clifftop, teetering high above a brilliant pure bay. Elation filled my chest like oxygen flushing out smoke.

It wasn't long before I understood that an "easy" New Zealand tramp was equivalent to a "killer" Ontario hike. Straight up, straight down, climb over huge boulders, scramble down rocky and root-torn muddy hillside, repeat. I felt blisters starting on my feet within a couple hours, and my bare shoulders were chafed raw from the canvas straps of my pack.

I sat on a log at a lookout to eat some trail mix. I propped my shredded feet on my pack, my damp back cooling in the breeze, my head tilted back. Branches of oversized leaves filtered my view of in-crawling clouds.

When I heard the buzzing, I tried to react with calm and turned my head slowly towards the sound. Two metres away, a rotted stump teemed with airborne insects, faintly yellow. I swore and jumped up. I had one EpiPen; multiple bee stings would be bad, very bad.

I've been terrified of bees since getting stung when I was little, but I didn't know I'd become allergic to them until my grade eight camping trip, and if the teacher hadn't thought quickly and used her own EpiPen on me, I would have ended up in the hospital, or worse. My hands had swelled, my throat closed over, air refused to respond to my faint sucking, until Mrs. Sudecki, who smelled like mint and onions, jabbed me hard with the needle. I'd never seen an adult look so scared. The next week David took me to the doctor and I got my own emergency injection kit for preventing anaphylactic shock.

My current EpiPen was in my pack, which lay between me and the infested stump and had attracted the attention of a few outliers from the hive. I walked back along the trail and then into the edge of the forest until I found a sturdy long stick. Creeping back towards my spot, I extended the stick as far out as I could and managed to hook it under a strap and coax my pack away from the hive. The curious bees soon lost interest and returned to their circuit around the tree stump. I took a few deep breaths, grateful that I could, then shouldered my pack and gave the stump a wide berth as I carried on down the trail.

THE STORM CAME off the ocean in a hurry, like it had somewhere to get to and I was in its way. Within seconds, a few fat grape-sized drops became an opaque, roaring wall of water.

Instantly drenched and rain-blind, I stood off the path and took cover under some trees. I cursed when I heard thunder, my words lost under its roar. Lightning came next. I felt like a deer in a minefield.

Lacking any other brilliant plans, I crossed my fingers and waited.

A loud snap of thunder was followed by a splintering crack and a long and rustling fall. It sounded too close. I wondered if the fried tree's roots might run as far as the ground under my feet. I started to shiver from seeping cold and terror.

Regretting once again having tossed my phone, I consoled myself that there probably wasn't service out here anyway. And who would I call? And what could they even do.

The back edge of the storm left a wake of dripping trees and flattened ferns. And mud. The trail was now a sucking, slippery thing, sometimes trying to pull the boots off my feet, sometimes rejecting them altogether, sending me sliding down rocks on my butt, my pack underneath me.

At about 6 p.m., on the shore of a wide, shallow bay, I reached the tramp hut, one of the basic cabins New Zealand places along its long-distance trails. It was mid-week, and not quite high season; so far, I had the place to myself. I made a fire in the wood stove, stripped down and hung my sopping clothes over a bench in front of it. My pack was mud-caked and sodden, the canvas heavy and stiff even after I emptied it. Only the things packed in the very middle were dryish, which meant I had one pair of underwear and a T-shirt. My food bag was wet, only a few things salvageable. My sleeping bag was rolled, the outer layer dripping wet and the inside barely damp. Cursing myself for not valuing waterproofing earlier, I hung what I could by the fire and boiled some water for my ramen noodles, hoping no one else showed up while I was still half-dressed.

I dragged a mattress from the bunk room over to the wood stove and stared into the flames as I ate, listening to the spit and crackle. Dryness was seeping up my sleeping bag, so I put one edge over my legs and lay down.

NIGHT CREATURES TAUNTED me. Lizzie, looking an age she never was, standing at the top of the hallway stairs, Look, she said, and spread her arms wide and took off, flying, but I wasn't sure she was Lizzie anymore, she was Char, and then she was gone, I heard a long and rustling fall in the distance, and then Mo-mo stood in front of me, holding Eloise, my stuffed elephant, asking me why the trunk was wet. I cried, I didn't know. We were just playing. What did you do? Mo-mo demanded, her face stretching ghoulishly, her voice echoing. I'm gonna call your mum, and she reached into the ocean and pulled out a cellphone. Then my Grandma Nan walked in, saying, Your mum can't make it, you're coming with me.

I woke up shaking and freezing, the fire now embers. My sleeping bag was still damp, but I pulled it up higher anyway and lay clenched against the cold. My heart pounded in the pitched silence. It was hard not to feel like I was being punished for something.

The dreams didn't help.

When I was younger, David had been there, often enough, when I woke. Or would come when I called. Later, with just Jules, I wouldn't bother to call. Jules would be too medicated in her sleep to rouse easily and was useless at offering comfort. Sometimes I would picture Lizzie as a person in my life, as the sister who shared my room, who knew when I needed her, who would slip out of bed, pad across the room and crawl in beside me, hugging me for a few kinds of warmth.

The sister that wasn't, the sister that was. And now Char, her immediate and blithe trust in me when she led me upstairs to her room. The look on her face when I suddenly left her there. The disappointment I would never stop delivering.

I'd seen that look before. The day I went to my Nan's house for the last time, with Jules. The power switched off, everything smelling faintly of mildew, the stale air coating my palate in dust. Nan had died in the hospital, but only after deteriorating in her three-storey house for several years, declining mobility first limiting her to two floors, then one. So that everything on the bottom floor had been sitting dormant for a few weeks, but the farther you ventured, into backrooms or upstairs, the longer objects had been sitting, unused, waiting for her to get better.

An old newspaper, unfolded and fading, lay on the bed, unmade. As though one day she had gone downstairs in the morning and never made it back up.

Jules had cried that day, for the second time in my memory, as she sat on the edge of Nan's bed. Her late ex-mother-in-law. I came upstairs and found her there, and just like the first time, it shook me to see her emoting so candidly. Jules saw me, hastily wiped her eyes and tried to smile. Your Nan was a real pain in the ass, she said, which I knew meant she'd really loved her. I turned and left her to it, not saying a word, pretending not to see the hurt on her face. Even now, the memory held as much anger as guilt. Anger that once again it was all about Jules's grief, with no room for anyone else's. Guilt—and regret—that the one time Jules had reached out to me emotionally, I'd walked away.

IN THE HUT, it was so quiet my ears rang, the ocean a distant under-hum, the night birds holding their breath, waiting for who knew what. I felt the endless space around me, the infinite distance of darkness and stars, night and solitude.

I got up as the sky greyed, and after instant coffee and a soggy peanut butter sandwich, I acknowledged aloud that two more days with wet clothes, damp sleeping bag and sodden food was going to suck. Especially if sleep kept getting away from me. I was sup-posed to hike twenty kilometres that day, but I already felt totally depleted. It seemed impossible.

The map posted outside the hut said it was seven kilometres to the nearest side trail, which would lead me three kilometres out to a park access point where I could catch a bus. Okay. I could do the half day to the early exit. Not that I had much choice.

I heaved my pack onto my back and started hiking.

A COUPLE HOURS in, I came to a long, flat beach, hard-packed in the sunshine, and I saw a sign for the access trail up ahead. Now, with my jeans almost dry and the burn in my leg muscles easing on the flat ground, I thought I could probably manage the extra day and a half it would take to reach the trailhead. But: if it rained again, my sleeping bag would never dry. And the remaining kilometres might be even more difficult than the ones behind me.

But wasn't that the point? To fling myself into the unknown, and be tested against its challenges?

I could hear Jules's voice telling me a million times, Just because you can, doesn't mean you should. Which rankled.

It's *good* to take risks, I said aloud, as though she could hear me.

I shoved my hands in my pockets, and my heart tripped as my finger tore through wet paper. I dropped my pack where I stood, carefully turned my jeans pocket inside out and peeled away the inky scrap bearing Lee's email address. It was smeared to illegibility, but it didn't matter. "Surfmonkey99" was burned into my brain.

Immediately, I wanted nothing more than to see her again. I cringed to remember my cold dismissal of her invitation to go north, my knee-jerk jealousy, my cruel comparison of her to Jules, and wondered if I'd still be welcome.

The obvious temptation was to take the access trail, get out of the park and go find her. But I winced to imagine telling her I'd given up after one night out here, when what I wanted to do, what she made me want to do, was impress her. Not just that, I wanted to impress myself. And cutting short something I had challenged myself to do, to go chasing down a girl, would not make me the person I wanted to be.

A shell caught my eye, glinting, perfect and blue as Neptune. It seemed like a sign. I pocketed it with lightness and a new resolve.

I was doing this.

I mock-saluted the sign for the access trail on my way by, and continued up the coast, my chafed shoulders, my blistered feet and the brutal hills less noticeable with every step.

THE SECOND NIGHT passed more easily, and by my third day I fell into rhythm with the trail. I felt the hike changing my brain, stretching it into new shapes, unexpected and inexplicable. Landscapes, inner and outer, rendered the familiar strange. My aloneness in the world took on the colour and shine of a brightly wrapped gift. I filled my lungs with air that tasted of lush forest, of succulent fruit, and released it slowly, reluctant to let it leave my body.

As I felt the mapping and marking of one, and then twenty, and eventually sixty kilometres in my very bones, in the torn skin on my feet and the sunburn on my neck, I thought about human smallness, the distances we must travel to find each other and the minute odds of paths crossing. Meeting someone like Lee was not something I should take lightly. Being away from her was bringing my feelings into sharper focus, making what I'd had with Jill seem insignificant in comparison. When I was with Lee, I felt like I might not be alone forever. Of course, everyone leaves eventually. But the very fact that I could feel that connection with someone gave me hope that I might have a place in the world.

I imagined apologizing to her, for everything, but even as I did, I felt the sinking, sick feeling I used to get when I thought Jill was into someone else. Lee hadn't gone north alone, she'd gone to some surfing competition with Talda. Maybe I'd already driven her away.

MY THIRD NIGHT, it was so warm I didn't bother with a fire. After eating the last of my damp bread and salami, I followed my flashlight beam outside to the clearing around the hut and turned it off as I lay across the top of a scarred picnic table. I had seen the stars from Lance's boat, but it was different to view them from here, days out from any human contact, the dark jungle around me. The moon wasn't up yet and the night was clear. At home I could have picked out Mars, but here it was only a guess. Picking out Neptune was pretty much impossible, but I imagined I could see it to the right of maybe-Mars. I thought of Char, drawing a spaceship to get us there. No matter how much of an ass I'd been, I couldn't deny that we were sisters, that there were things that connected us, and that by shutting her down, I was only doing exactly what my parents had both done to me. David repeatedly. Jules perpetually.

I thought about how many times in my life I'd wished I could have saved Lizzie, saved the house from falling down around me, saved Jules and David from everything that came between them. I heard Jill's persistent voice, or maybe it was that long-forgotten grief therapist, asking me: Who was there to save *you*? And I'd always answered: No one. I don't need anyone. My guilt preventing me from admitting otherwise.

Jules once told me—one night when I came home late from a game and found her with her laptop and a bottle at the kitchen table—that after Lizzie died, David had suggested adopting another child because he knew she couldn't go through another pregnancy, another childbirth. And he was right, Jules told me, I barely survived the first two. But he thought you should have a sibling.

David and Jules had both been only children and David thought it had made things harder, for him at least, socially.

But Jules said no to adoption. She thought he was trying to replace Lizzie. She just couldn't. And he never brought it up again.

You're telling me this why? I was tired and sore and had school the next day, and Jules's drunken rants could suck the energy right out of a room. But I felt a surge of resentment that he thought he could replace Lizzie like that, like all our grief meant nothing.

It's too bad he moved so far away, Jules had answered. He was the one who really wanted kids.

Only weeks after that conversation came the phone call from David, You have a new little sister.

I imagined Char being faced with what I had faced, and I ached to protect her, and seethed, consciously, for the first time I could remember, at the adults who hadn't been there for me.

I want to be better than them, I thought. That smart little kid needs someone better.

I DIDN'T DREAM that night. At noon the following day, the trail finally spilled me onto a grassy stretch along a park road, where a bus shelter and a few other hikers waited. I dropped my pack and collapsed onto a bench.

How's your head? someone asked, and I recognized two of the Belgians from the surf lodge in Kaikoura. They'd been hiking the northern portion of the trail, travelling south to this midpoint. Their friend popped out of the bushes a few moments later, zipping his fly. Oh dear, he said when he saw me. It was the kid whose board had brained me, and he offered a sheepish apology for the fifteenth or twentieth time since I'd come back to the hostel with stitches.

Dude, I said. I never said Dude, but it seemed appropriate now. It's the chance we take. We're both squids, right? So, whatever.

Yes, but I did not hit my head. He was my age, or maybe younger, and obviously still felt terrible about it. I felt bad for him, and was tired of other people's guilt, so I said he could totally and completely make it up to me by giving me one of his cigarettes.

See? I said, lighting it, inhaling. I'm responsible for my own self-destruction.

House.

—

hat the actual fuck?

Jules leaned forward between the front seats and thrust Declan's pamphlet through the gap. For two days, she'd been picking it out of the garbage, reading it, throwing it back in disgust. Finally, when Drew said they would take her to her house, to pick up some clothes and whatever else she needed (within reason), she'd pulled it out of the garbage one more time and shoved it into her purse. Now it was badly crumpled, and Farzan had to iron it out on his thigh to read it.

Ah, he nodded, and held it up so Drew, driving, could see what it was. Drew's fluid motion snagged for a beat. A quick eye-flick up to Farzan's face, to Jules in the mirror, and then he was suddenly concentrating very hard on exiting the highway.

Sensory deprivation, said Farzan. A big tank full of salt water, and you just . . . float. It's completely dark and soundproof and you're super-buoyant because of all the salt.

In a surge of motion sickness, Jules leaned back against her seat.

I thought he was an actual doctor.

Well, he is. An anesthesiologist. But he also does research into alternative pain management. He has like a PhD or something.

He said his wife used to do this.

Farzan and Drew glanced at each other, perhaps surprised that

Declan would have shared this with her. Right, Farzan said. Right. And it really helped her, right? I mean, she still . . .

Died, said Jules.

Right. But it eased her symptoms, I guess. Helped with the pain. So then he got on board at the clinic and now he's using it therapeutically. Says it's good for depression, PTSD. Addiction issues. Because you can't feel . . . *anything* . . . while you're in there. And your brain . . .

He spiralled a hand in the air to show where her brain would go.

It really helped me over the summer, when I was having problems with this. He rapped on his right shin, the hollow sound indicating his prosthetic. Drew reached over and patted his thigh.

Good thing, too, or we'd never have met.

Farzan flashed Jules a quick, bright smile. Declan introduced us.

Anyway, said Drew, we just thought it might help.

Jules rammed a thumb and forefinger into the tops of her eyeballs and pinched the bridge of her nose against a frontal lobe headache.

What would I find helpful? Not that anyone's asking. Is a diagnosis. Not some 1960s New Age bullshit. I want someone to tell me what the fuck is wrong with me. And make it better.

Jules—

And in the meantime, I really don't see why I can't have the only drug I've found that makes my fucking life fucking tolerable.

She did know why, but that wasn't the point.

Because you're not in control, Jules.

I am *always* in control.

Okay. Well. You have nothing to lose.

In the relative silence, she kept her eyes closed and tried to match the rounded growl of tires on asphalt with the pitch of her breath as it passed in and out of her throat.

She felt the car stop. Their collective mental sigh.

We're he-ere, sang Drew, not quite pulling off levity.

She opened the screen door, kicked away all the junk mail piled up behind it, unlocked the deadbolt and stepped through the tiny hallway into the living room. Drew, right behind her, let out a long, low whistle. She thought being in her own house would make her feel better. Or at least normal.

Oh, sweetie.

Oh my god.

She'd forgotten, or maybe hadn't before realized, the abandon with which she had wallowed in crisis in the days after Chloe left. Lying in bed, running out of drugs, her car in the shop, Rod angry. Withdrawal setting in.

The table in the front hall was invisible under unopened mail, more random flyers. Loose tangles of clothes grew like vines across the sofa, chairs and up the stairs, the pyjamas she'd worn all that weekend, the clothes she wore during the accident, the coat she wore on Friday night. The mushroom soup she couldn't eat Sunday night congealed on an end table, with an empty wine bottle and a residued glass.

Well, it's not so bad . . . Farzan brushed by her and picked up the dishes en route to the kitchen, where he reacted audibly. Oh man.

Jules followed and gagged. She hadn't closed the fridge door properly. The smell of rotten meat filled the room. After placing the dishes in the sink, Farzan swung the fridge wide open. The top shelf held a near-empty glass of milk and an uncovered half can of tuna. Both grey. Something unidentifiable festered in one of the drawers.

I guess it's good we came. Garbage?

His cheeks puffed out as he dropped the tuna into the black bag Jules pulled from under the sink. He turned on the hot water and started flushing the putrid milk down the drain. There were only a couple dirty plates, but every glass she owned was half-full

of something on the counter, and he started emptying those out
too. Jules had just opened the cabinet where she kept her booze
and spotted the half-bottle of eighteen-year-old Dalwhinnie when
Drew appeared at her elbow.

Let's go pack, he said. Jules sighed and followed him up the
stairs of her own house. The contents of her still half-packed
suitcase dominated her bedroom floor. More dishes and meagre,
abortively eaten meals, de-capped pill containers and an empty
Bowmore bottle crammed her bedside table. The bedsheets were
wound tight, like she'd tried to make rope.

Drew poked his head into her en suite bathroom. What happened here?

The cabinet over the sink hung open, shelves stripped, every
unfinished non-narcotic, non-opiate prescription from the last five
years strewn on the counter.

Jules eyed the pill containers the way she scanned data at work,
looking for a nugget that would offer her solutions, but was filled
instead with an odd mix of longing and shame. Drew intervened.

I got this, honey. You round up some clothes.

Jules turned back to her bedroom, faked a slow gaze around the
room, then sidled over to the bedside table to see—just *see*—what
was there.

I'm right here, honey. Drew, now behind her, put an arm around
her shoulders and veered her left, towards her closet. Reprimanded,
she shuffled her feet through the drift of clothes to snowplough
them back towards the gaping suitcase.

Didn't Marc say you might get probation if you met certain
conditions?

Jules didn't bother to answer. She heard the crinkly hits of small
objects landing in the shopping bag–lined bathroom garbage can.
She stooped down to scoop and stuff clothes manually.

I *know* you want to come back to work, Drew said.

She kneeled on the hard clamshell case to bring its edges

together, then zipped it shut. She loved the space-capsule look of the suitcase, its clean, impenetrable lines.

Perching on it, she watched as Drew opened the cupboard under the bathroom sink and started pulling out baskets full of old herbal supplements, minerals and vitamins from the early years of her long journey down.

You're no good to me in jail, or . . .

His silence like a grim punchline.

You don't like me, she thought. Not like this.

As he rifled through the baskets, throwing anything stronger than vitamin C in the garbage, he said, You're like a sister to me, Jules. I'm gonna help you get through this. His voice was muffled and he didn't turn around. Jules turned her suitcase up on its wheels and rolled it out of the room. Drew said something else, but she could no longer hear him.

Chloe's room was across the hall. She paused outside it, drawn. For the first time in living memory, it was the cleanest room in the house. As tidy as a cell, a sharp-cornered bedspread, the desk holding only lamp, laptop and framed picture. Suddenly needing to see her daughter's face, Jules crossed to the photo and picked it up. Chloe and that terrible Jill, printed right off Chloe's ink-jet printer, the two of them grinning devilishly, the camera obviously a cellphone held at the end of Chloe's arm. She recognized the background as the view of the city from the park along the escarpment edge. Something about the looks on their faces tugged at her, something just a little more familiar than it should have been. She didn't want to recognize in the face of her daughter the same thing she was just starting to recognize in herself—that glazed-over, dazed-out, empty-eyed— But no, Chloe didn't look empty. She looked . . . *elsewhere*. Dislocated.

She put the picture down and wondered, not for the first time, how much dope Chloe smoked, and what else she might do. She'd tried to broach the subject exactly once, last spring, and had been met with a sarcastic, Really? We're going to talk about drug use? Embarrassed, Jules had let it drop.

But the memory made her wonder what else she might find in her daughter's room.

If it was freakishly clean, it was hardly by accident. One of the worst battles during Chloe's last weeks at home had been about the state of her room. Battles in which, Jules could now admit, she'd made some tactical errors.

When she'd said, I might have house guests while you're away, you know, all she'd meant was she wanted the room left tidy. She didn't want to have to clean up after her daughter, or to make the housekeeping service dust around her things. But she could have said it differently.

What she probably shouldn't have said next was, Just get all your crap out of sight, I don't want to have to look at it. Meaning, of course, but possibly failing to convey, that she didn't know how long Chloe would be gone, and every object on display would only remind her of that absence.

But what she definitely should have stopped herself from doing was throwing the dismissive gesture at the trophy shelf as she said "your crap": this was the lit match, spiralling end over end to land on the powder keg.

Predictably, Chloe's face had frozen, then swollen, then erupted into a torrent of obscenities that started with a "Jeezusfucking-christ," included a "youfuckingbitch," and ended with an "everagain-youfuckingcunt" and a slammed door. In the hour that followed, Jules heard crashing and banging and broken glass, and loud, inartic-ulate grunting. She'd called to the closed door, Aren't you a bit old for a temper tantrum? And retired to her room with a drink and a book to wait it out.

Looking around now, she had to admit that however painful the process, the results were impressive. A single bookshelf held a top row of barely cracked math textbooks and five other shelves of well-ordered science fiction. The upper surface, previously an irritating rubble heap of teenage debris, was perfectly bare.

Which begged the question: where *was* all her crap? And did she leave behind anything interesting that couldn't, for example, be transported across borders? Jules started opening desk drawers. Pens and pins, little notepads and old pairs of earphones. Stray homemade DVDs, an old cellphone, an empty bottle of caffeine pills. Getting warmer, she thought. She opened the first of the two big file drawers and heard bottles rattling.

Uh-huh. Now we're talking. She remembered her own teenage years as full of subterfuge and the constant need to evade her mother's bloodhound-like sense for nearby alcohol.

But what she found, behind an old pair of hockey gloves, was not booze or empty bottles, but a small rack of test tubes and a stack of glass beakers nested into each other. Disappointed, Jules slid the drawer closed.

The second big file drawer stuck, and thinking it was locked, she gave an exasperated tug, which opened it a crack and revealed the jangle of junk inside. She rattled it open a few more inches: a twist of metal and wood, little brass hockey players and swimmers falling at all angles, feet rooted to inert blocks.

She closed the drawer abruptly. Or she tried to, but some of the trophies had shifted and something caught at the back. She jiggled it some and heard internal clunks as multiple objects fell. She shook the drawer harder. No dice. Slammed it repeatedly, and heard the sound of glued trophy parts cracking apart.

Oh, not good.

But still it wouldn't close. She pulled the drawer all the way out, set it on the floor and reached into the empty space to pull out whatever was blocking it.

It was a small book with a tiny lock, and a little metal box.

The diary made her feel oddly exposed, confronted with yet another piece of evidence about how little she knew her daughter.

Tangible proof of a whole other, inner life. And a paper diary, no less, when kids of her generation were barely taught to write cursive. Chloe could be so fucking old school. It was like she researched how to be anachronistic.

The metal box, though, made sense with the Chloe she knew. Drugs or private mementoes, she guessed. Her hands shaking lightly, she lifted the lid, glimpsed rolling papers—

That better not be what I think it is.

Jules slammed the box shut. She hadn't even heard Farzan come up the stairs. He stood at the door, head tilted, hands on hips, pained look moving between her face and the box, assessing the state of emergency. Extended a hand: Jules handed him the box, which he opened.

Like mother, like daughter, eh Jules?

She in fact felt a distance from Chloe so abrupt and extreme she could hardly bear it. She flung herself out the door, trying to sound unbothered. You're done down there?

Downstairs, Farzan had tidied the living room and cleaned the kitchen. Hung up her coats. Vanquished the dirty laundry. Neutralized the stench. She could hear him talking to Drew upstairs but didn't bother trying to make out the words. She sat at the kitchen table and turned the locked diary over and over in her hands.

She really didn't know why she'd taken it. But she had it now.

A sticker on the front said in a jiggly-lettered font: *i can't sleep*. One corner of the cover had been bent back, pages underneath bunched and torn, probably damage from the drawer slamming on it. She poked at the pages with her finger, trying to read their contents, but all she could manage was a word or two per page: *terrible, amazing, cool. Bitch. Physics. Sleep.*

She heard the sibilant whisper of plastic bags as Drew and Farzan came down the stairs. Drew appeared in the kitchen door, his face inflamed, slow rivulets of sweat from sideburn to jowl. He took a moment to look not just at Jules but around her, at her hands and feet, the bench beside her, the table in front of her. Blinked at the diary and dismissed it.

Ready?

Jules took a deep breath and followed him out. It seemed, she realized, like they were waiting for her, somehow. Like she was having some kind of tantrum and they were the tolerant parents, letting her kick and scream her frustration out until she just wound back down to compliancy. She wished they would stop being so fucking patient, because she knew she would ultimately disappoint them.

Help.

———

The worst thing was the therapy. The Crown attorney had recommended a court-recognized program, and Marc and Drew had concurred.

Jules told them to go file that under plan B.

Instead, the following Thursday, after ten days of decreasing dosages, increasing boredom, mounting irritability and diminishing patience (in general as well as with Farzan, who never left the house, and with Declan, the gatekeeper to comfort), Jules was back in the ugly brown office of Dr. Morrow, who was asking her yet another very stupid question.

Would you say you're depressed?

Jules stood at the window, stared out at the leafless trees, the low grey clouds that threatened early snow. Well, not that early. It was the first of December. Winter was just so fucking long.

I'm still taking the Celexa, if that's what you mean.

The problem was, she hated the tedium of breaking in a new shrink. They always read too much drama into the details. Until they got to know her and realized that she was fine, she hadn't been broken by her quote unquote difficult upbringing, there were no demons there to exorcise, it was just an unkempt apartment and the dark pull of her mother's resignation, and anyway, she had hauled herself out of there, had put herself through three degrees, borne two children, survived the postpartum depression, the baby dying, the divorce, the complicated daughter, all of it, and she was Fine. Everybody needed medicine sometimes.

And would you say it's helping?

What do you think?

For months she'd been calling the day before to cancel these sessions. She didn't want to talk. But if she had to see someone, and apparently she did, she might as well avoid going through the goddamned preamble of her whole life story, all over again, with someone else. The downside was, she thought Dr. Morrow was an idiot. She was too young for one thing, maybe thirty, thirty-five at most. She didn't know anything. How could she possibly. Every session another hour of her life she'd never get back.

Have you heard from Chloe?

Jules shook her head. It was cold and bleak outside; four thirty in the afternoon and street lights were blinking on.

She landed. She's alive.

Would you say you're worried? It's been . . . ?

Morrow waited for Jules to complete the thought. Jules took a deep breath and turned from the window. It was starting to snow out there, a few pathetic flakes wandering down from the sky, vanishing before they made it to the ground. She couldn't bear to watch.

Couple weeks. She's with David. I'm sure she's fine.

Dr. Morrow was leaning forward in her armchair.

You see what's happening here, Jules? This is what you *do*. Your *pattern*.

Jules looked at the wide mouth that was almost smiling, the brow that was just furrowed enough to show that she really *cared*. Dr. Morrow had the act of concerned shrink perfected, she'd give her that. But she never said anything useful.

My pattern.

Mm-hmm, yes, she said, her voice the consistency of molasses.

You tell yourself that everything is fine, and then you have to pretend that it is. Imagine the strain that puts on your *psyche*.

She's on the other side of the planet. David's there.

But can you admit that you're worried about her?

Jules sighed.

I'm sure she's fine.

Dr. Morrow wrote something in her notebook. Jules rubbed her face. She felt puffy and grey, her clothes felt too tight, her back hurt. And in her current state there was nothing she could do about any of it.

Anyway, Jules, I was only partly talking about Chloe. You've lost a child before.

What's that got to do with anything?

Dr. Morrow's dark eyes opened wide.

Jules. Sudden infant death is a devastating tragedy. For anyone. Grief like that never goes away.

She met the shrink's stare, kept her face slack. She'd heard this before. It didn't help.

I'm not here about grief. I'm here about pain.

Okay. What about David?

What about him?

Now they stared at each other, Jules refusing to show any of the thundering emotions ringing between her ears, Dr. Morrow searching her face. Something skittered across the back of her mind. Somehow, the shrink saw it.

You're still angry at him.

He's an idiot.

What makes you say that?

He's incompetent.

How so?

It took him over a week to get home, for fuck's sake.

She knew Dr. Morrow was baiting her, didn't fight the impulse to bait her back with oblique tidbits of revelation. But the shrink surprised her, put it together in less than a heartbeat.

When the baby died. David was away.

Finally, Jules sat down in the second armchair, let out a gust of breath as her mind went where she rarely let it, the phone call from the babysitter (the baby stopped breathing), her shortness of breath (she stopped breathing somehow), the panicked sobbing she couldn't stop until Monica slapped her in the face. Monica, her secretary.

He was in China. I couldn't even reach him.

Two days of frantic phone calls to his editor in Hamilton, to the paper's office in Shanghai, to a post office somewhere, who the fuck knew where, to a man who possibly recognized David's name but not any of Jules's other English words. Forty-eight hours before she heard David's voice, hours she had spent hysterical, numb, drunk, unconscious.

Another two days to even get to the nearest airstrip.

That must have been incredibly difficult, said Morrow.

Eight days, in all, before he was home to help her deal with the police, the morgue, the funeral director, Chloe's school. His parents, taking her away. The days alone in an empty house. Meeting him at the airport, expecting the sight of his face to make it all better, and feeling nothing, nothing but resentment that she'd had to face this alone. As though, in his absence, any affection she'd felt for him had just flickered away, a piece of code no longer relevant.

She had loved him, once. Not on purpose, but there you have it.

THROUGH EXAMPLE, SHE had early on come to believe that adulthood was a state of loneliness, that the choice was between being poor and alone, or not poor and alone. She had never dated much, deciding early on that casual sex was as much intimacy as she could handle. She was fully committed to grad school, working and sleeping around on weekends when David started coming into the grad pub where she worked.

He always sat at a table in the back corner in the afternoon, pecking away on his old laptop, drinking bottomless coffee for hours and hours. Kind of haggard and rumpled in that grad student way she'd come to associate with the arts faculties. The guys Jules studied with wore ties all the time and were intolerably boring and arrogant. But David made her curious. He tended to stare off into space, sometimes for such long stretches that at first she wondered if he was having some kind of mild seizure. Or sleeping with his eyes open. And if he wasn't, well, that was even more interesting. One afternoon when he was so rapt in thought he seemed catatonic, she wandered back to his corner with a watering can, hoping to inconspicuously peek at his computer screen while she pretended to water the plants by the window beside him. She was pretty much right in front of him when his eyes found her face, and slowly came into focus. She froze, then went into server mode.

Everything alright? she asked, and gestured at his half-full coffee cup as though offering him a refill.

He looked at the watering can, then gave her a small smile that was part smirk and said, None for me, thanks.

Flustered, but wanting to cover her embarrassment, Jules said, Suit yourself, and turned to walk away.

The plants might want some, though? David said.

They're fine, she said over her shoulder, and went back to the bar. She heard him resume the typing he'd abandoned twenty minutes earlier.

After that, she mostly left him alone. She always felt very aware of his presence and thought it was mutual, that there was tension of some kind between them. But that's all it was, for many months: every afternoon that Jules worked, he came in, drank nothing but coffee, and they barely spoke.

Then one evening he came in, sat at the bar and ordered a single malt Scotch, neat. It was so unexpected that Jules just poured it for him in silence, slid it across the bar and waited to see what would happen next. He picked up the glass, swirled it, sniffed it, took a sip and let it sit on his tongue for a few seconds before he swallowed, and then smiled at her. A very warm smile.

I'm done, he said. As a grad student herself, Jules had a pretty good idea what that meant. When his glass was empty, she poured him another and poured one for herself.

Congratulations, she said, and they touched rims, making eye contact as they drank.

As she refilled his glass again, she told him she approved of his choice of celebratory drink. Quality over quantity, she said. I like it. Her entire life she'd watched her mother choose quantity over quality, and this was a welcome juxtaposition.

He told her he'd finally defended his master's thesis in English literature after five years of procrastination and waffling and being cajoled through the final stages by his supervisor, and Jules appreciated his self-deprecating candour.

He asked her what she did besides bartending, and when she started to explain her research in data set management, she had to laugh.

Your eyes just glazed over.

They got to arguing about the value of scientific discourse (Jules) and the importance of art for negotiating moral clarity (David).

They fucked for the first time that night in the women's bathroom.

The next day, David brought her a cactus. It's supposed to be hard to kill, he said, looking unsure of himself. It doesn't need much water.

You don't think I can kill a cactus? she asked him. But she was touched. He asked her to go on a date. Amused by his earnestness, she agreed.

They had fun—fun in a way she'd never really had as a kid. They went on bike rides. They went to movies. They got drunk on patios. He brought her coffee in bed. They wandered home late on empty streets, feeling on the cusp of something big, a great adventure, an epiphany, a revolution. They felt like a team, and although her heart was as street-tough and well-defended as ever, she found he'd managed to slip through somewhere and get close to it. She felt dangerous. She felt safe.

Jules eventually found she was faced with a whole other matrix of life decisions to make: alone or not alone. She started to trust him.

She knew that was giving him the power to hurt her, and eight years later, he did. Even though she'd told him on the phone that the baby died, it was David's arrival home that was their worst moment. The moment she realized she couldn't forgive him for not getting home faster, for not being there in the first place. For letting down the team. They'd already been running on fumes for a while, but that was the moment she realized nothing would ever be the same.

Within a week, he said he couldn't be away from her and Chloe like that anymore, left his post as a foreign correspondent and took the job as a staff writer, and started working from home. But Jules knew he was just doing it to assuage his own guilt.

AND THAT MADE you angry? Dr. Morrow always tried to make things simple.

Jules nodded slowly, her eyes staring widely into her memory. Angry, yes. Angry for years. Years spent in a slow-motion crash, the engine on the plane long since dead and no stopping what was to come. Six, maybe seven years of spiralling towards the earth before its final impact.

He kept saying he wanted *us* back.

He said it again and again, but it was too late, and she knew it. By the time he clued in to the damage their marriage had sustained, there was nothing left but wreckage, nothing to be saved.

Dr. Morrow leaned forward in her seat, saw Jules notice, then leaned back and crossed her legs.

Sounds like he missed you.

I guess. Seems like he's moved on pretty well.

She had missed him too, missed the way she'd loved him once, missed being able to love him, being able to love. Maybe six months, maybe a year after the baby died, they had their first of The Conversations.

She'd been sitting up in the bed, home from work a half day early, already back from a lung-burning run, watching *Law & Order* reruns and drinking Scotch. It was still light out when David knocked on her door, leaned his head and shoulders through and asked to talk.

When she said okay, the first thing he did was cross to the window and open the curtains, let the late summer sun blast in, dust motes swirling in confusion. Jules had muted the television with a sigh. He sat at the foot of her bed, his hairline receding, his middle already soft, looked at her with his guileless brown eyes and listed all the things that made him think she was quote unquote suffering from depression: that she barely spoke to him or Chloe, flinched if he tried to touch her, slept all day if she wasn't at work, worked obscenely long hours at a job he knew didn't warrant it. She ran obsessively, barely ate, drank too much and never returned phone calls—although there were fewer and fewer to return.

She didn't really listen, keeping one eye on the silent television. She didn't need a list. And she didn't need help. She just needed him to go away and let her deal with her own guilt, without the added weight of his.

He did go away, each time, with varying degrees of reluctance and relief. But he always came back, always with the same suggestion:

Won't you just talk to someone?

But Jules didn't want to talk. She wanted to shut it all down, lay a concrete slab over her bottomless well of grief. Running, Scotch, mindless television: these were what helped.

Then, less than a year later, her first disc slipped. David seemed to think she would now have to concede that she needed him. But she didn't. She couldn't stand it, his palpable pining for her even though they still lived in the same house. Eventually she realized: she couldn't stand *him*. But he did the laundry and the groceries and the cleaning and he looked after nine-year-old Chloe before and after school, and all of those were things Jules couldn't do right then. She led him on, she could now, almost a decade later, admit. She let him believe that they would get to a place where they would be able to work things out.

But ultimately, David was not actually an idiot. Four years later, the baby then dead for seven and Chloe a terrifying thirteen, he left for good. At which point she did go into therapy, and eventually added antidepressants to her daily diet of muscle relaxants and naproxen.

Where was Chloe? Dr. Morrow was really digging today. They were five minutes over time, which never happened.

She was going to school, of course, playing hockey— But the shrink was shaking her head.

No. When the baby died. Where was Chloe that day?

She was at home.

She recalled pulling up in the driveway, seeing Maureen, the babysitter, smoking on the porch with shaking hands, telling her to go home, and then going up to Chloe's room, where her daughter was playing silently with her stuffed animals. Then Nan and Elliot arrived, David's parents, who always thought they knew what she should do.

And Chloe stayed in her room that whole time?

She shrugged. She didn't want to talk about it.

Did I tell you I broke up with Rod?

Dr. Morrow made a note, but she was not to be distracted so easily.

I'm just wondering if you see a correlation between Chloe leaving and your escalating dependency on the Oxy.

No. Things keep hurting, that's all.

Morrow sighed and looked at her watch. Finally, it was time to go.

DREW DROVE HER back to his house. Ten days since her arrest and four days completely clean, nothing but over-the-counter analgesics and a basic anti-inflammatory. She felt like shit and craved solitude.

Drew opened his front door and Jules headed straight for the stairs, but as she passed the living room, movement caught her eye.

Jules, honey, let's go in there for a minute.

She followed Drew into the living room, and Declan was sitting there with Rod, who saw Jules and stood up, moving quickly across the room to embrace her. She clenched her teeth, stood stiffly, willed herself not to recoil from the shirt that draped his angular frame, his stiff, mis-gelled hair. The faint antiseptic-and-sweat smell he failed to mask with unfortunate cologne.

He told her he'd been worried, had tried to call her cell, her home, her office, Drew's cell, and had finally driven here, to Drew's house, to look for her.

Then Dec here answered the door, and he's been filling me in. How are you, Jules?

Disturbed by Rod's ingratiating tone, Jules looked at Declan, who warily tracked Rod's movements but spoke to her.

I never told him anything, Julie.

Jules looked back at Rod. You had me arrested.

Oh, I think we can all agree you did that to yourself. Right?

He swept his arms around the room, trying to rope everyone into agreement.

But the point is, now you're getting *help*, which is what I was trying to—

Declan snorted and said, Julie.

I was speaking, Rod said, and Jules would have laughed if she'd had the energy. Rod wasn't used to getting interrupted. His neck was already blotching in agitation. But Declan had his eyes on her now and didn't even look at Rod.

Listen, Julie, I told you, I have a treatment I think might help.

I thought you said she was clean.

Yeah, no thanks to you. Cutting her off cold.

I didn't know how bad it was.

Oh, bullshit. You knew perfectly. I've got patients who've been to your clinic. I've heard about you. You give that shit out like candy.

I didn't realize you were licensed to give prescriptions, Declan.

Well, I haven't sold my soul to Big Pharma, *Doc*, but I also haven't had complaints filed against me.

Everyone gets complaints. And my patients get the best drugs available.

Jules thought for one crazy, exhilarating moment that Declan might lay Rod out, but then Declan said, Julie. It's up to you.

Everyone was quiet, looking at her, and she realized both that it was her turn to speak and that, ultimately, as Declan had said, she had to make a choice. But she wasn't entirely sure what her choices were, just that Rod somehow represented one, Declan somehow the other.

Why are you here? she asked Rod.

He worked his mouth open and closed a few times. I told you, I was worried about you.

He tried to put his arm around her shoulders, but this time she did recoil, moved away from him. His teeth made her think of accordion keys.

Alright. Well, I have to go to court, thank you very much for that, but otherwise, I'm fine. You can go.

Jules turned and walked out of the living room, started up the stairs. She needed some sleep. But Rod followed her out.

I know about this Declan, that clinic he runs. I mean, flotation tanks? Seriously?

Jules was halfway to the first landing, turned and looked down at him.

I'm not blind, Jules. I saw you. On the porch that night.

Jules shrugged. She didn't care anymore. Things with Rod were clearly over, and whatever he thought he'd seen was insignificant. The man she had been drawn to on the porch that night was now the man who had been her rock through a week of detox.

Bye, Rod. She turned and walked up the stairs. But Rod was a last-word kind of guy, and as she rounded the landing on the second floor, she heard:

He's a crackpot, Jules! The front door slamming shut behind him.

By the time Jules reached the third-floor sitting room, she was pondering the irony that Rod had just accomplished what Declan and Drew and Farzan could not. Suddenly, an hour of floating in the dark, where she couldn't see or hear or feel anything or anyone, seemed like a great idea.

And, after all, what did she have to lose?

Aftershock.

W hen I saw the news, I was sitting in the bar at the Picton hostel, having a beer while I waited for the dorms to be swept out. Jansen was somehow still staying there, hanging around me as if we were friends, but his disingenuous optimism, his constant undercurrent of judgment, not to mention the racism, sexism and homophobia he tried to gloss over with slippery charm, made mere civility towards him taxing. I'd been using the ATM in the lobby when his voice at my shoulder made me jump.

Chloe! Your hike took you this long?

Three days, yep.

I hope you are okay?

Yeah, fine.

I'd walked away. He'd followed me.

Now, as he sat beside me, I tried to tune him out, stared hard at the TV behind the bar. When a headline banner reported a **6.1 AFTERSHOCK IN CHRISTCHURCH**, I asked Nick to turn up the volume.

Aw shite, more of this, hey.

Nick had a surfer's ropy frame and sun-bleached hair, but he was probably twenty years older than the surfers I'd met. He shook his head at the TV.

Chandra's sister lives down there. Had their house on the market for over a year now, tryin' to git out. Got kids and everything.

I was down there a few weeks ago. *Ein Drecksloch*. Shithole.

I ignored Jansen. Nick gave an appalled non-laugh.

Blood thrummed in my ears, my breath stopped cold as I watched shaky, cobbled-together cellphone footage of a road rutting apart, water geysering up from concrete crevasses, people canoeing down flooded streets. A row of houses sunk in on themselves with rooftops ripped in half. But they said it was minor, compared with other quakes. There were power outages everywhere but no injuries, and minimal structural damage.

My dad's down there. And his wife and kid. I thought of Char and the rescue dog she had once asked me to draw.

Nick must have seen the worry on my face and said, Y'can try to call him, so I went behind the bar to the office. But phone lines were down all over Christchurch. Amanda's voice mailbox was full, and David didn't even have a cellphone. There was no getting through. Nick put a hand on my shoulder and reminded me that the city had an extreme degree of earthquake readiness.

Back at the bar, Jansen said, I am sure they are fine. Another beer, yes?

His glibness grated on me. Clearly, the money from his father had come through. My guidebook lay on top of the bar, and Jansen picked it up and started flipping through it, trying to make conversation and folding down corners to mark things he thought I should see, with no awareness that he might be crossing any sort of boundary.

I was sore and tired from my hike, filthy in a deeper-than-the-skin kind of way, so I went to grab a shower while I waited for the dorms to be ready. I hauled my duffle out of the storage room and piled clothes on one of the bar's sticky tables until I found what I needed—my towel was way down near the bottom—and left the rest of it piled in a corner while I went upstairs.

The hot water hit me hard as bristles, hammering on my back, making my skin feel flexible again instead of brittle with cold and grime, and I lingered long enough that Chandra pounded on the door to remind me that water wasn't cheap.

Back in the bar, Jansen was not so much nursing a pint as performing meatball surgery on a series of shooters with three other travellers, all German, all white guys in hiking pants. They were drunk and laughing like idiots, Jansen waving his arms around wildly. Uneasy, I tried to walk around them to my bags, but when I was within reach, he slung an arm around me, and I was pretty sure I heard the word *lesbisch*.

I was just telling them how you like to hike by yourself, he told me, and they all laughed again, kept laughing. Didn't stop laughing.

I didn't know you spoke German, I said. His new friends wore lascivious grins, their eyes darting down, returning to inspect my face, making eye contact that was both inviting and hostile.

It is very close to Afrikaans, he said.

Then Chandra came and said the dorms were ready, so I started to gather my things from the corner. Clothes were still spilling out the top of my duffle and I had to shove down a couple pairs of underwear with the Germans watching. One of them smirked, raised an eyebrow, and I wanted to punch him in the throat, but instead I just punched at my clothes even faster.

On my way out of the bar, Jansen grabbed my arm, fake-pouting.

Chloe. You are mad because I have a little fun?

I jerked away, narrowing my eyes at his grammar, which was more awkward than usual. His eyes were a bit glassy and he was swaying. I could feel the Germans watching me.

I don't give a shit what you do. And I turned, again, to go.

But Chloe, and Jansen again grabbed me by the arm, stepped in close, and touched my cheek with his lips before I could stop him. No hard feelings, okay?

Something around his neck caught my eye.

What's that?

I'd seen that knotted leather string before. Jansen looked startled but recovered quickly, pulled it out to show me.

From our friend. Remember? His fish hook.

He *gave* it to you?

I was sure I'd seen Tanga, our ride from Kaikoura, putting his good luck totem around his own neck. I was *sure* of it.

Yes. His *matau*. For good luck in my journeys, he said. You were there, you did not see?

I shook my head, disbelieving.

We had a special relationship, in the front seat, he said. Do not be jealous.

It was more than I could stand. You're such an asshole, I said as I turned away, and if nothing else, the look on his face would always be worth it.

I shouldered my duffle and went to my dorm, put my valuables in a locker, still felt unclean, had another shower, got hungry and went back to the bar. I'd hoped Jansen and his Germans would be gone, and they were. I saw the Belgians, also looking cleaner, heading out for dinner. They invited me, but I wanted to try David again.

I still couldn't get through.

Could be a few days, hon. But the worst of it's done with.

I thought about Char and wondered if she was scared or just used to it.

Nick placed a bowl of chicken stew in front of me. I sat alone, read a few chapters of a spy novel with half my brain while the other half wondered if I should return to Christchurch. I was worried, especially about Char, but I didn't see how my being there would help anyone. I would just be making the situation harder, like if they'd had to go stay at a friend's or something. I would keep trying to reach them, and I could just as easily do that from Piha. After I found Lee.

———

THE NEXT MORNING, I couldn't find my guidebook. It wasn't where it should have been, in the outside pocket of my pack. I remembered Jansen flipping through it the night before, so I went to look for him. But Jansen was gone too.

I'm sorry, love, he packed out last night.

Chandra was working at the front desk, Nick in the office behind her. I could see through the office to the empty bar on the other side.

Yeah, said it was real urgent, like. Some family thing? Took a cab to— Hey, Nicky, didn't that German boy take a cab to the airport?

Yeah, real late, like midnight, he left.

Not really an airport, Chandra said. More like a long driveway they fly tin cans off. But it's quite cheap, to Wellington. Now, you staying on?

I went to get my moneybelt from my locker and unzipped it on my way back to the front desk.

It was empty. Standing in the front foyer, I was slow-motion swallowed by a vortex of doom as I yawned it all the way wide open. All my cash, my bank card: gone. Only my passport remained. I felt sweaty and sick, the panicked vertigo of knowing something was disastrously wrong but still trying to grasp the extent of it.

You alright? Chandra asked from behind the desk.

I think someone stole my money.

Chandra's eyes searched my face, gauging crisis level. Aw, shit. Well, listen, hon, I can hold your bed for a couple of hours. You just let me know what you want to do.

Back in the dorm, I shook out my sleeping bag, lifted the mattress, took everything out of my locker and put it back again.

But I knew. I knew everything.

I'd left my moneybelt in my duffle, left my duffle in the bar when I'd showered yesterday afternoon. That was the only time when it hadn't been on my body or in my locker. And I'd left Jansen in the room alone. I kept going back to his abrupt kiss on my cheek. *No hard feelings.*

I've been angry at a lot of people at a lot of moments in my life, but his easiness, the obviousness and my own stupidity combined to seize me with a whole new kind of rage: it was physical, it jolted down my limbs. I pounded the side of the lockers with the heel of my hand, over and over, until I was scared one of us would break. Hot tears burned my eyes.

Then, as quickly as it had come, the anger rolled away, left me exhausted in its wake. I curled into a ball on my bunk and wished hard for my own disappearance. I could still see the glances between the Germans and Jansen, hear the laughter that was clearly at my expense. He must have already had my money at that point. He'd done exactly what he claimed had been done to him, when I'd met him: stolen from me while I was in the washroom, left me with virtually nothing. My sense of being utterly powerless to undo something catastrophic was achingly familiar.

I WAS STILL there, trying to breathe, trying not to breathe, trying to reorganize my mental universe, when Chandra backed her way into the dorm a couple hours later, pulling a vacuum cleaner and a cart full of cleaning supplies and linens.

Oh, hey, hon. I was just looking for you. Nick says the German bloke left this for ya. Chandra pulled an envelope from her jeans pocket, held it out. I felt a brief surge of hope that all my misery was moot, saw with lightning speed the redemptive scenario: Jansen's father had come through, here he was paying back what he'd taken. But I knew it made no sense, and when I opened the envelope I felt even worse.

I stared at the *matau* I'd first seen hanging from the rear-view in Tanga's truck. Stolen, obviously.

I need your bed if you're not staying, yeah?

I didn't move, couldn't speak.

Aw, love, did your guy go on and leave you without saying?

Oh god. I shook my head. *Not* my guy. But he stole my bank card.

I hated how pathetic I must look. Chandra hesitated.

And all my cash, I added.

Oh, hon. She sat down beside me on my bunk, placed a hand on my shoulder. He didn't break into your locker? She looked behind her at the bank of lockboxes, checking for damage.

I shook my head. He went into my pack when I was in the shower. I felt my core collapse. I folded in on myself, my shoulders on my knees.

I'm real sorry, love. Have you cancelled your card?

Not yet.

Did you give him your password?

As she asked, I remembered him coming up behind me in the lobby the day before. I sank even farther.

I think he saw me punch it in.

Aw shite, really? Money's as good as gone, then. Do you want to call the police? No telling what they can do, but good to have a record of it—could be he's done this before. Do you have *any* money?

My head rolled slowly from side to side.

Is there someone you can call?

Not really. Still can't reach my dad. So, that's great.

Oh, hon. Let me talk to Nick. Maybe we can let you stay here tonight, and you can pay us later, yeah? And you should cancel your card. He's already had it since last night.

As Chandra started downstairs, she said over her shoulder, What about your mother, hon? Can you call her?

Oh god. That was not likely to go well.

Tank.

_____

You gonna float?

The receptionist at the Whole Soul Healing Clinic wiggled bushy grey eyebrows at her.

I guess so.

It's interesting, he said.

Well, said Jules. Good.

Like going away on vacation. To another country, almost.

Great, said Jules.

It can even be like going to another planet.

Jules chuckled, surprising them both.

Even better, she said.

This seemed to encourage him, and when Declan arrived a few minutes later, the receptionist, who called himself Darwin, was telling Jules about a client who liked to spend entire consecutive days in the tank.

He's, like, approaching enlightenment or something. Talking to god and shit.

Oh, wow, said Jules, impressed that someone would make such an extreme claim.

Declan stood behind Darwin and rolled his arm through the air in a wide arc, a playful full-body beckoning. She followed him down a hallway that smelled of wood and chlorine. Sweat trickled down from under her bra.

Alright, Julie, here's our wee flotation tank.

It looked like a sleek sports car without wheels or windows, a gleaming white shell with chrome trim, the underside glowing a futuristic neon blue. Declan pointed out hooks, towels and the shower. He showed her how the lid simply lifted and lowered. There was no latch or anything, no locking in, no locking out. Her chest constricted, forcing her to take a deep breath that sounded like a gasp. Declan peered into her face.

You okay?

I think so. I'm just a bit . . .

She ground the heel of her hand into her solar plexus, its hard knot of anxiety. Declan squeezed her shoulder briefly.

This will help.

Jules inhaled deeply, trying to expand and loosen the knot under her palm.

I just . . . She motioned vaguely towards the tank.

Yep, it's all you. You'll know when it's over. Then come see me downstairs. Alright?

Jules gave a slow nod. She didn't understand why everyone—especially Declan and Drew—seemed intent on helping her. It made her wonder if she seemed like an abandoned kitten that people couldn't walk by without trying to save.

Her suspicion must have shown on her face. Declan shook his head, gave a warm half smile. Drew's real fond of you.

She shrugged. That wasn't enough.

Well, and I got a real soft spot for Drew. After my wife died, I . . . fell apart. For a long, long time. Like, I wound up in the hospital. When I got out, they sent me to a support group, and if I hadn't met Drew there, I probably wouldn't be here now. So. Guess I'm trying to keep my karma balanced.

Jules nodded at the weight of this. She wondered what a "long time" was by his standards.

Plus, if you gotta know, it's part of my research.

She made a face. That didn't exactly make her feel better.

I'm just a number to you, eh?

Declan chuckled. And left her to it.

JULES TURNED THE lights down low, piled her clothes on a chair, showered, dried only her face (gotta form a wet-dry barrier so the salt doesn't go in your eyes) and stepped into the tank. She still had scabs and open cuts where the itchiness from the Oxy and the withdrawal had made her scratch and pick herself to bleeding, and they all stung fiercely as the salt water found them, making her wince and stand back up. But she quickly started to itch again; stinging was always better than itching, so she lowered herself back down. It felt the way alcohol felt on a cut—or like mouthwash on rigorously brushed teeth—an antiseptic sting, somehow promising healing. Literally, salt in her wounds. The rash of sores across her lower back and hips, patches on her forearms and fingers. Even her toes. She concentrated on breathing through the burn. As the water settled, shaped itself around her body and held her there, she became still, and now her sores and scabs felt soothed.

She drifted imperceptibly, utterly calm. Every so often a toe or a pinky would brush smooth fibreglass, and with the slightest pressure she would push off again, lose all sense of space until another digit nudged the other side. Until even that stopped and she was completely immobile

and her mind slipped

floating

in the tank, a memory

part of a memory

how can you have part of a memory?

What makes it complete?

Or rather, is not all memory incomplete?

Our imperfect brains

Imperfect bodies

Soft rolls of uncontained flesh

Stressed bones strained ligaments

Soothed and cooled

All the molecules, every pore on the surface of her skin, drank in the darkness, the perfect counterpart, perfect antidote to the glare of day. Perfect temperature, the body, the air, the water, each a continuation of the other, the skin vanished, the edge faded, the force field between self and world lost all meaning, dissolved completely.

The only sensation by which she could measure her awareness of self was the feeling of her lungs expanding, so she took long, deep breaths, her ears underwater

hear your breathing from the inside

it rolls like a nighttime ocean

Chloe, breathing

Lying in my arms, legs folded over mine,

hair that smells like baby powder

I think she's crying

I can't help her

My baby is dead and I can't help her

Jules's eyes opened, an old reflex for ridding herself of hijacker memories. At least, she thought her eyes had opened, she could feel them blinking, but she could see even less than she could hear, there was no nighttime sky behind this darkness, only an internal space of imagined light, the inner screen of her mind almost palpable in front of her, a private show of her own inner vision. Eyes open or closed, there was no difference.

She felt no pain. How did she not notice that before? Nothing hurt in here. No muscles knotting or irritated nerves or aching joints. She could feel nothing at all. Which had always been the point of the Oxy, this absence of feeling. But the drug also dulled her thoughts, quieted her reflex to dredge up memories in the ongoing project of seeking perspective on one's life. It helped her avoid self-awareness at all costs, in fact.

Here in this chamber of mind, memories squeezed themselves into the darkness, shapeless phantoms that circled her, lay with her, stroked her with breathy ghost fingers.

She'd been to see Dr. Morrow again the day before, who had again poked around for Jules's sore spots.

the baby, the baby

Fourteen years ago, Lizzie had fundamentally altered everything. Jules's entire course of existence rerouted by someone who stayed alive for less than eight months. Even now, struggling to inhabit her creaky, ill-maintained, middle-aged rattletrap of a body without the magic pills, coming to terms with a drug habit that had stealthily ensnared her—even now, it all came back to Lizzie.

the baby died stopped breathing somehow

the baby died stopped that day, that day

the babysitter's voice from the speaker on her desk,

the terrible words, the blazing sunshine outside

brown bag lunchers around the fountain

daytime mums with Humvee strollers

Thirteen years and still it made her lungs constrict. Crumpling in the weightless dark, Jules pressed both hands to her chest to make sure she was still there.

She had hung up the phone and lost everything, lost all control, stood in her office and wailed, pitched and staggered, her vision darkening at the edges, until Monica came in and slapped her. Not hard, just enough to shock her, like swatting aside a frantic swarm of flies to see what festered underneath. All emotion had gusted out, left her numb and empty and exhausted. She heard talking but no words, only murmurs, she was crushed beneath a mile of ocean, paralyzed and sinking. Colleagues in their dark suits and fake concern hovered and muttered at the door, but she couldn't even look up from the carpet. A stain drifted into the middle of her gaze, shaped like a squashed cockroach, a dark spot of blackish brown that could have been coffee, ink or blood, on the floor just in front of her desk. This was the moment she remembered most often, the picture that came into her head as a sort of code word for that day, the dark days that followed, sometimes even for Lizzie herself: sitting on the couch and waiting to be swallowed up, sure she'd never again be able to rise, her eyes fixed immovably on the drab brown carpet of her office floor, the darker brown of that faded stain.

Low, TONAL MUSIC started inaudibly and grew, bringing her back to the cushioning darkness of the pod. A soft glow around the edge and a gentle chime let her know her session had ended. Jules pushed open the door of the flotation tank and climbed out.

Declan's clinic was more urban spa than medical facility. Low lighting, lush towels, a massaging shower awaited her. She towelled dry and dressed, noticing only as she finished how smoothly her body was moving, how bending over and stretching were actions she completed without awareness. Like a quote unquote normal person.

Declan sat in an armchair in his office, a file folder of printouts open on his lap, and as Jules approached, he gestured with his pen at a seat across from him.

Got your medical records already, no problem.

He'd sent an official request for these a few days ago, when they booked her appointment, but they'd both expected Rod, her primary physician of record, to resist and stall indefinitely. That Rod, or his office, had responded so quickly only made her wonder what he was up to. But wonder at a distance: sitting with Declan in matching blue armchairs, wood floors glowing around them as sun bounced through the fall leaves outside the window, and the smell of good coffee wafting into the room, Rod felt irrelevant.

Declan studied her face for a long moment, then said that, believe it or not, she already seemed more relaxed.

Did you like it?

I don't know if "like" is the right word.

Well, it's meditative, right? Produces theta waves, so your . . . subconscious, I guess, can rise to the surface, mingle with the conscious, more daily stuff. It can get pretty heavy.

They were locked in eye contact and suddenly it was too much. Jules tore away, looking for somewhere else to land her gaze. A wall of medical books and a large painting of a blossoming iris did not satisfy.

I guess so, she said. She could hear him flipping through her file.

Well, you have a lot of injuries, Julie. But they've run every test in the book, looks like. No rheumatoid arthritis, nothing like that. So I have to think there's something else going on. Like a different kind of stress, right? On your whole body—holistic stress. I feel like we should open you up so it can get out.

Open me up? She spread a protective hand over her breastbone.

Oh, you know. Declan waved his pen around, gesturing between them. You float and relax, and then we have a little chat. You and me. Alright?

It sounded a lot like therapy, and her immediate reaction was to resist. But a synaptic branch twitched and she saw in herself the stubborn refusal of her own mother to accept help. For years, not even denying that she had a problem, just not seeing the point in trying to live any other way. It wasn't a happy life, she admitted slurrily during one of Jules's infrequent calls home, but happiness was for other people. Jules could try to be happy in her place, she said. Then came the time that Jules had been summoned back from university when a bad fall on her apartment stairs had landed her mother in the hospital, and the clicking of the doctor's pen as he shook his head over wasted time: her mother had to stop drinking or die.

As her present started to reframe her past, Jules realized she was out of reasons to say no.

In the driveway, she rapped on the car window and Drew's eyes popped open. He stared at the car ceiling while his brain rebooted, slowly rolled his head towards the passenger side, saw Jules and popped the locks. She envied his seeming immunity to the cold.

They were halfway back to his place before he said:

So?

Her head felt loose on her shoulders, bobbing around with the movement of the car. Wind had picked up, quickly, and blew around snow, the sharp-edged gravel kind that clicked when it hit the windshield and cut open exposed skin.

I go back next week.

BACK IN THE third-floor sitting room, she watched the bare branches of the Last Tree Standing flail, the longest of its twiggy fingers tapping on the window. She'd been at Drew's just over three weeks. Funny how your perception of a room alters with the time you spend there. This would always be the place where she retched and writhed and cried while she came off Oxy.

She paced around, not wanting to sit. She'd spent too much time on that couch, wallowing, sweating into those sheets. She went out to the landing and listened for the TV downstairs. Drew had gone back to the office, and Farzan, she could hear, was where he seemed to spend every day, watching a very loud game of football on the five-foot television screen on the second floor. It was jarring to the point of fascinating to see this thin little intellectual so obsessively watching the iconic meathead sport, and if Jules had had more tolerance for it, she would have joined him just to enjoy that phenomenon. But football she just could not fathom. Soccer, maybe. But not this.

She could admit that the flotation tank had been very relaxing, like a full night's sleep in the middle of the day, but now she just felt cooped up again. Restless. Like there was something she was meant to be doing, but she couldn't get her shit together enough to figure out what it was.

She spotted her big leather handbag where she'd left it three weeks ago, slung over the back of a chair. It had been returned to her by the cops with a manila envelope containing her personal items. She'd taken out her wallet, dropped the rest of it into her bag and hadn't thought about it since.

She emptied the contents of her purse and the envelope onto the couch, then sat beside the pile and surveyed her life's minutiae: breath mints, heat patches, expired anti-inflammatories (too hard on her stomach), lipstick she hadn't worn in months, her cellphone and passport, a couple pens, two USB keys, a folded pile of pink message slips. A load of crap.

It wasn't until she noticed she was clutching a small pill container that she realized what she'd been looking for. But the container, small enough to tuck in a pocket and just big enough for six tabs of Oxy, was empty.

Which is good, she told herself. It's supposed to be good.

She unfolded the message slips and swore out loud: David. She'd never called him back. She'd forgotten, in fact, that he'd called.

She reached for her cellphone; the battery was dead. She untangled the travel charger, went into the bathroom and plugged it into the outlet over the sink. The cord on the charger was maybe two feet long, so she sat on the covered toilet seat. This would have to be a short conversation. She had a dozen new voice mails but ignored them for now, opened David's contact info and hit Call. Her heart pounded with a sense of impending conflict as she listened to the ringing. She tried not to look at her reflection. Her biggest complaint about the layout of the third floor was the mirror directly in her eye line every time she sat on the toilet. Right in her face. Tucked into the corner of the mirror was a copy of her own mug shot from the day of her arrest. Drew had put it there as a reminder: Whole lot of ugly, honey. Let's not go back there. She really didn't want to look at that either.

Finally, she heard the click of connection. A man answered and she took a deep breath.

David?

There was a pause, oddly muffled.

Sorry, love . . . Like to leave a message?

New Zealand accent, hesitation. A woman's voice in the background that Jules thought she recognized. Is that Amanda I hear?

Amanda? She could tell he was pulling the phone away from his face, to gesture maybe, or hand it off. But then his voice came back stronger. Ah, sorry again, love. Who's calling?

This is Jules. David's ex-wife? Returning his call.

Aw, yeah. He seemed interested by this information, but then said nothing more. Jules started to fume.

And who might you be?

Aye, I *might* be Lance. I'll tell 'im you called, then, yeah?

Wait—is my daughter there? Chloe?

Now there was a longer silence, a held-breath silence, no one moving on either end.

Ah, sorry, love, Chlo's not around either, hey. She's fine, though, everyone's fine. I'll pass your message on, yeah? Oi! Must go, sorry.

Anxiety pinging faintly, very faintly, on her less than optimal parental radar, she hung up and wondered what havoc her daughter was wreaking on her ex-husband's life that would lead someone to reassure her that "everyone's fine."

The rattle-bang of the back door let her know Farzan had gone down for a smoke. Unable to decide if it was to hang out with a guy she wasn't sure she liked or to bum one of the cigarettes she didn't really smoke, she went down to join him.

Work.

—

I made a series of phone calls: my bank in Canada, to cancel my card. A replacement would arrive in about a week. But Jansen had used the card twice, left my account over a thousand dollars short, which didn't leave me much. Not enough by far.

I called Jules, who didn't pick up. Typical. Left a message. Regretted it right away.

I called the police. As predicted, they couldn't do much. "Jansen" had checked in to the hostel claiming to have been robbed, so no one saw a passport, no one could verify his identity. Chandra and I couldn't even agree about where he was from. The cab company could confirm he'd taken a cab to the airport, but there was no record of anyone by that name getting on a flight. I asked if they would look at security footage, even offered to sit with a sketch artist, but was told the police resources for such a petty crime were pretty much tapped out.

There's guys like him who make a living off cons and such, a beefy and red-nosed cop told me. Preyin' on low-security travellers such as yourself. All we can do is tell ya to be more careful.

It had been stupid, I could now admit, to leave practically all my cash in my moneybelt. To use my bank card, enter my pass code, without looking over my shoulder. To leave all my belongings in the bar while I showered. I'd known he was a dick. I hadn't known he was a thief. Well, not until I'd seen Tanga's *matau* (the thought of which made me feel sick about my inadvertent collaboration). Regardless, it was stupid to rely on some unspoken travellers' code of honour when, as I knew, even your own mother can let you down.

But, it was only money. I hadn't been hurt. And I wasn't totally desperate yet, although I would be soon. I still had my credit card, but that was really meant for emergencies. Once I used it, I'd have to get Jules to make the payments, which, as safety nets went, was pretty shaky.

I was stuck where I was for at least a week waiting for my bank card. With low hopes, I emailed Lee to see how much longer she'd be at Piha, to suss out if she even wanted to see me again. And I kept trying Jules and David, but in total vain.

CHANDRA HAD PRETTY much saved my life, I thought as I climbed to the third floor with my broom and garbage bags. She took some kind of pity on me and offered me a couple weeks' work changing beds, cleaning toilets, sweeping floors. Horrible work, I thought at first. Jules had always had a cleaning service, so I had pretty limited experience with cleaning toilets, let alone scrubbing down showers or picking up other people's trash.

I had, however, spent a lot of time in locker rooms, and hockey players can be full-on disgusting, so I wasn't super squeamish about what Jules would call wet-mess: basically, anything organic in origin—bodily fluids, food, pieces of nature that made their way indoors. Jules would not have reacted well, for example, to the sunflower seed shells under the window in the boys' dorm. Or the pair of underwear, way at the back under a bunk. Or the chunks of dried mud, scraped off someone's post-hike boots.

I'll admit I was glad to have my rubber gloves as I used the broom to retrieve the underwear, flicking them into my garbage bag with a wrist shot and trying not to dwell on whether or not they were clean.

But I felt satisfied with myself, like embracing the dirt kind of connected me to the world, made me a part of it in a way I didn't always feel. Material objects meeting my own bodily boundaries. Which I knew was exactly what Jules would react to; I could feel my own latent reaction to the messiness of human beings, their tendency to leak beyond their containers.

In a weird way, I loved the job. I found myself developing an appreciation for the filth of travellers who had better things to do than worry about the artifacts they shed as they went about their lives.

I WAS BEHIND schedule again. By the time I got to the kitchen with my mop and bucket, people were already trying to unpack food into cubbyholes I hadn't yet cleared out, trying to make tea on a stove I hadn't scrubbed, putting dirty plates into a dishwasher I hadn't emptied. I tried to navigate the chaos and do my work, but then Chandra came in, and that was that.

Chlo! Hon, what on earth is going on in here?

I'm just trying to empty—

This whole kitchen should have been done this morning.

She shook her head, staring at me. I waited, in limbo, clean plates in one hand and dirty in the other, totally unsure which way to turn. Chandra took command:

Alright, everyone, just label your stuff and pile it on the counter till we get some space cleared out, right? Chlo, we'll talk when you're done.

I finished the kitchen under a spectre of shame, the new arrivals looking at me with pity and scorn.

When I was finally done my shift, I went into the office to check my email.

I logged on and held my breath when I saw a new message from surfmonkey99:

> Still at Piha, tourney got pushed, now competing the
> 15th-20th. See ya if I see ya. (Hope I see ya.) xo Lee.

I felt my heart swoop, soar and dive.

I was still staring at it a couple minutes later when Chandra came in, shut the door behind her and put on her serious face.

Chlo, hon, we have to— Well, you're smiling! What are you so happy about?

She's still there. I haven't missed her and she wants me to come.

I was gushing, but I didn't care. Chandra grinned at me.

Aw, you finally heard from your girl. That's great, Chlo!

But the only thing is, I would have to leave . . . like, tonight, I think. I tried to look pained, knowing I was about to leave Chandra and Nick in the lurch.

Aw, look at ya! You have to go. What's her name again?

Lee.

See, even the way you say her name—ya must go. She beamed at me for a moment too long, deciding something. Anyway, to be honest, Chlo . . . I came in here to tell you we'd have to let you go.

What?

You're too slow. And rather sloppy, if you must know. You know I like you, but this . . . Well, you're good at other things, right?

I snorted. Well, obviously.

The hurt on Chandra's face made me backpedal.

I mean, I like it here and everything, but . . .

I git that, hon. But this is our place, yeah? Mine and Nick's. And we . . . well, we like to look after it. I'm sorry, Chlo, but today's your last day. But listen, it all works out, yeah? I'll even add the bus fare to your pay. Oh and hey, this came.

She handed me an envelope, a flat and rigid rectangle inside it: my new bank card.

I went upstairs to pack. I started stuffing clothes into my duffle and got about half done before I stopped short. Feeling the thrill of impulse, I pulled everything out again, picked out what I really needed—my favourite T-shirts, underwear and socks, extra jeans, toiletries, a hoodie, flip-flops—and crammed it into my day pack. Everything else went back into the duffle, and I dropped the whole thing at the Lost and Found.

My load felt lighter in so many ways.

My bus wasn't till midnight. Before I left, I tried calling each of my parents one more time.

Call.

Hello?

    Hi.

    Groggy and disoriented, the line between dream and waking wavered.

    Chloe?

    Obviously.

    Well. Nice of you to check in. Jules knew she sounded angry, which wasn't her intent, but her worry had curled itself into a different shape and now came shooting out of her mouth in attack mode.

    She heard a sharp expulsion of air.

    So, I guess you didn't get my message.

    Funny, that's what I was going to ask you.

    She sat down on the toilet seat and avoided looking at her reflection by resting her eyes on her mug shot. Drew was right: she looked terrible. Black pockets under her eyes, greying hair unwashed and stiff. Wood-grain lines around her mouth and eyes that weren't there a year ago. Or was it five years ago. Who kept track of these things.

    You left me a message?

    At your dad's. Someone named Vance? Or Lance?

    So anyway, I was robbed, said Chloe, and Jules's eyes went

involuntarily to her reflection, which looked as alarmed as she felt, and not much better than the mug shot.

Excuse me?

Chloe told her the story, and later Jules would admit to herself that she did not react well.

Leaving your valuables unattended. Brilliant.

A part of her wanted to swoop in and scoop her daughter out of there, save everything, protect her always. But it was too late for that. Much too late.

After a silence came the sandpaper rasp of a deep, bracing breath, amplified by digitized signals sent to space and back.

I, like, *knew* the guy. Sort of. But the asshole was gone by the time I noticed.

How much money are we talking about?

I feel bad enough without you lecturing me.

Jules counted to five, mustering calm.

How much?

There was a long silence, and she wondered if Chloe was counting to five.

'Bout a thousand bucks.

Jeezus, Chloe. You've cancelled your card?

I'm broke, not stupid.

Oh! You want *money*.

Well. This could ruin my whole trip.

Bet school's looking pretty good.

I have a job, but it's not—

Chloe, if you had any idea what I'm going through—

What *you're* going through?

You have two parents. Try the one who's not ten thousand miles away.

Are you fucking kidding me?

I just can't deal with this right now. You'll have to—

Chloe cut her off with a tirade full of expletives and a reference to working the streets for money, which ended with the not-unfounded accusation, It's always about *you*, isn't it, *Mother?* Before she terminated the call.

JULES STARED AT her bedraggled reflection, breath rasping, tremulous in her fragile husk. She knew she'd lashed out, knew Chloe was likewise going for shock value, but it didn't help; between them, they had trashed the conversation, veered it straight into the realm of raw verbal assault that left Jules feeling desiccated.

The clock on her phone said 8 a.m. She knew Drew would be at the office. She'd been hearing football games playing downstairs for hours already. How there could even be that much football was a mystery, but Farzan seemed able to watch it any time of day.

Her phone was charged, so she unplugged it and dialed David's number again. This time a woman answered.

Amanda?

Jules stood at her window and watched the Last Tree, its bare, gesticulating branches.

Yes? Her voice was clipped, almost hostile, like she already knew who it was.

It's Jules. Is David—

But already she could hear the phone being passed off.

It's your *ex-wife*.

Bitch, thought Jules. The construction crews were in full force in the condo development one block over. The grid of iron girders mapped the tree branches onto a graph, lines criss-crossing in erratic patterns of growth and decline. Grinding and rumbling made the glass shake. Or maybe it was just the wind.

Hi, Jules, said the voice she'd once been married to for fifteen years. She slammed her feelings of nostalgia into a box, clamped it shut. David. I just spoke to Chloe—

Oh, good. That's good. Where is she?

That's what I'd like to know. Why isn't she staying with you?

Ah. She was.

She knew, just *knew*, thought she could even *hear* him dragging his hand over his balding head. She used to tell him that was *why* his hairline was receding, this constant wiping of his gleaming pate whenever he was embarrassed or didn't want to tell her something.

David. She heard herself using that acid-and-saccharine voice she didn't think she'd ever used on anyone else. Where is my daughter?

Well. She went sailing with Lance?

Who's Lance? Does he know where she is?

Sort of . . . Not sure. Things are a bit . . . weird around here.

His voice was drifting away, background noise submerging it. Nearby, a child spoke incoherently, and Amanda answered, melodious and sweet.

David, she started, but then his voice was suddenly stronger and faster:

Gotta go, Jules. Talk later.

Her phone beeped, then went silent as the call cut off.

Less than a month, and already David had lost track of Chloe. Jules was on the other side of the planet on fucking house arrest and she'd spoken to her more recently than he had.

She scanned through her emails until she found the one with Chloe's New Zealand cell number. Had David even tried calling it? Yes, he had, because she found all his emails too, his mounting concern that neither Jules nor Chloe was answering his calls. She dialed the eleven digits Chloe had sent her and waited, preparing to quote unquote be nice.

When it went straight to voice mail, she tried not to panic. She'd just talked to her minutes ago, and she'd been fine. She was fine. Like Jules had told Dr. Morrow: she wasn't worried.

Chloe had said she'd left Jules a voice message. Jules sat on a chair by the window and skipped through her voice mail until she found it. It was more than a week old, and she sounded utterly dejected, said she couldn't even pay for her hostel because she'd lost her wallet. She didn't know what to do; she had no money; she started crying.

I think I've really fucked up.

Jules froze, her hand locked onto her phone, as she listened to the grain of her daughter's voice. It had been many years since she'd heard Chloe cry, but she could still read the sound like a mystic, every hiccup loaded with meaning and nuance.

I tried Dad, but I can't get through.

Her voice was torn at the edges, a squeak of hysteria weaving around the upper register. Then she said:

I guess Christchurch is all shut down 'cause of that big aftershock.

Aftershock.

Jules tried to reconcile this new information with her conversation with David, his claim that things had been "weird," a claim she had chalked up to his usual stunned reaction to the world. He'd sounded more or less okay, and clearly the phones were back up, but it did not make her feel good.

And I've lost my phone, Chloe was saying as she broke into a racking sob and abruptly hung up.

Jules sat with the phone against her ear for several seconds, then lowered it into her lap, stared blindly out the window, wishing, for the first time she could remember, that she was a better person. That she even knew how to be better. That her reaction in this moment wasn't to crave, in the way she was suddenly craving, the pills she didn't have.

When the doorbell rang, she ignored it. It would never be for her. But it rang again, and again, the eight-note sequence persistently interrupting itself two or three notes in, refusing to take the implicit Go Away for an answer. Farzan probably couldn't even hear it over his football game. Jules went down to put an end to it.

She opened the door to Rod, literally standing there with his hat in his hands. In winter he liked to wear a fedora over his black scarecrow shag under the misguided impression it made him look distinguished rather than slightly shifty. He was holding said hat in front of him, staring hard at its rotating brim.

Oh no, not you.

Rod looked up, eyes puppy-dog pathetic—but also, ever so slightly, baring his teeth. Now why would you say that?

What do you want, Rod?

He smiled his best disarming smile. Invite me in?

Jules chewed on her lip—an old habit, for years kept at bay by lipstick, but not these days.

Alright. It was below freezing outside, after all.

Drew's house had an actual foyer, a vaulted front hall he swore was big enough for Ping-Pong. But when the door closed, and all Jules could hear, other than the faint sportscast upstairs, was the shuffling and breathing of the two of them, she tensed. It felt intimate and wrong. She planted her feet apart, shoulder width, and crossed her arms.

What do you want?

She watched as he cloaked himself in the charming but vulnerable schoolboy, with the twinkle in his eye that suggested only she could help him and only he could help her. But she felt a sudden keen sense of the passage of time, of time wasted and time running out.

You're alright, then? I sent your records to . . . He gestured, like he couldn't bear to name Declan or his clinic.

Yep. Thanks.

So how did it . . . how was it?

She shook her head slightly, narrowed her eyes.

What do you really want, Rod? Third time now, but who was counting.

So you liked it?

It was very relaxing. Turns out I need to relax more.

He made a sound like Huh, or Hmm, nodded his head and looked at her in what she imagined he imagined was sympathy.

Anyway, I'm kind of busy.

He pulled his head back, birdlike. Busy? With what?

Fuck you, she thought. But she told him.

I don't know where Chloe is. As she formed the words, their immensity racked her, adding a slight tremor to her voice.

That's . . . distressing, he said, sounding not worried at all.

She shrugged, not trusting herself to speak evenly, and equally not wanting to put into the air words—any words—that would stop him from saying what she knew he would say next. What she was waiting for him to say.

How's your neck, Jules? And your back? Do you need anything for them?

Because truthfully, everything hurt like hell.

I brought you a peace offering. Hat in his left hand, he reached his right into the pocket of his trench coat. Might help.

He held it out like a gift, the sample-size offering of little green pills with precise 60s carved out of each of them. When she didn't take them, he shrugged, stepped around her and placed them on the writing table under the stairs. She didn't stop him, didn't move, tracked the pills with her eyes.

I'll just leave them here.

Isn't that the exact drug you had me arrested for trying to get?

Uh, well, those are actually the OxyNEO. Free samples.

That's not the point.

Rod looked at his shoes, head bowed, as humble as she'd ever seen him. He seemed suddenly much younger.

I'm sorry, Jules, about the arrest. I am. I was lashing out. He looked up at her. I felt like you were just using me for drugs.

She conceded mentally that this was the truth but said nothing, still unsure of what he was doing there.

And then that Declan guy really got under my skin. Anyway, I'm told these aren't habit-forming. Just thought you might want to try them.

She'd done enough research in the past few weeks to doubt the claim, but at this point possible addiction was a moot concern. She managed to say I don't, but the *want them* wouldn't come out. The pills pulled at her with their own gravitational force. Stringing together words of refusal was like building a bridge out of Popsicle sticks in a hurricane. She kept her eyes on the prize, the solution in a bubble pack. It was so close. Too close.

I'm supposed to stay off the opiates.

She was numb and reeling, felt the struts of her very new resolve tremble and sway, the whole thing might collapse with a breath.

You need what you need, though, right? Guess I realized you can make your own decisions.

She couldn't argue with that. I need what I need, she repeated. He walked over to her, rubbed his hands over her arms, squeezing them gently.

I've missed you so much.

He pulled her into his arms, rested his chin on her head, rubbing her back, wholly oblivious to the clenching of her shoulders, the tension in her jaw.

Nothing is the same without you. He leaned back to look at her, his pale forehead flexed in a demonstration of concern, and then he winked at her, he actually winked, and said, Don't I always look after you?

It was the wink that did it, this new flirtatiousness of his reminding her of how understated he'd been when they met, highlighting everything about him that had changed. The roaring wind in her brain fell abruptly away and she could see the precipice on which she stood, the edge of the vortex that had swallowed so much time, so much of her life already, and she suddenly knew: it would take everything if she let it.

Whatever utter insecurity had led Rod to this point, she didn't need to be a part of it.

Okay, no. You gotta go.

She disentangled from him, his arms clinging like stretched taffy, and moved towards the front door, left him standing in the middle of the foyer, his stupid hat askew on a head cocked in confusion.

She opened the door.

But, he said.

She shook her head. She had nothing left to say.

She shut the door behind him, possibly a little faster and louder than she'd meant to. But not much.

And, of course, it took mere seconds after his Porsche drove off for her to remember—not that she'd forgotten—the sample pack of Oxy on the table by the stairs. As she crossed the room, Farzan appeared on the landing above. She froze, caught. But he didn't look accusatory, he looked struck.

They've had another earthquake in Christchurch. A big one. It's on the news.

Quake.

———

The news shattered her, the destruction, not just the destruction, but the commentary, a 6.4 earthquake hit the city of Christchurch just hours ago, so far eleven people are confirmed dead and hundreds injured, two weeks of escalating aftershocks, hardest hit was the suburb of— And that was it, the female voice went on to talk about flooding in the Philippines. Farzan rolled it back so she could hear it again, that ten-second clip that told her nothing.

That's David's suburb, she told him, and then she said nothing, took the remote out of his hand and watched it several times, but there was nothing, nothing new.

Is that where your daughter is?

Jules nodded, slowly. She was. At her dad's.

Chloe, Farzan added, as if knowing her name could somehow make her safe. Can you call? Make sure they're okay?

She felt herself sinking below the surface of things, this couldn't be happening, couldn't be happening.

I don't know where she is now.

It came out in a tight whisper. She'd said the same words just minutes before, but the earth had literally opened up since then, and she felt strangely far more comforted by Farzan's presence, his quiet watchfulness, than she ever had by Rod. She told him everything in an incoherent rush, felt the sobs locked up tight in her chest trying to punch their way out.

I told her to call her father.

She sat on the couch, Farzan with an arm around her shoulders. From where? he asked, and she recalled the buzzing that had woken her up.

My phone, she said, and went upstairs to get it. On the way up, she cringed as the shoulder that had been aching since Chloe's call sent fresh bladed fractals into her neck and arm. At the landing on the way back down, she veered left instead of right. Moments later she was halfway to the kitchen for some water. Oxy in her hand.

Whoa-whoa-whoa.

Farzan appeared out of nowhere, made her jump. Took hold of her arm, followed it down to her hand, uncurled her fingers to pry the bubble pack from her fist. He was surprisingly quick and strong and she was so tired.

I need that.

Okay, okay. He tucked it into his front pocket. Let's just talk for a sec first. He sat on the kitchen bench. Gingerly, Jules slid in across from him. She closed her eyes and tried to breathe through the Revenge of the Pain.

I just need one.

I know. But listen. She heard him rap his knuckles on the table.

I'm listening.

Where did Chloe call from?

Scowling, she checked: a long and unfamiliar number. Jules showed Farzan. He shrugged. She hit Dial.

Picton Backpackers, drawled a woman's recorded voice, followed by check-in hours and location, and a beep. Jules left a message, hung up and swore.

Okay, so. Farzan handed her his own phone, showed her a map of New Zealand. Way up there, he pointed, the north end of the South Island.

Way up there. She peered into the tiny screen, zoomed in, zoomed out, looked at the map in satellite photos. It seemed very remote. Desolate, even.

So at least you know where she is.

I know she's in the middle of fucking nowhere.

The earthquake was down there. That's, like, hundreds of miles away. He pulled and poked at the phone in her hand, trying to show her. She put it down in frustration, massaged the back of her neck.

She knew of only one way to deal with how she was feeling. She knew what he would say, but she had to ask:

Just one?

When he didn't speak, she looked up, found him glaring at her.

Whatever, Farzan. I don't need a lecture.

Drew stuck his neck out for you. And your daughter—

You just said she's fine. She has a credit card if she really needs it.

Really. That's your response. Why are we even trying to help you?

She doesn't need *me*, Farzan. And I never asked—

You're unbelievable.

You know nothing about me.

Right back atcha, sister. You need to get your shit together, Jules, or watch your life go down in flames. He stood abruptly. I don't have time for this shit, he said, sounding equal parts exhausted and furious as he went back upstairs.

You don't know what this feels like, she called after him, weakly and to no response. You don't know anything.

SHE SWORE. SHE wanted to leave, but she couldn't. The clamp on her ankle made sure of that. And where would she even go.

She tried to call David again, but whatever lucky connection she had found earlier was broken now. What would she say to him anyway.

She climbed the stairs to her room, feeling ancient and wrecked. She could hear, coming through a shut door on the second floor, Farzan's voice over a dampened football game. She outlined, and filed for later consideration, the strategic problem of how to recover her pills from his pants pocket.

The guest room felt more restrictive than ever. Her bed was a twist of sheets, her crap all over the couch and floor, clothes dropped anywhere she'd changed.

Since she'd left the apartment she'd shared with her mother, Jules had always kept her places of residence immaculate. (Although, judging by what she'd seen at her house, her account with her cleaning service was in serious arrears.) But generally, she made a point of being a very tidy person. The past few weeks, here in this room, habits had unravelled, and objects had ceased to find homes. Disorder had colonized her space.

She wandered around the room, picking things up and finding places for them. She hung up some clothes, put others in a laundry hamper. Maybe she'd wash them later. She made the bed, gathered up the newspapers she'd pillaged for crossword puzzles. Collected unwashed coffee cups to take downstairs.

As she restored the room to its clean lines of furniture and walls without the intrusive scribbling of her scattered belongings, she glimpsed a memory of what normal felt like. These were folded shirts and a smooth, calm bed. Books could be neatly lined up on a shelf. She could cope, she thought. She knew how to do this.

Straightening the sofa cushions, she found the little book she'd taken from Chloe's room, its cover bent back.

Oh.

Oh.

Dr. Morrow was right about one thing. She'd lost a daughter before.

It took her a paper clip and twenty seconds to pick the lock on Chloe's diary.

Diary.

———

Despite the backlash from the earlier incident, Jules had tried to track Chloe by accessing her Socialink account for a second time a few days ago, before she even knew she was "missing." But all that remained of Chloe's account was her public profile: a rather alarming screen cycling through several graphic cartoons of people offing themselves in various ways, bleeding text declaring that *Chloe_In_Net Is Dead!* And along the bottom of the screen, the flashing question *Do You Want to Kill Yourself Too? Click here.* So, instead, she had cyberstalked other people Chloe knew, starting with her girlfriend Jill. She was prepared to use some backdoor code to get into her private messages, but she didn't need to. Jill's privacy settings were non-existent, and her profile picture said it all: a typical Couple Status picture (smiling seriously in a close embrace in front of a tree—seventy-five percent of high school students posted at least six a year) with someone Jules did not know, dated two days after Chloe had left on her trip.

Jules had said her daughter's name aloud, feeling her heartache and a sad relief: Chloe's radio silence was about *Jill,* not about *her.*

READING HER DAUGHTER'S diary now, which started the previous April, midway through Chloe's last semester of high school, Jules found much of the adolescent drivel she considered typical. The perpetual overblown drama with Jill. Rage at her oh-so-villainous mother for not sharing her eighty-thousand-dollar car with her then eighteen-year-old daughter. Anxiety that the world might not hold a place for her; naive excitement at the prospect of creating one.

Then her eye popped to the word: *Oxy*. She sucked in and held her breath, let it out slowly like she was underwater and had to make it last.

Not a secret, then. Chloe had regularly gone through Jules's dresser drawers and bathroom cupboard, and had known for a long time about the pills. Certainly, she never seemed surprised by their discovery. Quite the opposite. At one point she was waiting, worriedly, to see if Jules would notice that she was missing some. (She hadn't.) And Chloe and Jill had taken Oxy together one afternoon, lounging by Jill's pool.

Mortified, Jules flipped several pages ahead, thinking: Okay, Guilty. She was, once again, violating Chloe's privacy, albeit, again, out of parental concern. But also, Not Guilty: because Chloe had apparently violated Jules's privacy, multiple times, out of nothing but self-interest, and surely that made it worse? Surely that put Jules ahead enough on the scale to outweigh the fact that Chloe had done what all the Public Service Announcements warned against: gotten high by stealing her parent's prescription medication.

But no, she knew she really was terrible at being a mother.

Maybe she could make up for it now.

In an entry dated a couple weeks after Chloe had started university, Jules read:

Dreams, under the surface. At night they try to drown me. My childhood bullies gathering round, haunting and taunting. Can't. Fucking. Sleep. Missed my morning classes all week. So not good.

Jules remembered Chloe's terrible nightmares. The worst part of which, for Jules, had been the waiting. The dreams happened with such regularity that she found herself lying awake, anticipating the horrible choked cries from Chloe's room.

Back then, Jules, who already had a tendency to self-medicate, did what she needed to remain unconscious for the minimal six hours a night. An extra Scotch or two. A variety of pills.

But Chloe's dreams would wake David, and David would wake Jules. And he was right to—she wasn't so terrible a person, or mother, that she didn't even want to know that Chloe was suffering. At least not at that point. Not yet.

When the dreams continued, became chronic over months and months, they finally took Chloe to grief counselling. Within a few months, they seemed to stop. Chloe never talked to Jules about her dreams, not once, but the grief counsellor had said she might not, so Jules hadn't worried. She had enough trouble looking after her own grief, and her daughter had seemed fine. So she'd thought.

But here it was, thirteen years later, and Chloe was still, or again, going through fallout.

That kind of grief never goes away.

October 1:

I can't sleep but I dream
I can't sleep I can only dream
wake up suffocating, 4 am.
Drugstore pills no help. Hafta go to Student Health.
bits of memory that waited years to get me alone
have got something to say

And the following day:

student health won't give me anything.
asshole fucker idiot doctor tried to call me "normal"
"overwhelming anxiety" kind of missing the point
every time I blink my eyes try to sleep
every time I sleep I think I'm dying

Then, just days before Chloe withdrew from school:

Dream last night
Mo-mo took Eloise and said it was all my fault
but no one needed to know
she'd look after her for me
I didn't believe her but I let her.

Jules wasn't really seeing words anymore, she'd slammed head-long into a wall of memory, a wall around her memory, years of truths appearing, climbing through the cracks. Mo-mo, Maureen waiting for her on the porch, trying to light a cigarette. Chloe playing with Eloise, her beloved stuffed elephant, up in her room. Before Nan and Elliot took her away. The bedroom, with the crib, that she could never use as an office again. The version of her life she could never live: everything that happened behind her, when she wasn't looking.

JULES.

Drew, breathing heavily, stood in the doorway to her third-floor room. A few stapled pages, envelope-creased, hung from his hand.

How ya doin'? The tone was casual, the frown scrutinizing.

She shrugged. Didn't know where to begin.

Farzan says Rod came by.

Oh. Yeah. He did. It felt like weeks ago, continents away.

Drew lumbered towards her. And brought you more Oxy. Fuckin' guy.

I didn't— Farzan took it. Jules closed Chloe's diary—a mistake, because it said *Diary* on the front of it, and Drew was now close enough to read it.

Jules. You can't read that.

I don't know where she is, Drew.

Well, she's not in *there*. He reached for the book. It's not right.

But she pulled it away.

I need to read it. She tucked the diary under her arms, out of sight. Drew sagged, disappointed. She'd hurt his feelings and felt a beat of remorse. She was no closer to knowing where Chloe was, and felt further than ever from knowing who she was, but it was the only clue she had, and she wouldn't give it up.

Alright. Well, here's something that is my business. He held up the papers in his hand. A certain B-class sedan? On your company account? The rental company is claiming you never brought it back.

I never brought it back. She thought about her beloved Benz, repaired and waiting at the dealership.

Drew flapped the papers again. I know that, Jules. Want to know how I know it? Because we also got a notice, at the office, from the *po-lice*, saying that that same car has been impounded and, for a not so small fee of fifteen hundred dollars, can be retrieved from the pound. At which point we can return it to the rental company, who, by the way, are threatening to sue us for the price of the entire car.

I'm . . . Shit. I parked it at the pharmacy . . .

Jules had never seen Drew this worked up, and it scared her. He was the one person who made her feel rooted. She worried that if he let go, she might float away.

The other partners want me to fire you. You're going to have to do a program, Jules.

She knew what he was saying. They all—Drew, Marc, Farzan, Morrow—thought she should do one of the court-recognized recovery programs, with support groups and urine samples and so on. It sounded like summer camp for junkies.

I just forgot, with the cops and everything . . . Give me those, I'll deal with it—

She stood to take the papers, but Drew pulled them out of her reach. Sorry, sweetie.

But I'm clean. And I'm seeing Dr. Morrow.

I know. Drew shrugged. But it landed on the wrong desk, and I had to tell him something. Raj and I have been partners too long.

Jules rubbed her thumb on the cheap brass lock on the diary, stared at its plain black cover, damaged by her frustration.

But listen.

Jules listened.

Stay clean till your court date, see what the judge says and we'll go from there. It could be just a relaxing couple weeks in cottage country.

The diary was so understated. Utilitarian. Chloe was doing what she needed to do in a world so separate from Jules's but so entangled in it, silent threads of memory stretched thin between them. She remained silent. Drew shifted his bulk slightly.

Farzan, you know. He's just trying to help.

Yeah. I know.

So don't be such a bitch, Jules. Make nice.

Masculinity.

A fter stewing for a solid twenty-four hours, Jules tried to make amends with Farzan in the same way she'd first started to be friends with him: she went down to bum a smoke. She wasn't planning to make it a habit, but a few times in the past few weeks when the withdrawal, the anxiety, the captivity, had driven her mad, she'd instinctively zeroed in on the nearest life form, and the closest thing to a drug.

You're interrupting my work, he'd protested weakly, the first time, and Jules had finally come out with it: How could watching hundreds of hours of football games possibly be . . . "work"?

Masculinity Studies.

What?

It's called a dissertation?

He didn't seem to mind the distraction, though, and usually went out to the back porch with her. And she'd started to really like him, which wasn't something that happened to her often.

She went down to the second floor, leaned on the door frame of the sitting room where Farzan sat amidst stacks of open books and stapled printouts, computer on his lap and remote in his hand. He paused the image on the massive television when he saw Jules, a life-sized huddle of three men in muddied jerseys and tights left frozen on the screen, their shoulders padded out to caricatures, their helmets touching intimately. One could clearly see that they all had their hands on each other's asses.

Hey, she said.

Farzan didn't say anything, just looked at her and waited, his jaw set, impatiently bouncing the remote.

Any updates on the Christchurch earthquakes?

The bouncing hiccupped, resumed. I'm sure your TV gets the news.

Right. She wanted to ask for a smoke but felt herself chickening out. Okay. She turned to go.

What kind of person *are* you?

She turned back, saw on his face a familiar hostility, only this wasn't her teenaged daughter, she wasn't his mother. But she knew what he was talking about.

Her *diary*, Jules?

I was looking for clues—

You violated her *privacy*—

What choice did I have?!

In seconds, it had escalated, a sudden violent storm that rolled away, left the air heavy. She stood still in the doorway. The remote continued bouncing in his hand.

Was it worth it?

It didn't make me feel better, if that's what you mean.

The remote slowed to a stop as he sized her up for several seconds. Then Farzan stood and grabbed his coat from the arm of the couch. Going for a smoke, he said, pushing by her, making her stand back. You coming? But he didn't turn, didn't wait.

After a moment she followed him down, out into the glaring day.

WHAT DID YOU find? Farzan flicked the filter end of his cigarette and catapulted ash into the bush. Is it going to help? His heavy eyelids hooded his eyes protectively in the bright sunlight, the actual hood of his black sweatshirt shadowing his forehead.

Help, she said, examining the word and its connotations. She took a long, deep haul off her cigarette and exhaled a mushroom cloud of smoke and frosted breath. I still don't know where she is. But maybe I'm starting to fill in some blanks. Or maybe figure out where the blanks are in the first place.

She had no words for how responsible she felt, how deficient reading Chloe's diary—both the act itself and the information she gleaned there—made her feel as a person and as a parent. And even if she found the words, how would this young guy, barely thirty, with no kids of his own, have the slightest idea what she was talking about.

Farzan studied her from under his cloaked brow. Uncomfortable in his gaze, Jules crushed out her smoke, intending to go inside. But then she stayed, trying to keep her back in the narrow rectangle of direct sun, tucking her hands into her armpits to keep them out of the wind. Farzan turned away, stared out at the world beyond the backyard fence, patchily snow-covered garages with netless basketball hoops, the top branches of naked trees.

I used to play soccer, back in Washington where I grew up. Right through my teens. I even got a scholarship for North Carolina, which—well, they don't give out many.

You must be really good. Jules was more impressed than she thought she sounded. She'd never, ever played team sports except under duress.

I was. Very good.

Chloe plays hockey. She had a whole bunch of trophies in her room. I didn't even know she'd won that many.

Farzan glanced sideways at her. Oh yeah? You go to her games? Sometimes.

She tried to remember one.

Farzan had smoked his cigarette right down to the filter, and now he ground it, hard, into the grimy plate that served as an out-door ashtray. See, that's my point, Jules. That's my bloody point.

That I should have gone to games?

Farzan faced her, his eyes fierce. That you *could* have. That you're such a cool person in so many ways, you could be *amazing*, but you just—you don't care. You just don't fucking *care*. He made a frustrated grunting sound and went into the house, leaving her there in the dazzling, frigid day.

She perched on the edge of a plastic chair, already grey-brown with wintry residue, and stared into the empty swimming pool. Wet snow had drifted into the deep end, and a bird or squirrel had made tracks across it that the sun had warped into shapeless holes.

She did care, she told herself. Of course she did.

But the truth was, she'd never really wanted to be a mother. At least, never planned on it. And once it had happened, never com-mitted to it in the way she probably should have. And the second baby, well. That nearly sank her.

JULES HAD BEEN seeing David for over a year when, somehow, despite ample precautions, she got pregnant. She was on the fence about what to do about it, but David, in an uncharacteristically proactive move, went and got a job at a newspaper, and then pro-posed. They sat on a picnic table in the park across the street from the grad pub, and it was in that moment, looking into his familiar brown eyes, both of them bundled up against the biting February wind, that she saw it all. Everything her mother had never had, everything Jules had never even considered available to her: a husband, a so-called normal life. Maybe a home, together. Maybe more than one child. She'd always known with unwavering foresight that she would have a career. Math had been her bea-con since childhood, showing her a way out. This, though, David, down on one knee in the snow, this was something else. In that one moment, as her fingers and cheeks went numb and her toes started to ache from the cold, she wanted it. She wanted it, and she said yes.

Three months later they were married, with no one but David's parents, Nan and Elliot, in attendance. Chloe came in October, and if Jules remembered one thing about that day at the hospital, it was the tidal wave of new understanding that crashed over her as she looked at her newborn daughter's slightly squashed-in face, red with an imminent scream.

She looks like an angry alien, she said, and she could sense the nurse tensing up, but she didn't care, she was laughing and crying as love and loss overwhelmed her. This little person, at the same moment she became the centre of Jules's emotional universe, had become her own discrete entity, separate from her and all the more powerful for it.

Jules finished school and worked from home for a couple years, writing code for the cash, and almost inadvertently producing some of the pioneering algorithms in a then infantile field called data mining, her twin master's degrees in computer science and information management finding their perfect union in her work.

Their marriage was not such a perfect union, however. And working at home, with an infant, who then turned into a toddler, turned out to be her private version of hell. Chloe was amazing, she understood that: a natural athlete, walking at ten months, talking at thirteen, insatiable curiosity and an insane laugh. Jules wanted to stare at her while she slept, to walk around with her in the stroller and play with her in the park. To watch her encounter the world and be amazed by it. But Jules didn't recognize her*self*. She struggled to concentrate, to work for more than ten minutes without interruption. David wasn't home to help enough, and when he was, he drove her crazy too. Slowly, at first, his dirty breakfast dishes forgivable as he rushed off to work, and the socks he shed like leaves all over the house a seemingly small nuisance. He was always late for a deadline, always apologizing for the mess he left behind him, but never found the time to clean up, never noticed her tension and exasperated sighs. Previously, Jules had believed herself incapable of loneliness, but now she missed their adventures and their adult conversations. She waited in desperation for Chloe to start daycare, thinking it would help. When David started going away on more assignments, she found herself looking forward to his absences.

She managed to get pregnant again—again, despite ample precautions—and then she let David convince her a baby was what they needed, a new life form running around to bring them closer together. But six months into the pregnancy she was miserable with regret, and the baby seemed to know it. *Lizzie* seemed to know. She fought to keep the baby alive and managed to carry her to term. But less than a year later she was dead, and Jules was never able to shake the feeling that the thoughts she had never uttered aloud had somehow poisoned her baby.

And now it seemed she might have poisoned Chloe too. She took a cheerful, smart, relatively well-adjusted child and turned her into a tormented, drug-experimenting insomniac. Good work, Self.

THE SUN GAVE way to a cloud and Jules shivered, realizing her hands and butt were numb with cold. Back inside Drew's house, she headed upstairs with the vague notion that she might do some laundry. It was probably time to stop turning her underwear inside out for the clean side.

On the second floor, the sitting room door was open, the groping huddle of footballers still frozen on the television. Farzan sat sideways on the couch, massaging his stump of a leg, his prosthetic on the floor beside him.

She stood in the doorway trying to think of what she wanted to say. There was no denying that he'd hit a nerve.

My therapist asked me a question last week that I couldn't answer.

Yeah? What was that?

His tone suggested he'd already heard a lot of answers to a lot of questions and no longer expected anything but disappointment. The sadness of it moved her forward into the room.

We were talking about when Chloe was a, not a toddler but, you know, a kid. Little.

It felt jarring to differentiate between Chloe as a child and Chloe now, although to call her an adult didn't feel right either.

Anyway, she asked me where Chloe was when . . . on this one particular day, and I realized . . .

She paused as he started to strap his shortened leg back into the prosthetic. He glanced up at her, saw her watching him.

You didn't know?

No, I knew.

He looked back down at his leg, grimaced.

Is that why you don't play soccer anymore?

He coughed out a bitter half laugh. Not according to my father. He thinks it's because I'm . . . how did he put it? Oh yes. A "fucking pansy-assed fairy faggot." Nothing to do with the drunk cabbie ploughing into my motorbike.

Jules sat down beside him on the couch. Farzan rolled his eyes and wiped it all aside with a broad sweep of his hand.

He sees me as broken, and he wants someone to blame.

He pulled his pant leg down and shrugged.

So, fateful day, you can't remember where Chloe was. Shrink asks and you can't answer, plus you don't know where she is *now*, plus you read her diary and found out what teenagers really do these days, so you're freaking out. 'Bout right?

It was about right. When Dr. Morrow had asked her where Chloe was the day the baby died, Jules had known without much thinking she'd been at home with the babysitter, knew she'd seen her playing with her animals when she got back from the hospital, and that somehow, several hours later, under the anaesthetic of a half-bottle of Scotch, Jules had sat on the kitchen bench and watched her leave with Nan and Elliot. She could remember Chloe's face, tight and pale, her refusal to cry or complain as she bumped down the stairs with her little suitcase, a stuffed animal dragging from one hand.

But there were hours in between, hours she spent losing her shit, calming down, losing it all over again, with Nan and Elliot trying to comfort her, trying to make practical decisions, trying to take Chloe home with them and Jules refusing to let them, over and over and over until her strength was gone and she finally relented. She spent hours on her bedroom floor, the bedroom she shared with David when he was home. Hours when she didn't lay eyes on Chloe.

Did reading her diary clear up that little mystery for you?

She leaned her head on the back of the couch.

No. It just made me think I'm a terrible mother for not thinking about it earlier.

Farzan looked at her with half a smile.

Well. At least you care that much.

Piha.

The shape of things to come.

Two dream-state days on buses, a ferry and more, very indirect, buses until the beach shuttle dropped me here, on this long curve of beach with its resident surfers, who lounged and laughed, waxed and waited. Standing on the damp side of the wavering line in the sand, surf coming at me in an endless procession of water walls, wonder walls, breaking, collapsing and finally crumbling into cool froth around my ankles, my feet burrowing as the ground washed away.

Surfers were practising out on the break. My backpack still on, boots in hand, I watched a figure slice up a great curl of wave and cut down the moving mouth of its tube, barely escaping as it collapsed behind them.

A cocktail of admiration and fear, like pre-game jitters, bubbled in my belly as I remembered those two seconds of flying, time stretching and suspended under my board, before the crash.

I had hurt the ocean, and it had hurt me back, and I craved reconciliation.

I TURNED, SQUINTED, and everything was only backdrop to Lee, walking towards me, the rage of her hair in the noon sun. We made eye contact at a hundred metres, and even if people cut through our line of vision, it was always there when the way cleared, steady and waiting.

She stopped a few metres away, glanced at the bus-height swells.

Maybe we'll start you out with somethin' more wee, yeah?

She pushed her aviator glasses up on her head as we stood there smiling at each other. She wore a grass-green wetsuit with the top hanging down around her waist, a long-sleeved T-shirt in the same colour. Sponsor logos curved around her muscled legs. I pictured dropping my pack and boots and running towards her in a slow-motion Hollywood embrace. Apprehension made my feet wriggle deeper into the sand.

Hey, I said.

You came.

I came. I felt a need to apologize, so I said, You gonna win this thing or what?

Lee took a step closer. You gonna be my cheerleader?

I thought you were mad at me.

Another step. Why would I be mad?

Cuz of what I said.

Yeah. That was nasty.

You're really nothing like my mother.

Oh, that. I thought you meant about Talda.

You *were* mad.

More like frustrated. It seemed like you didn't trust me.

I was shitty.

Yeah. You were.

But I'm here now. I took another half-step towards her, my insides quivering.

You're here. She smiled. And in case you didn't notice, Talda is with that bloke over there.

She pointed, but I didn't even look.

I don't care about Talda, I said. You were right about that Jansen guy, though. Fucking thief.

Aw, Chlo. I'm sorry, mate. I shouldna left like that. He was such a con.

Lee took another step, and now we stood very close.

Sorry, she repeated.

I'd been holding my breath but could smell the perfectly balanced mix of salt and sweat and sunscreen that was fundamentally Lee. You didn't do anything wrong, I told her.

Lee's smile widened. Not yet, she said. She took the final half-step.

Hollywood could suck it. I tasted ocean and toothpaste and lemonade, felt the coolness of damp neoprene under my palms, the wet undercoat of hair at Lee's neck. When a loudspeaker announced the Ladies' Over Forty, I laughed, and we finally broke apart.

Ladies, eh?

Aw, don't get me started.

Lee picked up my pack in one hand, grabbed me with the other and started pulling us away from the water.

You don't wanna watch—

No.

Back across the road and into a campground, we pushed and kicked aside packs in Lee's small tent even as she pulled my T-shirt up over my head. With her wetsuit unzipped and peeled off, a team effort, we toppled onto a sleeping bag. She tasted like the ocean and the ocean was the universe. Fingers twisted in hair, our mouths hanging on like kissing was breathing, our brains and bodies fusing, bare arms wrapped fiercely around backs, bodies straining to get closer, to be more inside each other. Everything washed over us in waves. Then I went over the edge, the pulsing shook my whole body and I cried out. Lee's neck strained back, the tendons in her throat standing out, and she looked so beautiful.

Photograph.

———

Later, we ventured down the beach, our beacon the bonfire where Sean and a few other surfer types already sat around drinking. Sean roared when he saw us and ran over to scoop me up in a hug.

I've missed you too, I laughed.

This one's been pining—

Lee smacked him playfully across the back of his head. Shut up about it, yeah?

I found a seat on a lopsided bench near the fire, and Lee sat on the ground in front of me, leaned back against my legs. Beer and cheap wine went around in travel mugs and plastic cups, and surfers trickled in like night spirits drawn to the fire. Sean and a gangly Argentinian named Jorge rolled a number of joints and passed them around, and we all lit up ceremoniously. I drew in deeply and watched the smoke wind and circle between us, rising. I felt the delicious tweak to my state of consciousness, a dimensional slip that added layers of perception and possibility. Lee's hand trailed light fingers down the back of my calf, and I thought, This. This is the moment I came for. No matter what happened—and I was so low on cash, my plans clearly needed to change, were changing by the minute—I had reached this place, and I could feel something fundamental shifting, the tectonic plates of my brain starting to realign.

Lights came on behind us, and the surfers cheered. A small building I hadn't noticed before squatted at the edge of the woods. A couple people beelined for it, and Lee leaned back to tell me it was a surf bar—cheap beer and free bathrooms, she said. Unpredictable hours.

Been here forever, Sean added. You seen the pictures of your dad yet?

I have not, Lee answered, with some trepidation in her voice.

He used to surf here, Sean told me, back in the day.

Sean sprinted over to the bar and came back holding a framed photograph. I'll bring it right back! he called to whoever was inside. They have this up on the wall, he said, as he placed it in Lee's hands. That's got to be—what?—thirty, thirty-five years ago?

Look at those shorts, I laughed, looking over Lee's shoulder.

A broad, lanky twentyish guy, with a tanned surfer's physique and neon-green-and-pink shorts, stood next to an orange surfboard that towered over him. I felt Lee go still against my legs, could only imagine what she saw: her father at an age she'd never known him, at the age she herself was now. But I knew what loss was, knew from the curl of her shoulders, her shallow breathing, that it was knowledge we shared.

Y'alright?

Lee nodded. Thanks. She reluctantly handed the picture back to Sean, and he went to return it.

I rested my chin on Lee's head, squeezed her rib cage gently with my knees. As she stared into the fire, her hand slipped into mine and held it, right over her heart.

He just loved *life*, she said. Loved it to the extreme.

I thought about Jules, clocking time and numbing pain. Working obsessively, always trying to make more money. Drinking herself to sleep, waking up to do it again. He taught me how to surf, said Lee. Every time I go out, he's right there with me.

I heard her voice rip and my heart ached for her. But also for myself, as I remembered that I too had once had a parent who'd doted on me, who was lost to me now and whom I'd been grieving for years.

I thought about the first time Jules took me skating. She and David had both scorned baby steps—no training wheels on my bike, no shoes without laces and none of those easily balanced two-bladed skates for me. At not quite four years old, I was straight into what must have been a tiny pair of hockey skates, my mum in snow boots shimmying backwards on the ice while she held both of my hands. The balance had come quickly, and it wasn't long before I started peewee hockey. But what I remembered about that day was the absolute and undivided attention: I was the centre of Jules's universe. The edges of my blades cut into the ice, and my legs figured out what to do, as I propelled myself forward, ever forward, into my mother's ever-retreating embrace.

You're amazing, Chloe, she'd said.

You're a natural, she'd said.

And the smile.

She'd scooped me right off the ice, held me in a brief but tight hug, my heart bursting.

Then she'd placed me back down, steadied me for a moment and let go. You don't need me at all! And she'd shoe-skated off to drink her coffee in the penalty box, leaving me to wiggle and slide across the now-vast frozen expanse by myself.

You don't need me at all.

Hey, said Lee, bringing both of us out of our respective reveries, did Chlo tell you guys how some *ass-hat* ripped her off?

I grimaced, still embarrassed I'd let it happen, that I'd been so naive. But when I told the story, Sean said, Fuck it, let's kill him, and I immediately felt exonerated. No one but me thought it was my fault.

It could have been worse, Jorge said. It's only money. The lit end of his joint etched slow red lines across space. Better to have friends than money.

Or *stuff*, I said. That is an excellent mantra. I liked how opposite it was to Jules's materialism, her tendency to use money as a tool of manipulation.

I knew she'd refused to send me cash when I told her I was robbed because I hadn't called more (not that she was ever nice when I did) and she was feeling sorry for herself (as usual). Jules withholding money was a gesture meant to hurt. She might call it Tough Love, but it felt like no love at all.

I had four hundred and some dollars left in my moneybelt. I already knew I'd have to cash in my round-the-world plane ticket and somehow find work again.

But it was exhilarating—every moment felt precipitous: I was about to take a flying leap, I had only to choose a direction, and I just didn't care how broke I was. I liked the idea of not needing Jules, and how possible it felt.

Fuck money, I said out loud. And Lee laughed, which was everything.

Court.

J ules woke at 6 a.m., tried to reconstruct her turbulent dreams: Chloe drowning, Lizzie wailing, Jules held down by men in lab coats, cutting open her brain and telling her to keep an eye on her blind spot. A little white hatchback, sinking in the ocean, a teenaged daughter waving from the passenger seat, Jules had no ears, she couldn't hear anything, she knew she should help but then her eyes were sealed shut too, and she couldn't get them open, couldn't remember how.

Siege mentality, Dr. Morrow had called it, when she had finally found a box she could check to describe Jules: Child of an Alcoholic. That's how you've been living your life, she nodded, as though it explained everything. You've built bunkers—barriers of drugs, booze, work, anything to keep your feelings at bay, and keep people at a distance.

Morrow's uncharacteristic directness felt like a reprimand, but then she'd softened it by asking if that felt about right. Jules couldn't say no but refused to say yes. It felt to her like all her barriers had recently been dismantled.

Their hour had ended, but the words had been dogging her ever since.

AT 7 A.M., she remembered it was Friday and got out of bed. It was still dark, night smothering day a little longer every morning, a little earlier every afternoon as winter approached. Killing spirits with its velvet pall.

She rummaged in the basket of laundry she'd managed to wash the night before, promising herself she'd fold it later. She branched out from the track pants she'd inhabited for the past week with jeans and a sweatshirt. Okay, the sweatshirt wasn't really branching out. Anyway, it was too casual for court. She started again with wool pants and a button-down. Better for court, certainly, but so conservative it chafed. She tried a skirt: no way. Went back to the jeans, and found a black T-shirt and a blazer.

She made a cup of coffee, relishing the chainsaw gnash of the coffee grinder. She drank it on the back porch, watched the sun come up, smoked one of Farzan's cigarettes and confronted the full awareness that she'd started a new habit. Well, if she had to go to jail, she'd already be one of the cool kids.

Ready?

Drew stood at the back door, his lined trench coat open over a lime-green suit, nectarine shirt and grape-juice tie.

What, now? It was only eight o'clock, and her hearing was scheduled for eleven. It really was a crazy outfit. It cheered her up.

Marc says early is better. Shows a good attitude. This judge likes it.

This judge better not examine said attitude too closely, she thought, but kept it to herself.

MARC MET THEM on the steps of the old courthouse.

Hello, darling. Drew gave him a hug and a quick kiss on the lips. Thanks for doing this.

Oh, my pleasure, said Marc, as he and Jules exchanged cheek kisses. Need more pro bono anyway.

Pro bono? This was news to Jules, and it irked her.

I told you, sweetie, the partners—

I can pay my own legal bills, Drew. I have money.

Drew's face turned cherry pink, and he stuttered. I just . . . at your house, I saw the stack of unopened mail—

Don't worry, sweetie. I need more freebies, and "unemployed recovering addict" is just what they like to see on my sheet. Marc winked and squeezed her arm.

I'm unemployed?

Ask me tomorrow, said Drew.

Great. Well then, thanks, I guess.

OTHER THAN THE bailiff who guarded the door behind the bench, they were the first people in the courtroom. It was eight forty-five. By nine o'clock, the room was packed with frazzled lawyers in cheap suits, sullen clients from a large cross-section of demographics, and their parents and wives and husbands, who had crowded in to witness these reckonings. Jules did a quick survey and thought that of the people she took to be defendants, she was probably the only middle-aged white woman. Well, there was one woman with bleached hair and a stretched-out tank top who might have been Jules's age, but her terrible makeup made it hard to tell. Jules wondered what she was being charged with, but then she tousled the gel-stiffened hair of a scowling tattooed kid about Chloe's age, who flinched and swatted away her hand, and Jules realized she was just somebody's mother.

Judge Enrique Mancuso entered, striking and in his fifties. Marc had explained that he had a first-come, first-served policy in his courtroom, so even though her hearing was officially set for eleven, the bailiff now read her docket number aloud from his tablet:

Stacie Julie Wright.

Jules was too busy cringing to hear anything else. The Wright was from David, that was okay, but she'd long ago dropped and amended the rest of it—never legally, though, and as she followed Marc and Drew to the defence table, she took a moment to regret it.

Good morning.

The judge was smiling. It was the beginning of the day. Marc said Judge Mancuso played squash every morning—sometimes with Marc, in fact—and whether he won or lost, the exercise always put him in a good mood. Jules had wondered about the vague ethics of working such advantages. But she wasn't stupid enough to shy away from proffered help when the possibility of prison still circulated in her universe.

Judge Mancuso consulted a file on his bench, then asked Marc and the Crown attorney to confirm that they'd reached a potential plea agreement, which they had. Then he turned to her.

So, Ms. Wright, for the sake of the record, how do you plead to the charges in question? That would be—oh fine, read them, then.

A communal chuckle moved across the gallery. The bailiff, a clean-cut young guy with smooth brown skin, suppressed a grin as he read Jules's charges, after which the judge again asked her how she wished to plead.

Jules stood up and took a deep breath, but kept it from turning into a sigh.

Guilty. Her voice crumbled like dried crackers as it left her mouth. But within her, it resonated like a fundamental truth, a hibernating monster stirring in the back of its cave.

I'm guilty, Your Honour. This time with more air, and it came out too loudly, made her shiver. Her ears rang.

May the record show it. Ms. Wright, I have a note from your Show Cause that says you were in pretty rough shape. Says you "exhibited classic signs of opiate withdrawal."

Jules nodded as he looked her over.

You seem better. Are you feeling better?

Somewhat, Your Honour.

Oxy, was it?

Yes, Your Honour.

No fun, withdrawal, is it?

It truly sucked, Your Honour.

This got a sympathetic laugh from the gallery.

Alright. Are you in a treatment program?

Marc spoke up for her:

Ms. Wright is being treated by a psychiatrist, Your Honour.

And how long have we been doing that?

Marc looked at Jules, who shrugged.

Years.

Marc rushed to clarify that it was years because of depression, not Oxy addiction.

Hmm. Prosecutor?

The Crown attorney was young, maybe thirty, and had an eight-inch stack of files on the desk in front of her. It was a first offence, she said. If Jules would commit to her current treatment, the Crown would be satisfied with one-year probation.

But the judge said:

Well, I'm not satisfied. Doesn't seem like your shrink helped you avoid this conundrum, does it?

No one answered him. Mancuso was rereading something in the file, maybe more details of her case, the charges that had been dropped. Jules held her breath, terrified the deal Marc had wrangled out of the Crown was about to poof away. Drew took her hand and squeezed. Mancuso continued:

I'm sure the Crown attorney is aware that the real risk here is that you'll turn to street drugs, and right now a great many of those are being cut with fentanyl. Which can kill you. It's turning up in heroin, street Oxy, any opiate not from a pharmacy—and that's where Oxy users are turning. And—I played squash with a narcotics detective just this morning, and he tells me that's not just street users, but people—well, like you, Ms. Wright, people who had prescriptions but somehow—you know how—got hooked, and need a substitute. Or a supplement.

Jules had a desperate sense of impending impact on her life. Your Honour, I'm not about to start doing heroin.

Don't knock it till you've tried it! someone called from the back of the room, and the judge hit his gavel to quiet the room.

Thank you, he said to whoever had yelled it out. I believe you've made my point.

More laughter. But not from Jules. Drew was crushing her hand, but she held on like she was falling out of an airplane.

Let's go with the year probation, that's fine, but contingent on your completion of an in-patient program, okay? Ninety days. The Crown here can give you a list of the court-recognized ones. Stay out of trouble, Ms. Wright.

He gave her a nod of encouragement and banged his gavel.

Happy holidays. Who's next?

NINETY DAYS?

Oh sweetie, it could have been worse.

Yeah, said Marc. I thought he was about to give you thirty days.

He gave me *ninety*!

I don't mean rehab.

Oh.

At least they took that thing off your ankle, though, right?

She stared out the car window, the melting and grey remains of an early snowfall, the hardy cyclists who sprayed through gutters of slush alongside the row of inching cars. Winter hadn't even officially begun and already the city felt grimy and hostile.

When do I have to go?

Fourteen days, so . . . by New Year's. I really think that's the best one for you. Pricey, I know, but super cush.

Jules looked at the brochure in her lap. Marc had "just happened" to have it in his briefcase. A big red-brick farmhouse in the country, with white trim and pillars, sat in the protective embrace of weeping willows and elms. But anything could look welcoming in summer. *Greenvalley Healing Centre*, dark-blue cursive print spelled out across a light-blue sky. *Your Journey to Recovery Begins Here*, in smaller yellow cursive scrolled across the immaculate front lawn.

It's like a vacation, said Drew. At a spa. If you sign on, I think I can persuade Simon and Raj to, you know . . . He didn't need to finish: To not replace you. To not fire you. He patted her knee.

The inside of the pamphlet showed well-dressed, relaxed-looking people lounging in a sunlit room for "Group Therapy: You Are Not Alone"; a white-haired but still handsome man relaxing in an armchair next to a serious, pretty young woman with glasses and a clipboard: "One-on-One Counselling: We're Here to Listen"; a yoga class ("Strengthen the Core of Your Being"); and a silhouetted figure passing in front of a tequila sunrise ("Rediscover Beauty"). There were also some more descriptive paragraphs, but one of them began with the words "You are Beautiful," and it hurt too much to read further.

I am *not* doing yoga.

Jules folded it back up and rolled it into a tube.

Her cellphone rang, the screen showing a long international number Jules thought was familiar.

Jules Wright.

Hey there, this is Chandra, I'm calling from the Backpackers here in Picton.

Jules recognized the thick accent as much as the voice.

Thanks for calling back. I'm trying to track down—

Yeah, Chlo you're looking for, yeah?

Yes, Chloe, my daughter. Is she there? She called me from there.

Oi, I'm afraid you've missed her, hey. She left, oh, I don't know, a while back, I guess. She was here for a week, like. More, maybe. Poor thing. That bloke took her cash was a real piece of work.

I bet he was, said Jules. You know, I called a few days ago.

Aw, yeah, said Chandra, distracted, noise in the background.

Do you think she was still there then?

Aw, she mighta been, hey? Can't say. Don't really check voice mail too often, everything's email these days, yeah? Technology, she laughed. Jules did not. She had also emailed, in fact, but there'd been no response to that either.

Well, do you know where she went?

Hey, Nick, where did Chlo say she was going?

There was mumbling in the background, then:

Not sure, but I know her friend was up in Piha, hey.

Hey, Jules said, her radar picking up a target for her universal frustration. I have no idea who or where that is, she said through clenched teeth.

Drew glanced at her quickly, shook his head; she was being rude, he meant, and it wouldn't make this conversation more productive. She flattened her tone, asked the woman to repeat herself.

Yeah, Piha. To meet up with someone named Lee, I think it was. Some surfing competition? Oh sorry, a whole busload just walked in, I gotta git— Good luck, though, I bet she emails you soon, hey.

Jules hung up, wondering how, when Chloe was the one she couldn't find, she could be the one who felt so lost.

Feelings.

When Chloe was little, they'd had a beehive under the roof of the garage that came back year after year no matter what they did. Chloe knew to stay away, or they thought she did. Jules and David were not exactly helicopter parents, but they tried to explain the danger to their daughter so she would know to avoid it. One summer afternoon, Chloe must have been seven or eight, Jules was sleeping when the sun reached her eyes, so she got out of bed to close the curtains and happened to see Chloe approaching the garage at the back of the yard, hockey stick in hand. Jules somehow knew what she was about to do and yelled at her to stop, but her window was closed to keep in the AC, so she banged on it, glass shaking. Chloe turned and looked up at her, her jaw set with determination. Even at this distance, her eyes were defiant. Jules watched as she raised her hockey stick to the hive, and she never saw the impact, never saw the hive splitting open, the outpouring of angry bees, never saw Chloe turn and bolt for the house, only heard the scream as she raced down the stairs to the kitchen, opened the back door and scooped Chloe inside, swatting away the last of the bees. Her own blood pounded and Chloe was hysterical as Jules looked her over, trying to distinguish injury from scare, and put ointment on the nine bee stings she found. (Stings the doctor later concluded were the root cause of Chloe's severe bee allergy, after that horrible call from the school and the fast-acting teacher with her EpiPen.) But that day, Jules's heart had broken at the sight of the welts puckering up on Chloe's back and neck, and she'd wanted to hold her tight, but every time she tried, Chloe cried harder and said it hurt too much.

Now, again, Chloe was unreachable, possibly in trouble, even danger, and Jules felt a visceral protectiveness that was both new and very old. An image, or maybe a memory: Chloe sitting alone, against a wall, knees drawn up, eyes wide in a worry that looked fundamentally wrong on her six-year-old face, then something had closed, her eyes, or a door maybe, and the image was gone.

And suddenly Jules had the answer to Dr. Morrow's question, maybe not an answer, but a clue. She popped that old home movie into the mental machine and scanned the tape for missed details, even though she knew every frame.

That night, that terrible night, already feeling the blame coming from Nan, why wasn't she home, what kind of mother was already back at work with an eight-month-old. Nan had never wrapped her coiffed blue head around the idea of postpartum depression. They wanted to take Chloe home with them that night, saying Jules was in no shape to look after her, but she couldn't let them, couldn't understand why they would want to take away the only person she had left. Maybe they thought she'd forfeited the right. Maybe she had. She only knew that to be alone in the house at that moment would leave her body empty of its heart. But eventually she was no longer strong enough or sober enough to resist. She didn't care anymore. It had taken hours, Jules drinking on the floor while they stood over her, berating, and finally what she needed most was for them to leave, whatever it took. Was Chloe in the hallway that whole time? Recalcitrant Chloe, watching, unblinking, while Jules sat on the bedroom floor and drank half a bottle of Scotch?

A few days later, Jules was falling asleep on Chloe's single bed. Chloe was home again and curled into her, crying softly and saying something Jules was never sure she'd actually heard. I'm sorry, Mummy.

But Jules was the one who was sorry, she should have been home and she wasn't, everybody said so. The smell of baby powder: two little hands taking one of Jules's and holding tight.

THEY HAD DROPPED Marc at his office and were heading back to the house in rush-hour traffic, meaning long and repeated intervals of waiting to move. Drew's neighbourhood was a few miles west, but to avoid the traffic he drove east, then south, and twenty minutes later turned to inch along the western waterfront until they would go north.

It really is faster, Drew said for the ninth time.

Three sides of a square. Makes perfect sense, Jules said. The city's dysfunctional infrastructure was a running public joke, and they both chuckled. Drew looked over at her and smiled.

What?

I just . . . haven't heard you laugh in a while. It's nice.

Lake Ontario rolled, ocean-like, the horizon endless water, the American shore too far to see. Today the sky was galvanized steel, the lake black as iron. It hadn't frozen yet, the whole thing rarely did, but mid-winter would see ice between the shore and the breakwaters. They reached a section of Lake Shore Boulevard where the city had put parking between the east- and westbound lanes, with an overhead walkway for beach access.

Can we pull in there? I just want to walk outside for a minute, without my— She tapped her ankle where the electronic bracelet had been until that morning.

DREW STAYED IN the car. The temperature had plummeted. The November wind came at her with teeth and knives as she fought her way across the exposed pedestrian bridge. It cut through her peacoat and stripped her naked, tore savagely at her face and bare ears. She grinned into it.

Along the edge of the lake, the bike path was ploughed clear of snow but almost deserted. A lone runner in earflaps and gloves puffed by, red-faced; a figure swaddled in a parka threw a stick for a dog oblivious to the cold. Jules walked right up to the shore, the strip of jetsammed beach. Dusk had set in, and with few lights down here, the water roiled, blacker and blacker. She felt her chest open up with the line of the horizon, the bite of the wind stripping away seven layers of grime, self-loathing and well-practised facade, and she had a moment—just a moment—of pondering how much it had cost her not to let herself feel. The smashing waves on the breakwater roared like monsters, clawing through the woolly fog of her perception in raw catharsis. She felt her cocoon of numbness start to split, the wind's frigid fingers prying wider its fissures, and felt something wholly new carving its way out from within.

And maybe, if she didn't fuck it up, something newly whole.

Breathe.

———

A hospital waiting room
the sound of a baby crying
a familiar unfamiliar face, Mo-mo but not Mo-mo, Jules but
not Jules, Lizzie but not Lizzie, all of them but none of them at all
a baby crying in their arms, I look down at my own hands, I
hold a stuffed elephant
I know why it's damp but can't remember
dead is dead, Jansen says, no hard feelings
Mo-mo laughing in a ripped-open way
I try to yell but
water fills me
pale-blue light and salvation
a million miles away
hey, a voice cutting through,
Hey, Chlo.
I woke up, sharp and sudden, to Lee, backlit beside me by green
tent fabric and pre-dawn glow.
Alright?
Her voice tight with worry. Embarrassed, I tried to smile. Yeah.
I reckon it's time you filled me in, yeah?
I knew she was right. My dreams had woken both of us every

266

night since I'd arrived. A familiar exhaustion weighed me down. Dark spots flickered in the corners of my vision, and the line between dream and reality wavered like a buoy line in a pool.

I wasn't quite ready to lay bare everything, so I started with half the truth.

Remember when you took me surfing?

Feel sick thinkin' about it.

So not your fault. I just . . . feel like the ocean is mad at me or something. For my phone. I know it's dumb—

Ah, Chlo. She'd been propped on one elbow and now lay back down beside me to stare up at the surface of the tent. It *was* a shit thing to do.

Is that supposed to make me feel better?

My dad, right? Lived his whole life on the water, helped *start* cleanup movements all over the *world*. He never did anything but worship the ocean.

Sensing what was coming, I draped an arm over her sleeping-bagged form.

And still it crushed him like a bug. Yeah? Because even though he practically lived on the water, felt like he was a part of it—and it was a huge part of him, let me tell you—at no point was it ever under his control.

She took a ragged breath. I had the sense that she was giving me a glimpse of her that few people got to see. I felt a deep pull of connection, and went right to the heart:

My baby sister died. I was there when it happened.

The words hung, awaiting judgment.

She turned her head to look at me. That what you're dreamin' about?

I nodded. When I can sleep at all, I added. Lee looked back up at the tent ceiling and was quiet for at least a minute.

You feel so powerless, hey.

And *guilty*, I said.

And guilty, Lee agreed. When I watched my dad go . . . Lee paused as her voice cracked. I was young, yeah? And I thought he was invincible. When I was real wee, he used to put me in a life vest and I'd ride on his back while he surfed—just small stuff, course—but it always felt like the wave did whatever he wanted it to. But when I got my own board and started going out, I realized he was just reacting to it, doing what he needed to, what the wave told him he had to. That's all anyone can do. And when I watched him go under that day, and not come back up . . . and then come back up, but not moving . . . just floating into shore with his board . . . that was my world ending. And for a long time after, I thought, That should have been me. I was the one who was vulnerable, who was small and had only a couple years of experience, not twenty, like him. But . . . Lee wiped her eyes. Anyway, that's why I nearly crapped my trousers when I saw you get hit. I thought, Oh no, not again. I'm constantly terrified someone else I love will get hurt.

I took her hand and pressed it against my cheek.

The previous afternoon, I'd watched Lee surf in the finals, riding monumental swells like so much flotsam, or like an orca, fearlessly flipping in the air, cutting down breaks. I got stoned on the beach with Sean and tried not to think about what could happen if things went wrong, tried to see the waves as impressive rather than deadly, tried to not imagine one crashing down on top of her, massively shattering.

Tried not to remember my own swim for the surface—primally desperate for air, the marbled light of being suspended and weightless, outside time. Between life and death.

On her final run, I held my breath as a swell raised itself up beneath her, a waking giant. But then she popped up to her feet, totally relaxed, just getting a lift from a good friend. When it finally broke, the wave was a twenty-five-footer, bent itself into another perfect pipe, and Lee carved a beautiful line down its underbelly

before she exited, spectacular, like a motorcycle escaping a collapsing mountain underpass—and making it look easy.

She did her high-fiving, backslapped Hero Walk along the beach
while my heart pounded with awe and love and terror.

So I knew what she meant. It was petrifying to see someone
you cared about take on danger. To know that all you could do
was watch and hope. To be waiting, always, for something to take
them away.

All my inner voices of caution sounded like Jules's, and I had
spent years arguing with them. But in this case, something actually
scared me. And I didn't want to be afraid of things, not for myself,
and not for anyone else.

But I'll tell you what, Lee said. It's 'cause of you I realized
that. None of us is in control. Things just happen. And I need to
remember surfing with my pa without all the fear and guilt. 'Cause
those are some of my best memories.

When I didn't answer, she turned on her side to look at me.

Chlo, she said. Let it out. If you want.

Fear and guilt, I echoed her.

They're tough things to make peace with. But they'll never let
you rest until you do.

I thought about my disjointed memories, the shadows that
stalked my sleep. Dead is dead, no hard feelings. Mo-mo and the
sound of Lizzie crying, then not crying anymore: the part of the
story I'd wanted to tell someone for most of my life but hadn't
known who or how. The thing that laced itself through my dreams
and made me feel crazy and deviant, and that I had never, ever put
into words.

So I told her. I told her how I'd been home from school, in
bed with a cold, the babysitter downstairs on the phone. How I'd
heard the baby start to cry, and how the crying wouldn't stop, and
finally I got out of bed, my stuffed elephant Eloise dangling from
one hand, and walked to the top of the stairs to see the edge of

Maureen as she moved past the kitchen door, her voice low and tense, then rising, stretching, cracking: Fight With Boyfriend. Do Not Interrupt.

So I tiptoed down the stairs to the front hall, where Maureen had parked the baby in a car seat by the front door.

Lizzie was wailing away; I couldn't figure out why. I tried to pat her and rock her and said *shh*, but nothing helped, I even made Eloise dance in front of her, which usually made her laugh, but the wailing only got louder and I only felt more desperate for fear of Maureen coming in and yelling. Or worse.

There was no soother in or near the car seat, so I put Eloise's trunk in Lizzie's mouth, to see if sucking on it would make her happy so she'd stop crying. And she did stop crying, she sucked a little and blinked a few times at me, then closed her eyes and fell asleep, just as Mo-mo's voice escalated to a hot rage, its apex the smash of the cordless into its cradle. I darted back upstairs before I could be seen.

A little while later, after the clatter of lunch dishes in the sink, I heard the quick rhythm of Maureen's footsteps, the flush of a toilet, the bang of the screen door as she went outside for a ciga-rette and again when she came back in. After all that came the rise of her voice in panic, followed by a quiet that made me cold with dread. I waited a long time, but the house only hummed, telling me nothing, so I crept back downstairs to see Mo-mo's back, out on the front porch in a weird hunched-over position, the car seat beside her. I reached up to press the latch on the screen door, still heavy for my small hand, and Mo-mo didn't turn around, but she must have heard me. Just go back to your room, she said. *GO.* I retreated, hear-ing, as I pulled myself slowly up the stairs, the murmured words. *This is all your fault.* A little while later the siren, the ambulance, the dark-blue uniforms carrying something away below my bedroom window. Until my mum came home and Maureen left, and Nana and Grandpa were there too, they were all in my parents' bedroom for hours and hours while I watched from the hallway and no one spoke to me, no one even seemed to notice I was there. Then my grandparents took me away without telling me why, even though I knew: my mother didn't want me around. She wouldn't even look at me.

I must have leaked some tears while I was talking, because by the time I was finished, my cheeks were wet. But I just felt numb. Lee curled around me and hugged me tight.

It's all so fuckin' random, she said. But it's not your fault, hey.

I shrugged, unconvinced and out of words.

I got you, she said.

Some memories will buoy you up, I thought, and some will drown you.

We lay there in silence while the universe spun around us.

Departures.

T his was the place. This exact level in this exact parking garage, the short-term lot connected by walkway to the international terminal.

Waiting, she was waiting, she had waited for David, standing right here, and when he didn't come and didn't come, she'd sat on that very curb, unable, possibly in response to his inability to get home faster, to go into the terminal to meet him.

She'd needed him in that moment more than any other before or after.

But then he did arrive, finally, his flight pushed back another hour, another hour, his short connector fogged in at Montreal, until six hours in the parking garage had her going out of her mind. She did try, at one point, to relocate to the terminal waiting area, figuring the twenty-hour flight prolonged into over forty was punishment enough.

But she barely made it. Emotions crackled like fireworks all around her as she fought her way through throngs of arrivees and greeters, departees and farewells: they assailed her, they had nothing to do with her. She ached for goodbyes she would never say and wouldn't be meeting her husband with any kind of joy. She took a few minutes of refuge in a bathroom stall to steel herself, then bolted back to the relative isolation of the parking garage.

Where, she remembers, the despair, the grief of the previous two weeks filled her head, her entire being, in an endless wailing song, a noise she couldn't quiet. She sat on the curb beside the luggage trolleys and keened, her back turned to the people unburdening themselves of their bags. She could hear them behind her, could sense their looks, but didn't care. Until she managed to re-submerge her emotions, to breathe past them long enough to focus on practicalities like letting Nan know she'd be even later than she'd suggested the last time she'd called.

Then David did arrive, stumbled his way dazedly out of the parking garage elevator, looking something far beyond exhausted: shell-shocked.

Which she understood now as totally expected, given the circumstances.

But at that time, she had sought in him a bastion, a sturdy structure to cling to when she thought she was drowning. When she needed to keep breathing.

And what she found, when they embraced, what she felt between her arms, was nothing. A fragile shell that crumpled under pressure, the pressure of her arms, the pressure of her need. Because he had his own grief, she knew, in her logical brain at least. The problem was perhaps less David's weakness and more her expectation in the first place that he be solid and strong, a brick house of sanctuary rather than a feeling, grieving, flesh-and-blood human.

As they leaned over a half wall and watched the runways that sprawled for miles, Jules had filled him in, blow by blow, with all the details of what had happened. What arrangements she'd been making, the nightmares Chloe was having, already, and the radiating disapproval of his mother every time she called. As she gave him the most detailed, detached account she could manage, trying to step up in the moment, trying to keep the debilitating heartbreak momentarily at arm's length, where it struggled, kicking, against her hold, she could sense, beside her, David coming apart. Which wasn't fair, and it made her hate him, in that instant and for a long time after, for not getting there sooner and, having finally arrived, being nothing but another vector of need.

They were broken, then. Both of them, separately and together.

Now, HERE SHE was again, sitting behind the wheel of Drew's car as she waited to be met on P3 of the short-term garage at Pearson Airport. Only this time she was the one leaving.

She'd waited until she was on the way there to call Drew at work, to minimize the possibility that he would talk her out of it. And when she'd told him he might want to come pick up his car, there'd been a silence on the line and she could hear the million reasonable objections loaded into it. But he'd said only, Fine, and she knew he'd be saving his reaction for the face-to-face.

All four of them came, piling out of Declan's Fiat with their intervention faces on. Drew, Declan, Farzan and Marc.

Marc, the lawyer.

Nothing like making it easy.

They wanted explanations, so she told them her plan, which they received about as badly as expected.

Drew was furious. He'd vouched for her, with the partners as well as the judge. He couldn't believe she was going on the lam.

Jules did something she hadn't done much in her life but sensed was going to loom large in her future: she apologized.

I've been an asshole. I really fucked things up. I'm so sorry.

Drew looked conflicted, like he liked what he was hearing but wasn't sure if he believed it.

But it's over. I'm done. I have fourteen days to start treatment. I'll be back, and I'll leave all the bullshit behind me, I promise.

But Marc cleared his throat and said that, technically, she was not supposed to leave the country. And by technically, he meant legally.

What's the worst that could happen?

Marc looked away, looked back. Well, you're on probation. You could go to jail.

By the time they figure out I've even left, I'll be done rehab—acting like a fully functioning member of society. They're gonna put me in jail then?

They could, yes, for violating your terms. Marc looked apologetic. They might.

Even though she'd known that, the words gave her pause. Hers wasn't the kind of life that could easily accommodate a prison sentence without things really falling apart. More than they already had, which was saying something. But her eyes followed the unwavering line of half wall as a plane lifted off in the distance, and she knew nothing else mattered.

I gotta find my kid, she told them.

I get it, said Farzan. I just hope you know what you're doing.

I'm cleaning up my act. She believed it as she said it.

Drew studied her for a long moment. Jules shrugged, uncomfortable but resolved.

However he chose to interpret this, he seemed to accept it, shook his head, and sighed. I'll try to cover for you, Jules, but you had better be back in time for treatment, or I swear to god I'll come and get you, and you will not like me after a twenty-four-hour flight.

I'll be back, she promised again.

I'll set it up for you at Greenvalley.

She thanked them all for helping her, which was a surreal moment, more testing out of words she wasn't used to saying.

You saved my life, she told them. I don't deserve you, any of you.

We know, Farzan said.

You can pay me back somehow, Declan said, and they all laughed.

Well, I know it too, Jules told them. Don't think I don't.

There followed a litany of advice from each of them—stay sober, stay clean, stay safe, stay calm—and when Drew asked if she had enough money, she said, Enough.

You still need to buy your ticket?

He wrapped her in a smothering hug.

Watch the neck. She rubbed at the knot that shot along a nerve into her shoulder.

Farzan put an arm around her and kissed her temple like a proud dad. You'll find her, he said.

He and Drew and Marc piled into Drew's car and instantly became rowdy teenagers, laughing and waving and honking as they toured around the half-empty parking garage a couple times before finding the exit ramp.

Which left Jules alone with Declan, who leaned back against his car and gave her a funny look.

Well, Julie. Seems to me you're at a real crossroads.

Am I? Jules felt like between the trip to find Chloe, coming back to do rehab and then getting her career and her house back together, her immediate future was a clearer and more direct line than she'd had in years. Or maybe she could just see it better.

I hope you don't give up on yourself, Declan said, which made her understand:

You don't think I can do it?

Do you think you can do it?

All I can do is try, right?

At this he laughed, and said maybe there was hope for her after all.

What he did next gave her something to think about over the following weeks. He reached out and took her hand and said, I hope I'll see you when you're back.

She assumed he meant at his clinic for more flotation therapy, so she said, Yes, I don't feel like I'm done with it either.

A slow smile travelled from his eyes to his lips. He hugged her, and she thought he held on just a bit longer than necessary. She felt something in her belly, maybe a small flame of hope, that she wasn't quite ready to acknowledge. She had other things she had to do first.

Jules shouldered her handbag and extended the handle on her suitcase. I have to go.

Good luck with your search, Declan said.

She turned and headed for the walkway. She hadn't bought a ticket yet and wanted to make that happen before she could chicken out.

It was only after she had cleared security and was waiting in the departure lounge that she realized her airport ghosts had vanished when her friends arrived. She wondered if they had just gone ahead without her, to lie in wait with David, a dreadful welcoming committee. Or if her forward motion had finally vanquished them.

Voices.

Are you serious? I asked.

Aw, it looks worse than it is. Lee took a seat on a rock. Go on, get it over with.

I hadn't been in the water since my accident, and Lee had convinced me I had to get back on the horse, so to speak. I'd agreed, as long as there weren't a couple hundred surfers around. So we had walked down a gravel road and pushed through some bushes to emerge on a rocky inlet, foaming and crashing, spiked and treacherous. The water had actual teeth.

It looks pretty bad, I said.

blue light, white shadows

an underwater voice

I had a vivid memory of walking home from the pool with Mo-mo. Plastic bag dragging in my mittened hand, heavy with my rolled wet towel and bathing suit. A frozen lock of hair bouncing on my cheek. I almost drowned at the pool, I told Mo-mo. How could you drown in the shallow end? she asked, and I didn't have an answer, was working hard to keep up with her long strides. But actually, Mo-mo said a moment later, you can drown in an inch of water. She'd heard about a guy who'd fallen unconscious in a puddle, inhaled enough water to fill his lungs, and that was that.

The raging cove brought back her words: Death is easy.

278

There was a bathtub-sized pool of stillness right in front of me that was partly sheltered by a natural breakwater. I peeled down to boxers and bra, walked up to the water's edge and prodded it with my big toe.

A wave smashed against rocks, and I flinched.

This is a test, I said under my breath.

You got this, said Lee.

I heard Jules's overly cautious voice clearing its throat, and I shut it down. Not every unknown represented imminent danger. The only thing holding me back was my own fear.

I forced myself to take a step forward, coolness up to my ankles.

I waded in a little farther. I crouched down behind the row of rocks, submerged up to the bottoms of my thighs, cupped some water in my hands and splashed it over my shoulders. It wasn't very satisfactory.

You missed a spot.

Ha ha, thanks.

I took three short steps forward, sat right down on the ocean bed, lay back and got my torso and shoulders and head wet, and stood up again. I saw a wave looming behind the closest row of rocks, and I lunged for the shred of beach, tripped and skinned my knee as I landed on sand and pebbles.

Lee was trying hard not to laugh, but failing. Good job, she said.

I wiped my face with my towel, half laughing, half mortified. I turned and looked back at the water I'd just braved as another wave roared in.

I felt like I'd slayed a dragon.

As we came down the beach towards the surf bar, Sean peeled away from the bonfire out front and jogged up to us. I faltered at the look on his face.

Another quake in Christchurch, he said, and Lee grabbed my

hand, pulled me into the bar, to the old TV in the back. To complaints around us, she changed it from a surfing show to an all-news channel.

Few days ago, I think, said Sean, who'd followed us in. The scroll along the bottom said six. And then eleven.

Six days. Eleven people dead.

The tingle of dread and the bile of guilt. The picture of the rescue dog I never drew.

Oh, fuck.

Six days and I hadn't heard. But, of course, I wouldn't have heard. I'd been avoiding hearing. I hadn't even tried to call in—well, more than six days, apparently. Beach life had transported me, let me forget to be worried.

Fuck, I said again.

Six days ago I'd left Picton to come find Lee.

Can she use your phone? Lee asked the guy who owned the bar.

WE SAT AROUND the bonfire smoking joints as a beacon moon rose.

What now, then? Lee stared at the fire as she asked.

Well, I have to go to Christchurch. Check in with my dad and my little sister. I know they're okay, but . . . I need to see them.

We were holding hands and she gave mine a little squeeze. I rolled my eyes and told her the other thing I'd learned from the call to David.

And my mother is flying in.

Aw, yeah?

What I didn't say was that I'd just met one demon head-on and felt like I was ready for more. Having Jules and David in the same room was too rare a chance to pass up. Of course, it might be a disaster. But at least it would be something.

I was just thinking, Lee said, that SCAB has work going on

down there. Cleaning up the sewage spills from all the quakes. Thought I might go help out. Volunteer, like.

What's SCAB—oh, wait, that clean beach thing, right?

Lee didn't answer, and a moment later I clicked into the rest of what she'd said.

Ha, ha, sucker. You get to meet my parents.

Arrivals.

———

Three airports, thirty-four hours and several glasses of wine later, Jules greeted her ex-husband in the Christchurch airport. They hadn't seen each other in five years, and she barely recognized him: he looked even smaller than she remembered.

Before she could speak, he rushed to tell her that Chloe had called and was making her way back to Christchurch. She would be there in a few days.

Ohthankgod! Exhausted, slightly tipsy and emotionally wrung out, Jules gave in to some decades-suppressed body memory and threw her arms around David. She wasn't quite weeping, but she was pretty close. David held his body rigid for a moment, then hugged her back tentatively. Mortified, Jules pulled away. A smile twitched under David's beard. The rest of his face looked surprised.

You look great, Jules. He took her bag and led her through the airport.

You still look like a rumpled grad student, David. She squeezed his arm to make sure he knew she was teasing. It was a funny thing to see him after all this time. She had so many levels of response, the most surprising a closeness and a sense of comfort she had long forgotten. Because no matter what she could say about David, he *knew* her as no one else ever had or probably ever would.

Less hair, he said. More— And he rubbed his belly like he was pregnant. They were joking around in a way they hadn't done since they were first married, but she saw the wary glances he kept darting her way, like she might transform into a lunatic with a chainsaw at any moment.

I GOT YOU a room in my hotel, David said. Down the hall. I think we'll be back at the house in a couple days, but right now the street's flooded, and there's no power or water or anything. When we do get in, it'll be a mess. But I don't know how long you're here.

I have to fly out on the twenty-eighth. A week.

His eyebrows wriggled. Quick trip.

As they drove to the hotel, Jules wondered if she'd even last that long. She'd never seen anything like it, except on TV. Emergency vehicles everywhere, people loading supplies off trucks, houses and streets askew like someone had knocked around pieces on a game board. Cars tilted sideways into rips in roads, rows of porta-potties blocked off wounded residential avenues. But they had it down to a science, David explained. They were used to it; they were organized. And a lot of the city was already empty because the last couple weeks of aftershocks had been so bad. There was rubble everywhere, no surface was clear of it, grit and dust and smoke coated everything, filled everything, gnawed at her eyeballs and nose and throat even through the car window.

Don't worry, we're not staying too close to the fault line. You should see downtown.

As in: this is nothing.

LATER, AT THE hotel, after checking in and passing out for twelve hours, Jules woke up in time for cocktail hour at the hotel bar. She had remembered halfway through her flight the court-ordered sobriety and decided it didn't apply once she was out of Canadian airspace.

She knew she shouldn't drink. She didn't even want to. Not really. She knew it wasn't good for her in multiple ways. The problem was, she still wanted Oxy. She still wanted to use. She was still thinking about using. She would've if she could've. She was just on the cusp. She was hanging on to a vibrating steel cord of unpleasantness— shame? disgust?—just hanging on to it, or rather grabbing it and letting it go, like touching a live wire repeatedly to remind herself just how badly it hurt.

She'd thought, recently, about how much of her life she'd spent in one state or another of intoxication. How close she'd been to a point of no return. She knew it was time to stop. She did. And she would.

But just one, she thought. What's the harm?

David joined her, saying he was kind of at loose ends without Amanda, who'd taken their daughter and gone down to work in her firm's Dunedin offices and stay with friends until they could piece things back together up in Christchurch. They might stay down there for a few months, he said. For the summer holidays, anyway. Christmas and whatnot.

I'm sorry to hear that, Jules said, surprised at her own genuine empathy. That can't be easy.

David ducked his head in a nod of thanks. The important thing is that they're safe. If something happened to Char . . .

Jules couldn't speak and didn't want him to go anywhere near the end of that sentence. What? she thought. It would be devastating? It would tear your life apart? You would want to shut down all feeling because letting any of it surface would feel like the end of everything? Try not to be a bitch, she heard Drew telling her. She slugged back half her Scotch, savouring the burn in her throat.

David took a swallow of beer and stared into an abyss behind the bar only he could see.

This past couple years, with all the quakes, you start to feel like . . . at any moment the ground could open up and swallow you. And it might, that's the thing.

Jules snorted. Bring it on.

David didn't seem to hear her.

Do you know we've had something like thirty thousand aftershocks? Well . . . they call them aftershocks, but what's the difference, really. It's just a quake that comes after another quake. More than half of them are four-point-fives and fives, so . . . You just end up . . .

Waiting for something bad to happen? Jules finished for him as she drained her drink. Sounds a lot like trying to stay clean. Or like, you know. Life. She pictured her own house, sitting empty, the only changes while she was away the accumulation of dust and mould.

Anyway, David said. Really forces you to live in the moment.

OVER LUNCH THE next day, trying to be nonchalant like they were just old friends catching up and not two people who'd spent fifteen years in a marriage, Jules let drop the reason her trip was so short. How else to say it?

So I have to get back to start rehab as a condition of my probation.

She stuffed her face with cheeseburger.

David's split-second laugh died in his throat.

You're serious.

Jules nodded, watching him over chipmunked cheeks. David studied her, then carefully placed his own half-eaten burger back on his plate.

You know, Jules, I was really angry at you. For a long time.

You were angry at *me*? Jules said, pointing at him then at herself, her mouth too full for the words to make sense on their own. David nodded, handed her a napkin and gestured at her right cheek.

Yeah. Which, I mean— Do you want to hear this? It's water under the bridge, far as I'm concerned.

Mm-hmm. It sounded ominous, but at this point, why the fuck not?

Okay. Well. He took a deep breath. That whole time, after Lizzie . . . maybe even before . . .

Jules swallowed her food and watched his mouth and strained to listen, holding her breath, trying to hear the words for what they were, she felt like she was falling.

I know you were struggling, Jules. He took another, bigger breath, then released the words in a steady stream. You were completely self-absorbed, self-indulgent and irresponsible, and we all suffered for it. Chloe especially. He crossed his arms, leaned back and waited. Jules waited too.

That's it? she finally asked.

That's not enough? You checked out of our marriage but didn't think to tell me about it for—what?—four years? Six?

More like ten, she thought, but he wasn't done.

You were my best friend, Jules. And then you were just—gone. Drinking alone in your room, for fuck's sake. Downright hostile— all the time. He looked around at the empty hotel restaurant, shrugged back at her. Good for you, I guess. Rehab. His face was tight behind his glasses and beard. She suddenly felt exhausted.

I'm trying, David. I know I made some mistakes.

Some?

Okay, a lot. I'm still making them, probably. But you know, I was mad at you too.

Does Chloe know? About— What are you on probation for, anyway?

Forgery. And no. And I'll tell her, but—just let me do it, okay?

David held up his hands, his eyes wide, glad it was none of his business.

But I was, I was mad at you too.

Yeah, so you said. He took off his glasses and pressed thumb and forefinger into the inner corners of his eyes. Jules had an unexpected jolt at how much older he looked without the frames to hide his deep-set lines.

You weren't *there*, Dave.

There.

When the baby died. It took you over a week to get home.

Where David had been building momentum, face tightening, voice rising, he now collapsed into the back of his chair, wilted and withered, a burst balloon. He stared at her so openly and for so many moments that she started to fidget with her napkin. She didn't want to meet his eyes, didn't want to be the first to look away.

What, she said.

You think I don't know *that*?

What do you think you know. Said as a statement, because she already knew: he knew nothing.

Well, he said slowly. I know *that*. And I know I'm sorry. I should have been there, and I wasn't. I know I should have found a way to get home *faster*, and I couldn't. I didn't.

She had wanted to relocate her self-blame onto someone else, but he was making it impossible.

But you should know I've been living with it ever since.

She'd been so, so angry, for so, so long. It felt familiar. It felt like habit. Or like home. When all of a sudden she felt it slipping from her grasp, she wasn't sure she could let go of it, wasn't sure she wanted to. What would she be without it? But what was she with it? Did it just gouge her out from the inside, leaving her a hollow husk of remorse?

It's one of my biggest regrets. David stared at his hands. I would have done anything to fix it, and you might not believe me, but believe me, I tried. At the time, and afterwards. For *years* afterwards. I honestly don't know what more I could have done.

She wanted to say, You could have just loved me, but she knew it was a lie, because he had, and in some way maybe still did, but she'd felt undeserving, so she'd torched it to the ground, and she knew that made everything, all the falling apart, in some way her fault.

And so, she was miserable. She felt like a monster.

I guess I'm sorry too, she said, not sure she'd heard her own words correctly. David looked equally surprised.

You never could have won, Dave. I was angry you weren't there, I was angry you were there too much, I was angry you loved me, I was angry you didn't love me enough. I was angry that you still seemed able to function and feel like a normal person, when I couldn't even get out of bed. So, nothing, is the answer. You could have done nothing. I wanted to love you, so badly, the way I once did. But I couldn't. I couldn't *feel anything*.

She took a sip of the wine she'd ordered with lunch, saw David's eyes flick to the glass and met his gaze, daring him to say something. He didn't.

I have to go feed my cat, he said. I'll see you later.

And he left her there to finish her lunch alone.

IN THE ELEVATOR back up to her room, she saw the sign for the floor with the pool, and it got her thinking. She couldn't even remember the last time she'd been swimming. Ten years ago? Twenty? She imagined the feel of water on her skin, the sound of her own breathing, her body moving forward under her own power. Later, she thought, she would see if the shop across the street had a plain-enough one-piece. Then she wondered if she could even do it. She knew she was weak, probably weaker than at any other point in her life. But she wanted to try.

Daughter.

———

hloe materialized out of the mist the next morning, a dark hooded shadow emerging from the dust. It was December 23, and Jules was smoking a pre-breakfast cigarette on her third-floor hotel balcony when she saw her arrive.

This is the moment, she realized, feeling it happen, feeling a slight tear in the tissue of her heart. This is the moment when everything shifts. The compass needle has swung right around, the opposing twin burdens of needing and being needed reversing positions. Now that she wanted to hold on, she would have to let go.

She put out her cigarette and went downstairs to give her daughter hell and cash.

David beat her to the lobby and had Chloe in a bear hug when Jules walked in.

As soon as she saw her daughter, all the caustic comments that had been bouncing around her brain dissipated completely. She would have said some weird primal need took over if she believed in such things, but of course she didn't. She grabbed her daughter and hugged her fiercely for as long as she could—which was a few seconds, at which point Chloe pulled away, practically sputtering.

Oh my god. Melodramatic much?

Hardly, when you've been missing for weeks.

Oh, please. Her nose wrinkled. You're smoking now?

Could be worse, trust me. I thought we agreed you'd carry a phone.

I lost it.

Now, kid, that's not strictly true, said David. Not from what I hear.

He told you?

He did.

Who did? Told him what?

Oh fine. I didn't lose it. I threw it.

From a boat, David added. He seemed oddly proud.

Chloe shrugged. It sank.

Jules laughed, deeply, from her belly, and David laughed with her. Chloe looked alarmed, then smirked. I'm getting you a new one tomorrow, Jules said.

She felt herself dissembling, as she looked at Chloe's face. Felt the burn of tears as her vision blurred. This is what it is to demythologize yourself in front of your child, she thought. This is the face that used to look at her like she had created the world, that had radiated unquestioning love, and Jules knew she was now less in Chloe's eyes. She would always be less. But the truth was, she'd been less for years, and maybe that self-awareness bore within it the tools for some kind of salvation.

Jenga.

O ver blueberry pancakes, I told David I thought I'd stick around and help him with the house. Or whatever he needed. I was focused on my food, but the silence lengthened and I looked up at my parental units, sitting across from me in the booth, which was in itself surreal, both of them smiling proudly, which made me incredibly self-conscious.

I don't have to. I just thought you could use a hand?

Well, maybe. But right now I can't even get in.

Wow. Bad, eh?

David nodded.

Where's, um . . .

Amanda took Char to Dunedin, he said. Safer there.

Lance?

He shrugged, gestured towards anywhere but here. On his boat, back up north. Helping with more beached whales.

With a sudden release of pent-up air, Jules asked, Remember Maureen? What did you call her, Chlo? Mo-mo?

I narrowed my eyes at Jules, wondering where this was going, and if she was about to bring up the very thing that I had resolved to bring up myself.

Jules looked different, clearer than I'd seen her in a long time. Sharper. When she looked at me, her eyes were more focused, and she moved her head more quickly in response to shifts in conversation.

Yes. I remember Mo-mo.

Vaguely, said David.

Well, you wouldn't, really, Jules told him. I saw him flinch slightly. It's weird, she continued. I never saw her. Not even once after . . . after.

There was a long, squirming beat during which David looked like he might bolt from the table, and I considered following him if he did.

I hadn't thought about her in years, Jules was saying. But she was *there*, for one of the worst things that ever happened to us. To any of us. That we've all been carrying around this whole time. Am I wrong?

She looked back and forth between us. She was not wrong.

And I got to wondering if she felt culpable somehow, Jules went on. I mean, I would, in her shoes. I do anyway. But we all know it's just a random act of nature, right? SIDS is a *syndrome*—as in, they haven't got a clue. They just stop. The babies. The light goes out. It's no one's fault.

Jules's voice was steady, her eyes shining at me.

I looked down at my half-eaten pancakes. Thought about an elephant's trunk, damp from the baby's mouth. I listened as Jules went on to explain about the mandatory autopsy, said again that no one could have predicted it or stopped it. But still I held in my mind images I'd only recently spoken of out loud, to Lee, and relentless dreams of a responsibility that both terrified me and felt like my own. I put the words in a queue in my head, stood back and saw them: ridiculous as clowns, a child's retelling, illogical and imaginative. I meant to keep them to myself, to take them out later, alone, to decipher how I had so long mistaken them for truth, but instead, thinking it was now or never, I took a deep breath and told my parents: I thought it was my fault. When Lizzie died. And abruptly, we all occupied the moment where it couldn't be unsaid. That's what Mo-mo told me, I added. That it was all my fault. I guess I believed her.

I was startled by the display of emotion on Jules's face, my mother's pain more visible in that moment than any other before it, making me wonder if her general inability to express it was actually a sign not of its absence but of how deep it ran. Something taut panged through my core, but I kept going.

I know it wasn't, I added. Now I know. And I don't think you were punishing me.

Punishing you? Chlo— Jules's voice cracked. She looked away, composed her face, looked back at me. You did nothing to deserve punishment.

But. Well, when you sent me away. With Grandpa and Nan.

I was just getting things off my chest. I certainly never expected an apology, from either of them, for anything. But Jules was making serious eyes at me like she was trying to show me her soul, and when she said, I shouldn't have done that, which was not something I'd ever heard her admit about anything, I knew that, in one way or another, for one thing or another, she was sorry.

I think I'm going to sell the house, Jules said next, and the centre of everything shifted.

David was nodding, which made me wonder what they had talked about before I arrived.

I felt a flash of deep resistance, or maybe resentment. We'd lived there when I was born. Lizzie had lived and died there. Those two things were the barest details, the broadest strokes, of what bound us all together. Just as I was preparing to excavate my memories, the house that contained them all would be gone from our lives.

But then Jules pointed out the flip side. It's time to move on, she said. I need to move on. And that house. She shook her head.

Bad mojo, said David, and Jules said, Something like that.

I saw her point. We would never be together that way again. This way again. Because what bound us together had also driven us apart. My parents' marriage was ancient history, and I was an adult.

Jules reached over and squeezed my hand. I was slightly disconcerted, but didn't pull away.

You can still come home, she said. Wherever I live, any time.

I sometimes think about what happens to the timeline, David said, when one whole future life just drops out of it, and the rest of us are left to fill in the gaps. To move that timeline forward without that one, integral piece that was intertwined around all of us.

The memory of the shape of a life, I thought. A shadow on my retina I couldn't quite see.

Like that game, pick-up sticks, David continued, fiddling with his fork. You had to pull one out and hope the whole pile didn't cave in. And you never knew if the one you were pulling was just resting on the others or was central to the whole thing. Without it, all the other pieces would just collapse. And scatter.

I hadn't meant to say anything, but out it came: Isn't that what you did, though, Dad? The nickname made him blink. You up and left—and I get why, but you left *me* and moved to the other side of the world. Don't you think that left me with a pretty big "gap"?

David widened his eyes as though wary I might blow. I thought about earthquakes, and how ground you thought was stable could suddenly cleave open, bringing the walls down around you.

I guess I resented that you could just go start over, I added, and leave me there with this mess. I jerked a thumb towards Jules. No offence.

None taken. My mother half laughed and wiped her cheeks with a palm.

I'm sorry, kid, David said, looking smaller and more sunken than ever. Truly. But you have to know—

I know it was never about me, I finished. Clearly.

He looked sad then. I guess I missed a lot of things, he said.

Anyway, we play Jenga now. I'd aired my grievance and now I felt bad and wanted to move on.

That tower game? David wasn't impressed. So hierarchical.

Jules rolled her eyes. Where are you staying, Chloe? Should we get you a room? Where's your stuff?

I have a campsite just out of town. We're— I paused, thinking this was either a great idea or a terrible one. Actually, if you can't get into your house anyway, why don't you guys come and see what we're doing?

DAVID CALLED A hotline and was told he could visit his house. I said we could all go, but he strongly discouraged it, giving me the distinct impression that my parents had had enough of each other. He squeezed me tight before he left and quietly slipped me some cash. Lance will be proud, he said. He told Jules to stay out of trouble.

Oh, and I forgot. He still had his wallet out, and he took from it a folded piece of paper. Char wanted you to have this.

Feeling like I knew what it was, I unfolded it: the spaceship Char had started drawing in her room that day, with two stick figures standing in the middle of it—one small with dark curls and one taller with bright-yellow spikes.

She says she hopes you can be her big sister again sometime.

I didn't know what to say, but I had a deep urge to send her something back in return. I had Tanga's *matau* in my pocket, but the thought of giving her something Jansen had stolen made my lip curl in disgust. I was planning to go to the post office and send it back to Tanga; how many men with that name could live on that one stretch of road where he picked us up?

Instead, I pulled from my other pocket the deep-blue shell I had found on the beach on the second day of my hike. I was meaning to get a hole drilled in it for a piece of leather around my neck.

Or Lee's neck. But this seemed more important, so I placed it in David's hand.

Tell her I'll see her soon.

It wasn't exactly an outpouring of sisterly love, but it was a start.

THE BEACHES OF Christchurch were closed for swimming, but this one was as busy as any summer day, crawling with volunteers in rubber galoshes and gloves and masks. The latest earthquake had ruptured another pipeline, and raw sewage gushed into the ocean. Figures in haz-mat suits moved floating bulkheads around in an effort to contain at least the solids on the water's surface, while volunteers trolled the land with spears, rakes and industrial vacuums.

We're camping down the road, I told Jules. But we're volunteering here for as long as they need us.

Finally, Jules asked, Who's "we"?

I grinned, then turned and waved at Lee, who handed off her rake and came striding over in her black galoshes.

Hey there, she said, and I introduced them. Lee didn't waste time.

So, I don't know if you want to stay around and help at all? She looked back and forth between us. I grinned more.

Help? Jules asked.

Lee knew some of the organizers of this surfer-driven relief effort, and bringing Jules here had been her idea. I watched my mother squirm, clearly not liking the idea of getting her hands dirty, but perfectly cornered.

HALF AN HOUR later, I ambled down the beach beside her, both of us breathing through masks and by unspoken agreement not talking about the smell. Jules worked the vacuum, sucking black sand and muck through a screaming accordion tube with a filter over the end. I carried a bright-yellow plastic bag marked with bio-hazard symbols, stabbing at solid objects with my spear and dropping them into it.

It was disgusting.

So anyway, I yelled at her over the noise. As you can see, I'm totally fine.

What?

I'm totally fine! Broke. But fine! I impaled a used maxi-pad, shook it off into my bag. Wondered who would flush that down the toilet.

I put money in your account already, Jules yelled.

You did? Seriously, who the hell? I had to use a gloved hand to dislodge a diaper from my spear.

Well, I'm going to be away! Jules shrugged, resigned to this.

I nodded. I wondered if the rehab would take. I nudged her hose to a pile of sludge too wet to pick up by spear.

Anyway, I'm sorry you came all this way for nothing.

I didn't. Jules shook her head, then said something I didn't catch.

What? I yelled.

It's not for nothing!

She gestured around with her eyes, her elbows.

I knew what she meant. Behind my paper mask, I smiled.

Acknowledgements

‑‑‑‑‑‑‑‑

would never have arrived at this point without Zoe Whittall, who not only gave me invaluable feedback on an early draft, but also connected me to Samantha Haywood at Transatlantic. I am incredibly grateful to both of them for believing in me, and in this book. My editors Janice Zawerbny and Iris Tupholme and the entire team at HarperCollins Canada, with their brilliance and generosity, pushed me to make it better, and I learned a thousand times over the truth of the adage that the editor is always right.

Research was a key component of writing this book, much of it done in informal conversations, with too many people to list here. My sister Janet and my mother, Mary, both shared memories that resonated with me and inspired parts of the story. Judy Taylor provided moving insight into the anxiety of living in an earthquake zone. Colin Kay of the Toronto Police (since retired) endured many nitpicking email inquiries from me in the early stages of writing. His explanations about arrests and Show Cause hearings were taped on my wall for months. In the end I'm sure I took a fiction-writer's bulldozer to the reality of everything people told me. Needless to say, any errors or omissions are completely my own.

Deep gratitude to my early readers Sarah M. and Jenn B.; and to David Bergen, my mentor as I wrote that first terrible draft; to my café comrades, both in Toronto and Fredericton, who are too

many to list here: writing can be very isolating, and you all made it less so. Thanks for engaging in parallel play with me. And Jack, for letting me take over his studio for three weeks every summer—you are badly missed.

I wouldn't be anywhere without my chosen family. Angela, Cathy, Róisín, Vanessa and Yasmine, all the best friends a human could ask for. And Sabine: thanks for always holding my hand in the dark.